THE PALM TREE CHRONICLES

A Los Angeles Love Story

Manuela Gomez Rhine

The Palm Tree Chronicles is a work of fiction. The characters are imaginary, and any resemblance to actual persons is accidental. However, many aspects of the story are based on real historical events, things, and places. These include the South Central Farm, the Huntington Library, Art Museums, and Botanical Gardens, and the novel *Ramona*, by Helen Hunt Jackson, all of which the author has first-hand knowledge and personal experience.

Cover design: Ramona Gomez
Illustrations: Michael Rhine

ISBN: 978-0989919456

Tampicopressbooks.com

For Michael and Ramona. For everything you are.

May 1, 2006
Pasadena, California

Chapter One
Always Date a Suicide Note

Pomona Sandoval was driving east across the Colorado Street Bridge when a sudden glare from the rising sun bounced across the car windshield and hit her square in the eye. Driving too fast to reckon with the momentary blindness, she swerved across the center dividing line and slammed on the brakes. The car jolted and stopped. The book and canister of ashes lying on the passenger seat flew to the floor.

"Mama, I'm sorry," Pomona cried. As she reached down to retrieve the fallen items, a horn blared behind her. Pomona glanced in her rearview mirror to see a woman emerge from a car that was now kissing her bumper.

"No, go back," she called through her open driver's window, motioning the woman away. Pomona rolled up the window, locked the door, and slouched low in her seat. The woman peered in through the car window.

"I almost rear-ended you," the lady shouted, rapping her fingers against the glass.

Pomona lowered her head so that her long black hair shielded her face. "Sorry, just trying to park."

"Missy, have you been drinking? You can't park on a two-lane bridge. You'll kill someone."

"Sorry."

"Thanks to me we didn't crash but you're a menace on the road." She turned and left. A moment later her car passed Pomona with a honk.

With jagged breaths and trembling arms Pomona continued driving along the empty bridge. The San Gabriel Mountains filled her view to the north. Puffy clouds drifted across a blue Pasadena sky. But the beautiful day meant nothing.

She turned onto Orange Grove Avenue and directed the car onto a residential cul-de-sac that bordered the bridge entrance. Here she pulled Pearl alongside the curb and parked beneath a palm tree. Her mother's 1988 Volvo 240 station wagon had 210,000 miles on the odometer and still purred like a kitten.

Pomona leaned her head back against the black leather seat, cracked and crumbling. The lingering smells of burnt sage and clove cigarettes filled her nose. A hint of Yves Saint Laurent Opium perfume. Orange blossoms and spice. The familiar aromas of her mother permeated the car. With every whiff, Pomona sank deeper into the treacherous waters that had flooded her life since Nora's death. She barely remembered calling the morgue and ordering the cremation. Her only life raft had been Nora's small stash of Valium, which became her nighttime friend.

She squeezed the slender green tin canister that was mottled with flecks of rust. It featured the painted head of an Indian Princess in full headdress and, beneath this logo, a festive garland of pink roses. Its fading label read: *California Perfume Company: Natoma Rose Talcum Powder.*

"Genuine history," Nora had exclaimed with delight after unearthing the tin from a box of second-hand kitchenware at the Pasadena City College flea market. "The California Perfume Company became Avon."

Pomona recalled that the Forest Lawn Mortuary attendant shared none of this excitement when she presented the vintage tin as the receptacle for her mother's ashes.

"May I suggest a simple pewter urn with an air-tight cap? For only $85, you'll have a beautiful vessel in which to cherish your beloved mother. I will even engrave her name for no extra charge."

Pomona's face reddened. "It's what my mother wanted," she had replied. It wasn't exactly, but Pomona had not wanted to reveal the deeper truth, that the $300 cremation cost had cratered her finances and she had to watch every penny. Pomona had nothing. Not a mother or father. Not a job or any way of making money anymore. No real friends. Not a boyfriend who could bring her some comfort. Certainly not the faintest hope that she could rebuild her life into anything worth living.

Nora was right. They were cursed in love. Pomona would spend the rest of her life alone, just her and Delilah, her mother's cat. Pomona's eyes still burned from the morning glare. The heat intensified the strains of sage and clove that seemed baked into the car's cushions and floorboards. She could no longer ignore the smells any more than she could ignore the book that lay on the seat beside her.

Ramona.

The book that had started everything. The book her father loved and mother hated. The book that had torn her family apart. The book that went missing for twenty years and weirdly reappeared only the day before her mother's death.

The cursed book.

Certainly its reappearance when Nora had pulled it out from beneath her pillow had marked the beginning of the end. Staring anxiously at its faded cover, Nora had said in a trembling voice, "Oh, Pomona, something about this book scares me. I don't remember, but I think there's a message in the story, a secret message of some kind. That's why I hid it."

Hid it? Pomona regarded her emaciated mother with shock. For twenty years Nora had insisted the book had been lost in their move from the house with the tangerine tree to the apartment on Mentor Avenue.

The previous day when Pomona had left the mortuary with Nora's ashes and crossed the bridge she had hatched her plan to scatter Nora's ashes from the bridge into the Arroyo, then climb over the railing and jump herself. This simple solution solved so many problems such as how she would manage to empty Nora's book-filled apartment, find a new job, and start life anew.

She had forgotten it was her thirtieth birthday until she wrote a suicide note that morning. A suicide note feels like something you should date. When Pomona did she realized she had picked the same day to die as the day she was born.

Wednesday, May 1, 2006
Not coming back. Donate all books (If Possible!) to the Pasadena Public Library.
Thank you,
Pomona Sandoval
(PS: if you see a black cat please feed and/or find her a home. Her name is Delilah.)

She considered adding a few lines apologizing for the mess to whoever found the note (could only be the landlord or his wife – no one else would bother looking), but after some deliberation decided it didn't matter. She would be dead. Pomona did, however, add one last sentence:

FYI - The signed first editions are worth some money. Look in bedroom armoire under winter coats. East of Eden, Land of Little Rain, Ask the Dust and others should not be thrown in trash!

Steinbeck, Austin, Fante. Nora had a thing for books about California and for buying rare volumes they could scarcely afford. Growing up Pomona had eaten too many boxes of macaroni so that Nora could collect her prized books, culled from antiquarian bookshops, flea markets, and estate sales. Shame if they were all tossed out. She really wondered if anyone these days cared about first editions.

During Nora's last year of illness they had read many books together. Her mother had been hungry for books, furious she had been cheated of the time she thought she had to read them all.

Every day Pomona brought stacks of volumes to Nora's bedside. Nora brought no rhythm or reason to her requests and choices—a bout of Jane Austen then on to F. Scott Fitzgerald, *The Great Gatsby* and *The Beautiful and the Damned*. They delved into Graham Greene, Joan Didion, Joseph Conrad, Eudora Welty, and Carlos Fuentes before moving on to John Fante, Charles Bukowski, and Shirley Jackson. These readings enlivened Nora. Brought back her spark as she listened to stories and ideas that she loved. But with each passing day her ability to focus shortened as her cancer made clear it would have the final word.

After writing the note and leaving it on the kitchen counter, Pomona had fed Delilah her last can of Savory Chicken Stew. She picked up the purring cat and held her close. "Now you're an orphan like me. You were on your own before and can do it again, so be brave."

Poor Delilah. Leaving her behind was Pomona's biggest regret, far beyond the books. She left open the bedroom window so that the cat could make her own escape when Pomona failed to come home that evening. Pomona knew that Delilah would climb down the pine tree from the second-floor apartment and, once outside, she would hang around the front door mewing until another tenant let her in.

Maybe Stacey would bring Delilah into her apartment. The landlord's wife had always liked the cat, had let her stay when Nora had brought her home from the SPCA, despite the lease's No Pet clause.

"That black cat's got secrets," Stacey used to say with a wink. "I'd like to hear the stories that cat's got to tell."

Only Stacey would wonder why no one was taking care of the cat. Delilah might be the only clue to Pomona's disappearance. No one would miss her otherwise. No one had taken much notice when Pomona had all but vanished from the world a year ago to take care of Nora. Not a riend or coworker had been in touch since she moved to her mother's apartment.

With a deep breath, Pomona opened the car door, pushed herself to stand, and stepped into the street. She smoothed the skirt of her full-skirted sundress. Plump red cherries popped against a crisp white linen background. With its fitted bodice and circle skirt, a $10 bargain from the Salvation Army, it accentuated her small waist and minimized her shapely hips and thighs.

"No one can wear vintage like you," Nora always said. "With your height and olive skin, why, you look like Dolores Del Rio."

Was she still so desperate for Nora's approval that she worried what to wear when jumping from a bridge? Fine. If her mother liked the dress so much then she would wear it to plunge head first into the Arroyo.

Pomona grabbed Nora's ashes from the passenger seat and slammed shut the door. As she did, the book seemed to sigh, "Don't leave me."

"Shut up," she muttered. She had planned to throw *Ramona* into the Arroyo with the ashes before jumping herself but holding the book and scattering the ashes at the same time seemed like too much trouble.

She walked back toward the bridge, cradling the tin. She left *Ramona* in the car because she would never read the book and she didn't feel guilty. People make deathbed promises to the dying all the time that they don't intend to keep.

Pomona leaned against the bridge railing. A sob rose in her throat. She couldn't help remembering what she'd read in a book she'd found under Nora's bed: "Lung disorders are the result of unreleased sadness and grief."

A part of her yearned for that last horrifying year, holed up with Nora and watching the cancer eat her alive from the inside out. The cancer that had started in Nora's right breast a year earlier had, by the time she died, metastasized to her lungs.

Chinese medicine says grief and sadness settle in the lungs.

This explained why a woman who had never smoked cigarettes died of lung cancer. Pomona wondered if Nora had read this too. She must have. Why else was the book under the bed hidden beneath a stack of old *Vogue* magazines?

Pomona reached the midpoint of the concrete arch bridge that curved gracefully over the riverbed, known locally as Suicide Bridge as so many had thrown themselves into the Arroyo. Built in 1913 by the J.A.L. Waddell firm of Kansas City, local lore said the bridge was haunted.

Nora didn't love the Colorado Street Bridge for its tragic stories or Beaux Arts beauty, but rather because literary heroine, Mildred Pierce, had driven across the bridge from her downtrodden and unhappy Glendale home to rendezvous with her Pasadena playboy boyfriend, Monty, in James Cain's noir classic *Mildred Pierce*. Nora had taught the novel in her literature class at Pasadena City College and counted the protagonist among her favorites. Mildred Pierce left her no-good-cheating-lazy husband and made her own way as a successful businesswoman who dressed with great flair.

While that was only part of Mildred's story, it was her independence that mattered most to Nora. The image of Mildred Pierce motoring from Glendale to Pasadena as an independent sexually-liberated woman was the reason Pomona thought to scatter her mother's ashes from the bridge in the first place.

Pomona hoisted herself onto the low bridge wall and grabbed hold of the metal railing that rose from its concrete base. "Such a foolish barrier," she muttered. "So easy to scale the metal posts and drop over to the other side." Staring down 150 feet into the scrubby landscape of oak trees, rocks, and shrubbery, a tiny bubble of excitement rose in her belly, a strange sensation breaking through her pain. Balancing on the wall, she patted her dress pocket to feel the outline of Nora's canister.

A car rumbled by, but Pomona kept her gaze to the south, across the span of the Arroyo Seco, a beautiful view into a sea of oaks. Exhilaration took hold. As she stepped from the concrete wall onto the metal bar that ran along the bottom of the barrier, she had the sensation of floating up and out of her body.

"Throw one leg over, then the other and simply let go," she whispered.

It was sheep-shearing time in Southern California.

"Leave me alone," she screamed as the book flashed before her eyes but this time it was cradled within her papa's elegant nicotine-stained hands. She was leaning her head against her papa Francisco's warm chest.

It was sheep-shearing time in Southern California.

"When I come back, we'll read *Ramona* together," Francisco had said the day he drove away in his Volkswagen Beetle. "Keep it for me until then." That was the last day she saw him alive.

"I tried but Mommy hid it and lied," she wailed into the air.

Pomona was now balanced on the low wall, clinging to the metal posts and ready to jump when she remembered the canister of ashes. There was no way to take the tin from her pocket and open its lid with one hand. She would have to jump with Nora's ashes in her pocket.

It was sheep-shearing time in Southern California.

The sentence was spinning through her head and picking up speed. She stared into the Arroyo. She had to aim straight down to avoid being impaled by an oak tree branch. She would surely be killed on impact.

Grief and sadness settle in the lungs.

"I don't want to stay here, Mama, not without you," Pomona sobbed down into the waiting trees. " I have no one. No one to love me."

No one, no one, the Arroyo echoed back.

Pomona was now straddling the railing, her breath hard and fast. She wobbled and loosened her grip on the post, shifted her weight forward until a baby's breath would have pushed her over.

But sheep shearing was late at Senora Moreno's.

Francisco's voice, forceful as a Santa Ana wind, blew through her head as he read this second line to an entire story, a lost story that he had wanted to share.

From the corner of her eye, Pomona noticed that a car had stopped on the bridge. A person was getting out, waving his hand and calling. She squinted into the distance and realized with delirious relief that it was Francisco, his black raven eyes flashing. He was coming toward her in his mint-green leisure suit, first walking, then jogging, his arms pumping up and down.

"Papa, I'm here," she called, taking her hand from the railing and frantically waving back. Of course Francisco would return in the eleventh hour. They always had that special bond that made Nora a little jealous. Even as a little girl she was all too aware of Nora's displeasure when Francisco gave her too much attention.

"Aren't you two peas in a pod," Nora would say with visible scorn.

Papa was back. He would understand her difficulty in caring for impossible Nora. Together they would forge ahead and her life would begin anew.

Together they would read *Ramona* as he had promised they would twenty years earlier.

She could hear him shouting as he ran even faster towards her, shouting not to jump. Pomona realized he was angry that she hadn't read the book as promised.

The man then said: "I'm a priest. I can help!"

"No!" Pomona screamed. The man wasn't Francisco at all. She could still jump before this strange man reached her but whirling in a cyclone of thoughts about Francisco and Nora, the book and her stupid deathbed promise, Pomona pushed herself back off the railing and fell to the sidewalk, onto to her hands and knees. Then quick as a cat she sprang to her feet just as the man approached. Just as he extended his hand.

His fingers brushed her arm. "God loves you," he said.

Pomona turned and ran back across the bridge, the slippity-slap of her leather sandals hitting the sidewalk. Only when she was safe inside Pearl did she look back.

The street was empty. With fumbling fingers she found the keys where she had dropped them on the floor. She pounded the dash with her fists.

"Shush my darling," she heard her mommy sooth. At that moment all Pomona wanted was for her mommy to hold her close and tell her together that they would face the world as they always had.

She looked at the book waiting patiently upon the seat.

"I knew you'd come back," it whispered.

She had made promises. To Nora. To Francisco. He would not return. Neither would Nora, but she had to read *Ramona*. Then she would return to the bridge. After dark was better anyway. Pomona didn't want another Good Samaritan attempting to wrestle her down, ruining her perfect swan dive into blackness.

Chapter Two

The Righteous will Flourish Like a Palm

Parker Wilson hugged his favorite neighborhood palm tree and laughed with relief, knowing that with each step he took upward into the predawn sky his dread and anxiety would fall away. He shrugged off his backpack and dug out his safety belt, rope, and climbing spurs. He strapped the spurs around his boots so they extended inward from his ankles. He tethered himself to the palm by hooking the rope around its trunk and snapping it to his safety harness. He began walking up the tree's slender trunk by digging his spurs into its sides and shimmying the rope higher with each step.

So many ways to climb a palm and Parker could do them all. One foot after another he walked straight up the palm tree until several moments later he was seventy feet off the ground, his head brushing against the fronds, as high in the sky as the rooftop of a six-story building.

Washingtonia filifera, commonly known as California Fan, is the only palm tree native to the Western United States. This California Fan, the tallest in Elysian Park, was his dear friend and greatest refuge. How many early mornings and late nights he had come to be alone in the fronds, just him and the birds and bats and insects. Alone at the top of a palm with a view of Los Angeles, Parker could begin to untangle his jumbled thoughts and focus on his dilemma: What to do about the arrival of Virginia. He was still in a state of shock that his ex-girlfriend had knocked on his door the previous day, almost a year to the day that he had left Kansas. A whole year. He had believed he was home free. Free of Virginia. But she had destroyed his mistaken notion as her Cadillac idled at the curb.

She had stood like an exotic pink flamingo that had crash-landed on his front porch. "I know you hate your daddy but this is ridiculous," she drawled with arms crossed over her pink silk dress.

He gaped, his stunned mind silent.

"Honey, you don't know the whole story by a long shot and I'm the sorry one left behind," she continued, not seeming to register his shock. "Who in this sick crazy drama is even thinking about my needs? Believe me, I have all the sordid details."

Parker's first impulse was to wrap his hands around Virginia's lovely neck and throttle her into oblivion so, of course, he was angry with himself for giving in to his second impulse, getting into the car and driving to her room at the Hotel Chateau Marmont.

Her skin was warm and soft. He hadn't touched a woman his entire year in California. The palms had given him enough, or so he'd thought, but the moment he lay with Virginia in the cool white cotton sheets that smelled of gardenias, he lost himself.

Virginia meant home. Maybe there's no real escaping the place from which you come.

More than that, Virginia was unadulterated sex. For years he'd been hooked like an addict to his opiate. Until he came to California. Until he found his palms. Maybe she was the one drug he could not quit.

No, he could not believe that or he was dead.

"Don't you want to hear my news," she had cooed as she lay naked in bed and stroked his back with her magic fingers.

He smiled. "Not now. I don't want anything to wreck my high."

From his solitary perch Parker looked over the still sleeping city. All around him palms stretched to the heavens. A blanket of fronds extended as far as he could see. A whole world of palms spread across Los Angeles. Across Southern California. It thrilled him to be part of this lush natural universe, this canopy of life with its own thriving ecosystem. From his special vantage Parker had witnessed so many astonishing things — nests of robin chicks pecking their way out of baby blue shells. Flocks of red-crowned parrots whizzing by as they screeched and squawked. He had been entranced by the charms of hummingbirds and surveilled by a murder of crows. He had watched hawks on telephone wires shake squirming mice in their beaks, shake them to death. Coyotes had loped below as if late for important meetings.

"The righteous will flourish like a palm tree, they will grow like a cedar of Lebanon," Parker whispered. Psalm 92:12. It was the only Psalm he remembered from Sunday school. In his heart Parker knew why it was good for a man to live like a palm. The palm grows slow but steady, from century to century, unmarked by the changing seasons that affect other trees. It does not rejoice in winter's heavy rain, nor droop under the drought and the burning sun of summer. Nor does an urgent wind sway it aside from perfect uprightness. There it stands, from generation to generation looking calmly upon the world below, patiently yielding its large clusters of golden fruit.

Parker had read those words in a book and had made them his mantra. If only he could live with such steady assuredness. If only he could temper his impulses.

Now at the top of the palm, his private cathedral, his mind drifted from Virginia and his father and his younger brother, Caleb, and floated to that special day when he was fourteen and had come with his family to California to visit an elderly aunt stricken by illness and ready to die.

This was when he first fell in love with the palm trees swaying on the shores of Redondo Beach. The majestic trees offered a life beyond slaughtering cattle. On that day fifteen years ago, Parker had found utter peace. The sounds of the waves lapping the sands. The smell of coco butter wafting off the groups of girls in bikinis. The golden light that

touched every surface. This all soothed his fourteen-year-old soul
consumed by anger. Sitting beneath a palm with his cowboy hat shielding
his eyes from the glare, his boots pulled from his feet so his toes could
wiggle in the sand, Parker had listened to the call of circling seagulls and
the ever-present anger he felt at home melted away. At home he courted
chaos. In the California sunshine Parker's self-defeating behaviors
diminished. He came alive in the Los Angeles landscape, so different
from the wide-open Kansas prairie that stretched so far you could watch
a lightning storm move for hours. There he could never escape the
prairie dust that filled his nose and covered his boots with brown soot.

But what had surprised Parker most among the lush and exotic flora
blooming and blossoming all around in this Garden of Eden was the sea
of endless palms that lorded overhead. Palms gave shape to the open air
and aroused his imagination. He had never seen anything like these
feather dusters. At night, sleeping on the foldout couch in his aunt's
living room, the palms had swayed like hula dancers before his eyes.

He noticed how the San Gabriel Mountains to the north were
shrouded in fog. How pink light warmed the sky. A breeze rustled
through the fronds. A family of sparrows began their morning chirps. A
woodpecker, level with Parker on the next palm over, started his day's
work in earnest. Rat-tat-tat – the woodpecker's red head was a blur as it
drilled a hole in the tree's trunk in which to store his acorn.

As if a gift from heaven, a flock of green red-crowned parrots flew
across the sky. He counted twenty, maybe thirty squawking as they landed
in the tree above his head and began scratching out a breakfast of insects.

Parker hugged the palm. He could not imagine a place more
beautiful than the paradise that stretched around him. He wasn't blind.
He saw the freeways and snarls of traffic, the cancerous concrete that
smothered the region. Tenacious life still pulsed beneath the urban cover.
The earth was fertile with a cosmic force that bubbled to the surface and
ignited the trees and plants. Los Angeles had a powerful energy field and
palm trees were the antennas that pulled in this energy from the ground

and the sky. Parker closed his eyes and listened to the determined woodpecker.

Rat-tat-tat.

The sky brightened. It was time to go. He had plenty of work and many more palms to climb. He had to get rid of Virginia, once and for all. The palms would calm his soul. They would help him resist her.

Chapter Three
The Huntington Palm Garden

P omona put Pearl into drive and began traveling east on Colorado Boulevard, past its long expanse of shops, banks, and restaurants. She was only dimly aware of her throbbing hands and knees, of traffic passing all around, of honking horns and morning sounds. She knew enough to heed red lights and stop signs but her mind was in a fog. She passed the city college where Nora had taught freshman composition and literature classes for almost twenty years. She drove aimlessly, veering off Colorado Boulevard, moving through neighborhoods of small bungalow-style homes before re-entering a business district where she caught a reflection of Pearl in a storefront window.

A flash of memory hit and she saw Pearl, newer and cleaner, gliding along the Baja Coast, her turquoise paint twinkling in the light, twinkling with the same radiance of the ocean.

Exactly five years earlier, Nora and Pomona had driven Pearl to San Felipe to celebrate Pomona's twenty-fifth birthday. The Mexican resort town on the Sea of Cortez was a six-hour drive from Pasadena. Nora had proposed the trip with great fanfare.

"C'mon, mother-daughter adventure. A celebration to end all twenty-fifth birthday celebrations. What you got going on otherwise?"

Pomona had been wary. She had always hated her birthday and she knew Nora's propensity for bad planning. But her mother was right that she didn't have a friend throwing a party or a boyfriend taking her to a romantic dinner. Nora was saving her from another lonely birthday. Anyway, who could say no to Nora once she had a plan?

It had been great at first. They spent four days lying on white sands, drinking beer, eating lobster, and laughing. Nora was her most beautiful then, her lean, athletic body still at ease in a bikini. Her strawberry blonde curls a mess of tangles, freckles grazing her fair Scottish cheeks. Her mother radiated light, attracting children and men like fireflies to a flame.

Nora twirled on the sand in a green and white polka-dot bikini while Pomona had worn a stupid one-piece black swimsuit with a little skirt to hide her full hips and fleshy thighs.

The image buzzed around Pomona like a hungry mosquito. Nora twirling on the sand, laughing into the sky, Pomona slouched on her towel, marveling at her mother's natural radiance.

On day four of their Mexican holiday, Nora made an announcement at breakfast. "We spent our last pesos on these huevos rancheros," she said with a rueful smile. "Blew a lot of money last night." Nora's raised eyebrows seemed to suggest it was Pomona who had insisted on the fancy dinner at La Fonda. That it was she who had ordered steaks and margaritas.

"Cadillacs," Nora had informed the waiter, as if him serving anything less would have been an insult. "Double Cadillacs." She had also, in a haze of tequila, over-tipped the mariachi band as they had played *La Paloma* over and over.

"You must have more money in the hotel room," Pomona had said.

"I turned over my purse and nothing came out but bottle caps and receipts. Good thing I already paid for the room or we'd really be screwed. Sadly, the gas tank is empty. I meant to fill it before we started drinking. But… oh well…"

"What kind of mother takes her daughter to Mexico without enough money?" The dinner had only made Pomona bloat, the sugary Margaritas still percolating through her gut.

Of course, as easily as Nora got into trouble, she found a way out. Nora always knew how to work an angle and find her advantage, as slight as that advantage might be.

They traded the spare tire and seat covers for a tank of gas. The owner of the Pemex station gave them Tequila shots and placed his hand on her mother's ass as they danced to Mexican ballads playing on the radio in the cool station garage. The swarthy man with sinewy arms was a good dancer and Pomona wondered what more Nora would have done with him had she been traveling alone.

"Don't be such a prude," Nora had laughed as Pomona sulked in the car. "We got the gas, didn't we? Always so serious. What's the worst that could happen? Life is fun!"

Nora heard music in the air. She made friends with strangers, with grease-soaked men in garages who shared their grimy bottles of tequila. But when the party ended, when the boyfriend stopped calling, she expected Pomona to be there – to stay by her side and hold her hand, make her tea and put her to bed. Whether nursing a broken heart or caring for Nora when sick and dying, Pomona was always by her side.

But Nora could not charm and seduce death as she did men. Fighting death wasn't hooking a man. It wasn't getting a teachers' discount from a bookseller. It wasn't convincing a landlord to disregard his pet policy by befriending his wife.

Pomona turned right onto Allen Avenue. She crossed the Pasadena city limits and entered the rarified world of San Marino with its long blocks of grand mansions perched above manicured lawns. After a mile, Allen Avenue dead-ended at the gates of the grandest estate of them all, the Huntington Library.

Her heart jumped at the serendipity. It was perfect. Francisco had loved the Huntington.

She passed through the entrance gate into the institution's sprawling parking lot. She guided Pearl into a shaded spot beneath a Jacaranda tree budding with purple springtime blossoms. With new resolve Pomona touched the book's worn cover. The Huntington Gardens were the perfect place to read before returning to the bridge. Francisco had brought her to these public gardens when she was small, to walk the grounds and see the Koi swimming in the ponds of the Japanese Garden. Together, they had wandered the estate's old orange grove. He told her stories of picking oranges as a boy in Riverside with his itinerant farmer father, who had been a Bracero.

"A Mexican guest worker to the U.S. in the 1940s, who could do the hard labor, could work in the heat and sun when others wouldn't," Francisco told her. "They called him a wetback but that's not true. He didn't have to swim across the Rio Grande. He entered through Texas with a work contract from the U.S. government and was sent to work on the farms in California."

Francisco and his father had worked the fields of Stockton. They had picked lettuce, and even strawberries in Camarillo. But this was later, in the late 1950s, when Francisco was a teenager. Pomona had never met her Abuelo Pedro, who'd died long before she was born. "Worn out before his time by the backbreaking work under the beating sun," Francisco said.

With Nora's canister ensconced in her pocket and *Ramona* in hand, Pomona crossed the long parking lot to the Huntington's open-air entrance pavilion and bought a ticket with the 20 dollars she had in her wallet. The only money she had left. She passed the gift shop and entered the gardens where she was greeted by a towering stand of one hundred-year-old bamboo. In the distance, due west, loomed the grand Huntington mansion where Henry and Arabella Huntington had once lived their expensive and luxurious lives.

Pomona's plan was simple: she would speed-read the book in the Japanese Garden, then return to the bridge. Though several hundred pages long, it wasn't *War and Peace* or *Anna Karenina* and if she just read one word after another without losing focus, the words would add up to sentences, which would stack into paragraphs. With some luck she could finish its three hundred pages in four or five hours. If Helen Hunt Jackson had written an overwrought love story as Nora asserted, it would be heavy on the long-winded flowery prose. To save time, she would skip long sections of description or rumination that didn't forward the plot. And then she would have fulfilled her promise to Nora and she could get on with her plan.

Pomona walked toward the mansion, beyond which lay the serene Japanese Garden. But her knees, scraped and achy from falling to the sidewalk, resisted. Her gaze settled upon the top of a palm tree that rose a short distance before her. Its fronds reached out and tickled the sky. The fronds seemed to beckon.

Pomona had never before been to the palm garden. Mr. Huntington had created all sorts of gardens on his magnificent estate during his lifetime. She had over the years, spent time in the rose, Shakespeare herb and desert gardens. She had never been the least bit interested in palm trees.

Why would she bother when palms lined the streets?

The palm garden was hidden between the desert and the Australian gardens. It functioned more as a transitional garden that one walked through to get to another more interesting setting

I shouldn't deviate from my plan, Pomona thought, and yet she found herself stepping off the well-worn path and heading for the palm.

Chapter Four
Land of Sunshine and Flowers

As if pulled into a vortex, Pomona veered into the palm garden. The garden was situated on a grassy slope, beyond a stand of bamboo. Entering the congregation of towering palms, she looked around and did not see another soul. It was quiet, serene, inviting. Pomona regretted overlooking this quiet spot in all her years of visits. She would never come again.

She chose a beckoning palm and sat down upon the manicured lawn beneath. From her purse she pulled out the book. She stared at the cover. First published in 1884, this was a 1913 Little, Brown and Company edition, with a cover illustration by the artist N.C. Wyeth. It depicted lovely Ramona with her glossy black hair sitting horseback and being led down a canyon trail by a handsome Indian man. She wore a full black skirt with a red shawl. The man, Alessandro, wore white pants and a white tunic with a turquoise blanket resting over his broad shoulder. Ramona's head was held high but her face was turned. Her eyes were full of sadness and hooded in despair. Alessandro, tall and dignified, gazed in the opposite direction, toward the mountain canyon.

The scene was filled with romance but tragedy loomed over their stoic faces as they walked from sunlight into shadow. As a girl Pomona had always imagined that she was Ramona, just as beautiful and just as loved. Even their names sounded similar.

Pomona. Ramona. Ramona. Pomona.

Of course she was neither although her father told her that she and Ramona had the same black hair that he loved. Pomona held the book to her nose and inhaled a scent of cigar smoke pungent and sweet that took her back to a long-ago night in their first family house, the old Spanish duplex. There they spent evenings sitting beneath the backyard's tangerine tree. Pomona saw the red glowing tip of Francisco's cigar, heard the clinking of ice cubes in his glass.

Had his mother already given him the book then? She must have. Abuela Maria only came to visit once, when Pomona was a little girl, so that must have been at that same time.

Without warning, a vision of Francisco flashed before her that she did not want to see from that terrible day when she was ten. There he was, throwing his battered suitcase into the backseat of his Volkswagen Beetle. After he and Nora had argued all morning. After Nora had heaved *Ramona* at his head and he had retrieved it from the dirt patch beside the Oleander bush.

"We were once like them, running away together, believing we shared something special. I love you as much as Alessandro loves Ramona," he told Nora. "Don't throw away our love. You must fight."

"Fight for what? More misery? I hope I never see you again."

Pomona shuddered at the memory and flipped ahead to the table of contents:

Ramona, A Story By Helen Hunt Jackson.
With an Introduction by A.C. Vroman.
Boston
Little, Brown, and Company 1913

Each chapter was marked with Roman numerals and decorative ink-drawn headings, the first depicting the interior of the Camulos Chapel within the Rancho Camulos, the supposed home of Ramona somewhere in Ventura, California, so the text said. Pomona squinted to see the delicate illustration of saints and religious figurines filling the chapel alongside plants and floral bouquets perched upon small tables.

She began to read the introduction:

The story of Ramona has become so well known on this continent that few who visit this land of sunshine and flowers but take an interest in the location of the story and the points and incidents that Mrs. Jackson has so vividly pictured. As is generally understood, every incident in this story has fact for its foundation, even down to the minutest detail of the house of the Morenos.

That horrible day when her parents had fought, Pomona had cried and begged her father not to leave. Francisco had wrapped Pomona in his muscled arms that smelled faintly of fresh cut grass. Without thinking, she reached around her neck and unclapsed the necklace Abuela Maria had given her. It was a long metal chain from which a silver pendant with the Virgin de Guadalupe hung.

"She will watch over you, mija," Abuela Maria had said when she had hung the necklace around Pomona's neck. In that moment, the last time Pomona ever saw her father, she had hung the necklace around his neck and said the same. "She will watch over you, Daddy."

He handed her the book. "If your mother doesn't want *Ramona*, you keep it. It once belonged to your abuela, my mother. Don't cry, Pomona. Your mommy needs me to find a way to make more money. I'll come back and when I do, we'll read the book together."

"I'm reading the book now. For you, Papa," Pomona whispered as she continued:

It was sheep-shearing time in Southern California; but sheep shearing was late at Senora Moreno's. The Fates had seemed to combine to put it off. In the first place, Felipe Moreno had been ill. He was the Senora's eldest son, and since his father's death had been at the head of his mother's house. Without him, nothing could be done on the ranch, the Senora thought. It had been always, "Ask Senor Felipe," "Go to Senor Felipe," "Senor Felipe will attend to it, ever since Felipe had had the dawning of a beard on his handsome face.

Pomona raised her eyes, unsure if she could penetrate these antiquated sentences about a certain Senora and her son Felipe on a California Rancho. But desperate to keep turning pages, she plowed on:

In truth, it was not Felipe, but the Senora, who really decided all questions from greatest to least, and managed everything on the place, from the sheep pastures to the artichoke-patch; but nobody except the Senora herself knew this.

So, this Felipe had a pushy mother too. Just as she wondered about Felipe's mother, a long shadow fell upon her.

"That Phoenix Canarias is spectacular," a voice said. Pomona glanced up to see a man standing before her. Startled, she clutched her book to her chest and stared at this man casting his long, mid-afternoon shadow upon her. Towering over her, unruly brown hair fell across his forehead. Muscular thighs pushed against his blue jeans. He was busting out of himself. He stared at the palm tree that rose above Pomona like an overgrown pineapple top.

"That tree is in fruit," he said. "See the heavy clusters of date-like fruit between the leaves?" He gazed at the tree with open adoration, as if it were a favorite child.

Pomona said nothing. She only heard her heart pounding against her chest. She had hardly had a conversation with another human being for a week, except for the Forest Lawn lady and the angry driver on the bridge. She had never considered that a person might try to talk to her today, that she might need to guard against human intrusion. She had believed she was invisible to the outside world, already a ghost. Flustered and nervous she kept reading:

An exceedingly clever woman for her day and generation was Senora Gonzaga Moreno,—as for that matter, exceedingly clever for any day and generation; but exceptionally clever for the day and generation to which she belonged. Her life, the mere surface of it, if it had been written, would have made a romance, to grow hot and cold over: sixty years of the best of old Spain, and the wildest of New Spain, Bay of Biscay, Gulf of Mexico, Pacific Ocean,—the waves of them all had tossed destinies for the Senora.

The man was undeterred by her reading. He stepped in close and circled the tree. Pomona lifted her head to see him caress its rough trunk. Suddenly, the man was standing unbearably close in his dusty jeans and worn sneakers. Pomona was about ready to get up and slink away to the rose garden when the man jumped at the tree and wrapped his legs around its skinny trunk. Hands and feet reaching and pulling, he moved up the tree until his hands grasped its sturdy lower fronds. Within seconds, he was twenty feet above her head.

"Hello down there," he bellowed in a voice that could surely be heard in the gift shop. "You're a beautiful sight, reading your book beneath this palm. What's your name?"

Pomona stared back dumbfounded. Her name? Why? What for?

"I said, what's your name," the persistent man called.

"Pomona," she called, blushing like mad.

"Pomona, Pomona," he mused, his legs still embracing the palm's trunk. "Pomona as in the Roman Goddess of fruit trees? Your right hand bears a pruning knife and you care for orchards, leading streams of water to them so their thirsty roots might drink? That Pomona?"

She nodded, dazed by his answer. People always thought Nora named her daughter for the City of Pomona, out by Ontario in the Inland Empire, or for the 60 Freeway. No one in California, land of fruit and orchards, knew anything about the goddess Pomona of fruitful abundance. Nora had plucked the name from a Roman mythology book while pregnant.

With nimble feet, the man pushed back off the tree and dropped to the ground, rolling over the grass and stopping at her feet.

"Are you hurt?" Pomona exclaimed.

"No," he laughed. "I've trained myself to take jumps like that. I usually climb into palms a lot taller than this one."

The man folded his legs crossways and picked up the book she had laid in the grass. Pomona reddened. What gall for this stranger to pick up Francisco's book. She wanted to snatch it back, but her arms stayed frozen by her side. She could not move a muscle, could scarcely breathe.

"Excuse me. That book is special to me," Pomona finally managed.

"I'm sorry. My name is Parker." He looked up from the page. "Parker Wilson. I'm from Kansas, but I guess I've already lost my Midwest manners."

Pomona had never known anyone from Kansas. She had to think. Dorothy and the Wizard of Oz came to mind. Tornadoes, ruby slippers, small dogs. "You live there?"

"Used to but came to Los Angeles a while ago." Parker's gaze moved around Pomona's face and body in a friendly, easy way, as if he found every angle and aspect of her agreeable. His eyes stopped on her underarms where the warm day had induced sweat to seep across the seams of her sleeves. He acted as if he had never seen perspiration on a woman before, and yet found it admirable. "I've never seen you in the palm garden before."

"I've never been here before," Pomona stammered. "I mean, I've been to the Huntington lots of times, but not to the palm garden…. Usually the rose or Japanese…the cactus."

"The palm garden is the best part of the estate," Parker exclaimed as if making a proclamation for the ages. His blue eyes glistened. The air around him rippled.

Then Pomona knew. Parker was a dream. While reading, she had fallen asleep in the grass. She remembered going into strange dream states when Nora was close to dying and Pomona could only sleep in two-hour bouts. They were often weird and scary nightmares with Nora writhing in pain, begging for more morphine. This dream was more Alice in Wonderland. She stared back at Parker, sure at any moment he would vanish like the White Rabbit.

"Even before I came to California, I read about Henry Huntington and how he planted his palm garden in 1905, four acres of palms from around the world. Most palm trees in L.A. aren't indigenous. Many were planted early in the twentieth century when this palm tree craze took hold. Cheap to buy."

Why was this stranger giving her random facts about palm trees? Pomona wondered if he was one of the Huntington docents on break from giving garden tours. But docents climbing into trees was surely frowned upon by management.

"In the 1920s Pasadena planted so many on Colorado Boulevard city officials considered renaming it 'Street of A Thousand Palms.'" Parker broke into a sheepish grin. "I go a little overboard with palm tree trivia but it's so fascinating. Someone once said that if God hadn't created palm trees, L.A. would have. What about you, Pomona? What brings you to read a book beneath a palm on this beautiful day?"

Pomona opened then shut her mouth as she tried to make sense of the bewildering turn of events. Something about this man sparked a desire to share some aspect of herself. She considered confiding that she planned to jump off the Colorado Street Bridge, but that she first had to read this old-fashioned story because her dead mother had believed it was the only way to remove a curse that kept them both from finding love, which would release her so she could die in peace.

A melting sensation warmed Pomona's chest. She could tell him that maybe she really did want to read the book and understand why her father had been so drawn to the story. She might even confess that she had done her best to forget her father after he disappeared twenty years ago but now she missed him with an unbearable ache that burned through her heart. She had not had a friend to talk to for so long. She had only had Nora, who, in the end, was sick and demented, vomiting day and night and babbling about curses, missed opportunities, and lost love.

"What is it?" Parker asked. He knelt down so that she was looking directly into his sun-strained eyes that seemed to brim with heightened sensitivity. "Your secret is safe with me."

"It's my birthday," Pomona said. The words slipped from her lips and hovered in the air like a hummingbird startled from a bush.

At that exact moment, a tiny blonde woman in red heels strode over and stood between them.

"Parker, I thought I'd lost you for good," the woman said with a frown. "I looked everywhere. One minute we're in the Library, looking at the Gutenberg Bible, and the next minute I'm standing there alone. Why'd you even bring me to this boring place?"

As the woman spoke, Parker continued staring into Pomona's eyes. Embarrassed, she broke her gaze and looked at the woman standing before them, arms akimbo, sun glinting off her armful of gold bracelets. Her buttery hair glistened. She had beautifully painted blood red fingernails and Pomona saw them running along Parker's back as her white skin melded with his in the dark room of her imagination.

Then the dream became stranger.

"Calm down, Virginia. You know I came to see the palms," Parker said, slowly standing. "Go appreciate the bible and I'll stay here in the sunshine with my friend, Pomona. I'll wait here until you come back."

Pomona wondered if Parker would tell this Virginia that it was her birthday and together they could laugh at the obvious and unfortunate fact that she was all alone in the world and would always be alone. But Parker did not say a word. The woman's presence had turned his friendly manner ice cold.

Virginia glared at Pomona and squeaked a nervous laugh. "Shut up, Parker. I'm not doing anything without you." As Virginia spoke, she lost an inch of height as her spiky heels sank into the soft grass. Even with her shoes stuck in the ground she was able to grab Parker's hand and look straight at Pomona as if to say, in no uncertain terms, he's mine.

Somehow Pomona managed to stand, unfolding to her full height of five-foot-ten-inches as this jealous woman clutching Parker's hand sank deeper into the grass. Virginia had those improbable legs, tiny calves hard and round as unripe peaches and thighs skinny as twigs. Pomona leaned against the palm, her head spinning. A flush of desire rippled through her body. She had never felt so seen by another person, as if she were an open book. Rivulets of sweat dripped down her back. Pomona glanced at Parker. Both he and Virginia stared back.

"Don't mind me," Pomona said. "I've got to go." Without a backwards glance, she stumbled from the palm garden, back through the entrance pavilion, and to the parking lot. When she reached Pearl, her shaking hand could barely guide the key into the lock.

Finally, the door opened, and she slid onto the seat. Tears began to fall. They would not stop for almost an hour. Pomona cried as she recalled the entire day and night after Nora had died. She had lain beside Nora's dead body, unable to move a muscle to call anyone – even the mortuary. The moon drifting across the sky, she had kept a firm hand on Nora's chest, the warmth draining from her mother's body one degree at a time. For twenty-four hours she had lain beside her dead, cold mother, petrified with fright that she would have to get up and continue her life.

Pomona cried that she had come so close to jumping off the bridge, that she did not know a single person who cared, and that even if she read *Ramona* she would never know her father. She cried that even if she read the book and broke the curse, it was all now too late for love.

Pomona cried for what lay before her now.

Something had happened in the palm garden when this strange man looked at her with his piercing blue eyes. A quicksilver life force had moved into her soul and rattled her bones. His gaze somehow upended her despair and turned the worst day of her life spinning on its head. Nothing made sense anymore—not even returning to the bridge.

Chapter Five
Roman Goddess of Orchards

Virginia stood rigid. "Tell me again, how do you know that bizarre woman?"

Parker shrugged. "I just met her, Virginia. She was sitting on the lawn and I said hello."

He thrust his shaking hand in his pocket. He couldn't explain. He was thrown by the dark-haired woman sitting beneath the tree in the Huntington's palm garden reading a book. The moment he saw her, he wanted to know her name. Hear her voice. One look at her face and he was tantalized by the arc of her eyebrow. The curve of her neck. At the same time, the deep sadness in her brown eyes disturbed him. Pulled him in deeper.

When she said her name was Pomona, Parker thought maybe he had actually stumbled upon a real Roman goddess lost in the urban garden of Los Angeles with no more orchards to cultivate. That would explain the sadness, wouldn't it?

Sad, because she had lost all her orchards, cut down and covered by asphalt, buildings, and parking lots. California certainly did not have the orchards it once had, the sweep of fruit trees that Parker had found when he'd come from Kansas, the first time as a boy.

Maybe this solitary woman was a Huntington garden statue who'd come to life. Parker imagined her breaking out of plaster that had encased her soul for hundreds of years, jumping from the pedestal and strolling through the gardens. She seemed lost in time. Born in the wrong century.

He had been racing to his favorite palm when this woman stopped him short. A beauty sitting beneath its canopy of fronds with a rare elegance. The first thing Parker wanted to do was show Pomona his strength, his talent, his swan dive. So he climbed into the palm to impress this stranger, so beautiful in her dress covered with cherries.

Then Virginia, with her impeccable timing, showed up and ruined everything.

As Virginia chattered on, Parker's gaze lingered on the spot beneath the tree where this mysterious woman had sat moments ago. *Ramona* lay on the ground. The hardcover book seemed to emanate light. It pulsed with life. It was clearly from another era, like his grandfather's prized encyclopedia volumes that lined his maple bookcases back home.

Virginia was now cleaning dirt from her stiletto heels, muttering as she wiped them with a hankie from her Hermes handbag. Parker sat down hard in front of the book. In the moment of Virginia's distraction, Parker glanced at the book's jacket to see a beautiful woman sitting upon a horse being led down a steep mountain path by an Indian dressed in all white. The title read:

Ramona, By Helen Hunt Jackson. The Greatest Story of California Ever Told.

Parker had never heard of this story. He was struck by how much the woman sitting on the horse looked like Pomona. Both had the same black hair and wistful expression, a sadness yet inner dignity.

Ramona. Pomona. Even their names rhymed.

Pomona. Ramona. Both exotic flowers sprouting from the earth.

Parker slipped the book under his shirt as Virginia stepped back into her shoes.

Virginia pouted, clearly not convinced that his exchange with Pomona was innocent. "These Jimmy Choos cost $300, not meant for slogging through the mud."

"This isn't mud. It's just dirt, and your damn shoes cost almost as much as my rent." Parker knew it annoyed Virginia to point out the vast discrepancies in their spending habits.

Virginia ignored the bait. "What were you talking about that she would run away like a frightened ostrich? This is supposed to be our day together. You know I have something important to tell you."

"I really don't want to know." Parker knew he sounded like a fool.

Virginia turned away. She pulled a compact and lipstick from her purse and painted her lips an unnatural shade of pink. She was plotting her next move, Parker knew. Virginia turned back around; her bright pink lips twisted into a forced smile.

"Let's order Champagne in the tea room and I'll tell you there."

"I can't," Parker said with a shrug. "Just remembered I've got things to do."

He wouldn't let her corner him.

"Fine then," Virginia huffed. "Two can play this game. Go ahead and be an ass. You're still mad that I tracked you down, but you'll thank me later." She strode across the grass, her stiletto heels sinking into the ground. She pulled them out with determination and continued on as she quickly disappeared behind the stand of bamboo.

Parker had no desire to chase Virginia, not with this mysterious book in his possession. It changed everything. He took it from beneath his shirt, opened its cover, and flipped through the yellowed pages to the introduction. The first line read:

The story of Ramona has become so well known on this continent that few who visit this land of sunshine and flowers but take an interest in the location of the story and the points and incidents that Mrs. Jackson has so vividly pictured.

This land of sunshine and flowers had already captivated Parker. He understood the appeal. He studied the fragile cover. He should take the book to the main office and leave it in the lost and found box. Pomona could find it there. But Parker did not trust leaving the book with anyone else. Also he could not bear to part with this essential link that might somehow bring them together again. He slid the book into his backpack and headed for the exit.

He left the Huntington and walked over to Oxford Road that led him through the surrounding exclusive enclave of San Marino mansions down to Huntington Drive where he headed west. Huntington Drive was a major east-west thoroughfare that traversed San Marino and the City of Alhambra before it merged with Mission Road and continued into Downtown L.A.

Parker took big strides, feeling the weight of the book in his backpack, the anticipation of opening its pages. It was eleven miles from the Huntington to his house near Dodger Stadium in Elysian Park. He had walked it before and would walk it again. He loved walking through Los Angeles, especially in late afternoons when the city was bathed in its famous golden light. The magic light poured through the fronds of hundreds of palms that he passed on his walk home. It filled him with elation. Each tree sang singing its own song and he heard the chorus all around.

Something had happened in that palm garden, a bewitching confluence of events. He had met a lovely and enigmatic girl and, if he believed in love at first sight, which in that moment he did, he had just met his soul mate. His salvation.

The day had taken an unexpected turn and it filled him with a wonderful rush of hope and renewal that he desperately needed.

Chapter Six
Delilah Had Always Been True

P omona drove in circles around the streets of San Marino, down Orlando Avenue and onto Rosalind Street, up to Arden and across Lombardy. It was easy to get lost in the narrow, winding streets edged with lush gardens (English gardens that had no right to thrive in Southern California's arid climate) and large graceful houses set back behind rolling verdant lawns. This was the rarefied world of well-to-do families, enterprising fathers, doting mothers, private schools, and sleep-away summer camps.

Swimming pools and tennis courts. Not movie stars. Those were across town, in Beverly Hills and the Hollywood Hills, but still, a fantasy world. How many times she had driven these streets imagining this perfect life, a father in a suit with a good income. A mother who stayed home and cooked meals.

The last outing she had taken with Francisco had been a daylong excursion to the Santa Anita Racetrack. He had placed $5 in her name on Ferdinand and she had won $100, a fortune that made her swoon for a month.

During lunch in the clubhouse she had matched his whiskey sours with Shirley Temples and they had laughed and laughed.

"We're the same, you and me," he told her on the drive home. "I know your Grandma and Grandpa Donnelly don't like me much but we must be proud of who we are. We may be brown but we're brown like the earth and the earth is what's real. The rest is bullshit."

"Does Daddy know our new address," Pomona had repeatedly asked Nora after they had moved into an apartment on the other side of town, a few months after Francisco had driven away in his blue Volkswagen bug. They had moved because Nora could no longer afford to rent a three-bedroom house on her income alone.

"Yes, of course, darling."

"Why hasn't he come to see me?"

"I don't know, but let me dial his phone number for you. Here, listen. It just rings and rings. Guess he's too busy for us. Well, we don't need him. I know it's hard to understand but you're better off without his erratic ways. You'll see what I mean when you're older. Not a positive influence, taking you, ten years old, to the racetrack for goodness sake."

Now Pomona wondered just what phone number Nora had dialed and what information she might have had about Francisco's whereabouts.

When Pomona turned onto Lombardy Road a third time, a white cat darted from beneath a parked car and ran into the street. She slammed on the brakes, missing the cat by inches.

"Stupid cat," she cried as the animal skedaddled across a lawn.

Delilah.

Suddenly, more than anything in the world, Pomona wanted to hold the cat. Bury her face into its black fur. Delilah had always been true, had come home each night, and had watched over Nora with her soulful green eyes.

Without thinking, Pomona had thrown the feline out on its head. How could she have done that? She turned around and headed north on Allen Avenue, back towards Pasadena. She parked Pearl outside the apartment on Mentor Street and ran to the building.

"Delilah," she called, peering under the pink and white oleander hedge that bordered the building. "Come here, kitty. Come home."

Pomona let herself into the once grand but worn lobby of the Spanish Revival building, an elegant madam with its pink and turquoise deco floor tile and wrought iron banisters. "Delilah," she called as she kneeled below the row of mailboxes lining the lobby's smooth plaster wall.

The cat was huddled in the corner beneath the mailboxes.

"Dear Delilah," Pomona murmured, scooping the black ball of fur into her arms. She carried Delilah back into Nora's apartment that she had never planned to see again. Her note was still resting on the counter in the small galley kitchen, waiting to be found. She crumpled it and threw it into the trash.

If not for turning into the palm garden instead of going straight ahead into the Japanese garden, Pomona would be standing on the Colorado Street Bridge now. She glanced out the kitchen window. The sky had darkened to the color of a ripened purple plum, the exact time she had planned to return.

Instead she had met a man who had climbed into a palm tree and called her his friend. Who had looked at her so deeply he seemed to have seen all of her in a way she'd never before been seen. Except maybe by her lost father. Her stomach churned with desire for this palm climbing stranger.

Delilah in her arms, Pomona crawled into her bed and fell into a deep sleep.

Chapter Seven
Working the Kill Floor

That night Parker dreamed that Pomona was harvesting corn. She was bathed in a golden luster as the late afternoon sun sank into the shimmering Kansas fields. In the sheen of the light he took her hands, stroking them with his fingertips as one does with fine silks and brocades. Suddenly tall green thunderclouds swooped in. In the distance came a funnel of blackness. A tornado about to touch down.

He woke with a start and stared at the ceiling, its paint flaking and peeling every which way. He glanced at his bedside clock – 4:30 a.m. Sitting up, Parker took *Ramona* from beneath his pillow and squinted at its cover. He imagined Pomona as Ramona, sitting on the horse and he as the Indian, her protector, leading her down a steep mountain path, just the two of them together, safe and happy. In that moment he wanted this more than anything. Even more, perhaps, than the palms.

Wherever they were going, they weren't in Kansas. Not many majestic mountains there. Garden City, Kansas, was definitely misnamed. There was nothing garden-like about it. Filled with meatpacking plants, its annual Beef Empire Festival brought folks from all over the region to celebrate the slaughtering of cows. His father's 5,000-acre cattle ranch and slaughterhouse was the biggest and most profitable around. It employed more people than any other in the region. Amos Wilson was king of the Beef Empire Festival. He was also notorious as brutally tough and obsessively hardworking. He was hated by his workers for squeezing from them all their blood, sweat, and dignity.

Parker grimaced at the thought of Amos Wilson and his authoritarian power that silenced any room he entered. Everything his father stood for made him sick. As he swung his legs from the bed a familiar cloud of claustrophobia overwhelmed him.

Growing up in Kansas had filled Parker with trepidation for its wide-open dusty spaces where he felt fully exposed with no place to hide. When he first got away, three years ago, to New York City, he discovered the power of anonymity. He loved the urban chaos where he could hide in plain sight, walking through crowds all day and never encountering a familiar face. This was total bliss after living twenty-six years in Garden City, population 25,000, where everyone regarded him as Amos Wilson's wild older son who wouldn't play by the rules. A dreamer with a reckless temperament who possessed the most beautiful girl in town, the beguiling Virginia Brooks. He knew how people regarded them; they both knew the power they wielded together. How it opened doors and excused their excesses. No one dared complain about their fast driving and rowdy partying, causing a scene at the country club pool as they threw beer cans into the bushes. That he once sowed mayhem with that power now filled him with shame.

Parker made his way to the bathroom, his bare feet padding along the scratched oak wood floors. His house was small and worn, held together by spit and a prayer, as his mother used to say. It consisted of a living room, bedroom, and kitchen. The paint chipped. The bathroom linoleum peeling. Parker didn't care about the appearance of the place. He loved that he could sense the life that had unfolded in this house for a hundred years. It was deep in the plaster walls and creaking floorboards. Marked by deep nicks in the kitchen sink's porcelain.

Back in the bedroom, Parker threw on his pants, t-shirt, and shoes. He headed out the front door.

Parker loved the old neighborhood of Elysian Park surrounding Dodger Stadium with its rickety wood houses, its mix of people and its palms. Before Dodger Stadium was built in the 1960s the area was known as Chavez Ravine. Its three neighborhoods of La Loma, Bishop, and Palo Verde were filled with hundreds of Mexican-American families. In the 1950s they all got kicked out in the name of progress. Poor, brown people always got the short end of the stick. Parker had seen that play out in Kansas, especially in the meatpacking industry.

In Elysian Park at this time of day it would only be him and a few homeless guys. Sticking *Ramona* in his backpack, Parker ran down the street and into the park, to greet his favorite California Fan palm.

At the tree's base Parker took off his backpack and dug out his safety belt, his rope, and climbing spurs. It was comforting to feel *Ramona* tucked into a side pocket. From his high perch he planned to read some passages from the book, hoping they might reveal clues about its owner. He had already checked the pages for a last name or phone number, a business card tucked close to the spine, but he found nothing that could lead him back to Pomona. Only on the back inside cover did he find a nameplate of heavy card-stock. Hermoine Delphina Gregorio Sandoval was written in a flourish of cursive. The handwriting was clearly from a long ago time.

As Parker climbed into the palm he could think only of the enigmatic woman sitting beneath the Huntington palm with her dark, unsettling beauty. Hers was not the kind of beauty that came with perfect blonde sameness, Virginia's kind of beauty, celebrated on magazine covers. Pomona was instead perfect as a palm tree. Also rooted to the earth. He was filled with a similar awe and wonder.

Parker realized that their chance encounter might only have been a single moment of grace. And yet a moment is a moment and he could not ignore its arrival. Why couldn't a woman like Pomona love him? Parker's stomach tightened. With such a gentle accepting love he would no longer crave Virginia's addictive high. He could begin anew.

Perched on the palm with his head in the fronds, Parker was ready to take out *Ramona* and begin to read when, looking out north toward the mountains, a shadowy vision startled him. He rubbed his eyes as cold crept through his neck. Stretching before him were not the streets of Los Angeles but the dusty ranch with its endless pens of restless cattle mooing, stomping, and snorting. The cows were crammed together, besieged by flies and reeking of molten feces that had once accosted him every morning when he went to work. He gagged. Bitter bile filled his mouth. Until now death had not followed him up into the palms.

Now Parker was no longer in the palm but back in the dusty Kansas yard behind the slaughterhouse. When he had first started working the kill floor he'd been scorned, even hated, as the boss's son. At first he had been surprised by this, then depressed. He had been wrong to think the workers would be friendlier because he had joined their ranks. In fact, they seemed to hate him even more, as if by working alongside them he was mocking their low station in life. Why would he work the kill floor otherwise? Once he grasped the unchanging force of the workers' animosity towards him, he'd wanted off the kill floor. But his pride refused to concede defeat.

Parker's arms and legs tensed. Sadness filled his gut as the old loneliness and confusion returned. He remembered how everyday he'd watch the guys file out back to the dusty yard for cigarette breaks. He watched them follow Incencio who was their commander, their true jefe. It was Incencio who stared right through him, ignoring his presence.

Incencio, the man from El Salvador who swaggered into work every morning at 6 a.m., a cigarette dangling from his lips, had intimidated Parker at first. As the knocker, it was Incencio's job and only his to stand at the knocking box and shoot each cow in the head with a captive bolt steel gun. It was the knocker who killed all day, one cow every twenty seconds. It was only after the knocker did his job that the eighty other kill floor workers could begin the hellish work of dismembering dead animals. Of course the workers considered Parker a freak for doing the worst possible slaughterhouse job of bleeding out, skinning, gutting, and carving animals. This was work reserved for the most desperate and poor. Parker didn't have to. He could instead file reports and make calls in his air conditioned office, same as his brother, or treat clients to meals of prime rib and filet mignon washed back with a double martini.

"You don't have to do this," Caleb repeated daily, pity clouding his earnest eyes.

Every day that Parker worked the kill floor he hated his younger brother even more for his ability to kiss Amos Wilson's powerful ass. Parker wanted the workers to know that he hated his father as much as they did.

Friday at 5 p.m., after the workers retired their knives, changed their bloodied clothes and washed death from their hands and arms. They gathered in the enclosed yard behind the slaughterhouse to drink beer. Shunned, Parker never joined them, until one night when, overwhelmed by frustration, he followed the guys out into the cemented square where they always smoked. For an hour Parker stood alone to one side, sipping one beer, then another, as the men carried on in Spanish. It was after his fourth beer that without warning, even to himself, Parker pushed himself into the center of the group.

"Who wants to fight," he shouted, holding up fists. "I'll throw a hundred bucks into the betting pool. I'm talking standard bare-knuckle boxing."

A hush fell over the group.

Parker knew he sounded like a fool. As soon as he'd said the words he'd wished he could reverse his challenge. Yet, instinctively he knew that he could only earn the workers's respect through such a risky move.

Shocked faces turned and stared. No one uttered a word.

Finally, a voice, clearly amused, said, "Sure, white boy, I'll fight you."

Chapter Eight
A Beautiful Oasis

As Parker sprinted back up Baxter Street he caught sight of Manuel's straw-brimmed hat.

"Buenos Dias," he called to the man sitting on his porch steps.

Manuel stood and removed his hat. "Buenos dias, jefe," he said with a smile. His face crinkled into a thousand wrinkles, a parched desert. His brown eyes shone bright like polished stones.

"I went to climb my palm," Parker said, trying to forget the tormenting flashback to the slaughterhouse yard.

"Nice day to climb a palm, but now we work?"

"Four Mexican Fans in La Canada. But first I'll make coffee."

It was 7 a.m. If they worked quickly they could finish the job by noon. Parker could then head over to the Huntington.

Manuel held out a canvas bag. "Mi amigo, I brought you papaya from the garden, bananas, and nopales."

Parker nodded. "Always so generous with your harvest, Manuel. What's going on at the farm?"

Manuel shook his head. "Terrible. Ever since the judge took away the...what's it called again? Injunction? That gave us the right to stay on the land. Now everyone is desperate because Señor Horowitz can tell us all adios any time. The sheriff too, he can kick us out any day." The man stood and followed Parker into the house. "Some people say we still have a chance," he continued. "That Horowitz might still sell us the land. But I think we will all be thrown out. Irma says, 'have more faith.' She thinks just believing that the farm will be saved can make it so. But I am not so believing."

"Why not?"

"We've been fighting this hombre for three years and even if he finally says, 'Okay, I sell the land,' where would we get such money? They say he wants five million dollars. Parker, five million dollars!"

Parker opened his window and spit into the yard with disgust that one developer could tell a hundred farmers they had to leave the land they had been cultivating for twelve years. He had been to the South Central Farm several times. It was a beautiful oasis in the middle of Los Angeles' most industrialized and polluted neighborhood, where yard-less apartments were squashed together between factories and warehouses and diesel smoke choked the air. Right there in the worst urban blight was the country's largest urban garden, fourteen lush acres growing an incredible assortment of unique plants, some which Parker had never before seen. On visits he had seen corn stalks standing tall against the sky and endless fruit trees – oranges, grapefruits, lemons, pomegranates.

At the farm he didn't notice the terrible habit of some of his clients to ignore the fruit heavy on their trees and let it rot on the branch or fall into their yards for their gardeners to gather and throw away.

"How can city politicians let one rich guy kick hundreds of people off land that grows so much food, gives so much green space, so he can build warehouses," Parker muttered. "It's insanity to think anyone needs more warehouses in a neighborhood covered with them."

Manuel pulled two mangoes from his canvas bag and held them out. A swirl of orange and yellow, the fruit were burning suns. "Come to the garden Sunday, Parker. The farmers want to gather as many people for another rally, to show we still will fight. The mayor says he's our friend and the farm should be saved. Many people say the garden is important because we grow food, teach others to grow food, keep the land natural for the whole city to enjoy. Still, no one stop Señor Horowitz from building a warehouse?

Parker laid his hand on Manuel's shoulder. His worker, his friend and teacher, who had taught him so much. Parker loved the palms, understood them, but Manuel spoke their language, as if he himself had sprung from a palm seed.

"I don't know, man, but I'll definitely come." He wanted to tell Manuel that he fantasized about beating the living lights out of the developer, knocking him around, rubbing his face into the ground and making him swallow a mouthful of dirt. But he refrained. He wasn't that guy anymore. At least, he was trying really hard not to be that guy.

As Parker ground coffee beans Manuel sat at the kitchen table, calloused hands resting on his heavy cotton pants.

Parker had only been in California a few weeks when they had first met. Those were crazy early days when he slept on the beach and tagged along with a group of palm trimmers traveling up and down Pacific Coast Highway, hitting the trees from Malibu to Manhattan Beach. They did not mind his company because he worked for free in exchange for lunch pail handouts. With the little money Parker had, he purchased his first pair of boots and spurs, a safety belt and rope.

The first time Parker climbed into a palm and began hacking with his machete he was happier than he'd ever known. It was hard sweaty work just like on the kill floor. He needed to use all his muscles and keep focus. Daydream or let your mind wander and you'd get badly cut, break a bone, snap your neck, fall, end up dead. But the payoff was the best high he'd ever known. The best sex. The best wine. The best fight. Work right and by the end of the day he had used his whole body and exhausted any energy that made him think crazy thoughts about hurting himself or others. Thoughts that filled him with hate and confusion.

The palms filled him with life, not misery and death.

At first the foreman had chased Parker away. But then one smart guy realized Parker worked harder than anyone and gave him a job with a crew contracted for city jobs along the coastline of Venice, Santa Monica, and Pacific Palisades, where thousands of palms rose into the sky.

Parker had noticed how the small Mexican man, older than everyone else, had watched him like a hawk as he shimmied palms and cut fronds.

The second day on the job the man introduced himself and began working alongside Parker, giving him tips and telling him secrets about each palm as if he knew them personally.

Parker set down a cup of steaming coffee in front of Manuel. "You were four when your father first took you into a palm."

Manuel laughed. "This story again. You are a little boy who wants only Goldilocks, the girl who tricks bears. Or was that Rapunzel?"

"You were so lucky, having a father who took you into palms."

"Four years when I first climbed. Some boys in my pueblo were only three so maybe I was a little big." Manuel's face lit up when he talked about his village in Southern Mexico, in Chiapas, though he had not been there in ten years time.

"Your father taught you to cut fronds with the machete."

"Sure. We had to cut big fronds to sell to the Americanos and their churches for Palm Sunday. You think this was fun, but me as a little boy worked hard so you Americanos could be with Jesus in your church."

Parker laughed. "I have a religious experience everytime I climb a palm."

Chapter Nine
Where Was Ramona?

Pomona woke with a start to a mechanical roar. She covered her eyes against the sunlight pouring through the window. Delilah slept on the pillow beside her, the canister of Nora's ashes a lump beneath the pillow. She laid her other hand on the cat's soft black head. The roar outside grew louder. It was trash day. A trash truck was rumbling down the street. She rolled over and glanced at the bedside clock. 11:48 a.m.

I'm still alive, Pomona thought. Still alone in Nora's apartment. Still breathing.

Damn.

I should be lying dead in the Arroyo beneath the Colorado Street Bridge, dusted with Nora's ashes, the canister by my side. An early morning jogger may have stumbled upon me. I might already be in the morgue.

But she had been thrown off course by a chance encounter with a man. A shudder ran through her body. That was the story of Nora's life, not hers. A flash of resentment at Nora's weakness for loser men stabbed her heart. Pomona slid her hand beneath her pillow and touched Nora's tin. No matter what, she had loved her mother and been loyal.

I still need you, Mommy. I'll scatter your ashes when I'm stronger.

Pomona bolted up in bed. Where was that damn book? Where was *Ramona*? Kicking back bedcovers and sending Delilah running, she stumbled out of bed and found her purse sitting on the kitchen counter. The book was surely inside.

But it wasn't.

"No, no, no," she cried. She wrapped a robe around her trembling body and ran outside to the curb.

The trash truck erupted in a roar as it violently grabbed and shook trashcans lined in front of the building. The truck rumbled away as Pomona searched Pearl's seats, under the seats, in the glove compartment and the trunk. She looked in the street and under the car. The book was nowhere.

Pomona slumped onto the sidewalk as a horrible dawning took hold. Had she left the book in the palm garden? Was her father's copy of *Ramona* lying forgotten in the dirt?

Maybe some visitor had chanced upon it and given it to a security guard who had taken it to lost and found.

Maybe it got caught in the sprinklers and was now a soggy mess.

Or a gardener threw it into the trash.

Then another thought bloomed in her mind. A thought that gave her reason to sit up. Maybe Parker had the book. An exciting possibility.

If Parker had the book, maybe he would try to find her. Maybe the book would bring them back together. Pomona jumped up and ran into the house. She had to return to the Huntington immediately.

Arriving at the Huntington an hour later, Pomona marched straight to the palm garden. She searched all around, but *Ramona* wasn't lying beneath the tree. She returned to the entrance pavilion and checked lost and found, but the book wasn't in the box filled with umbrellas, sunglasses, and sweaters.

Maybe Parker hadn't noticed the book beneath the tree, or maybe that ridiculously misnamed girl Virginia found it. There wasn't anything virginal about her. She could have found it and thrown it in the trash.

Pomona flopped onto a bench and massaged her throbbing head. How could she have lost Francisco's book? Maybe someone had picked it up and, deciding it wasn't for them, left it in another garden.

Pomona began to to look. With an aching head she tripped through the Desert Garden, into the Australian Garden and beyond to the Japanese Garden where now, utterly despondent, she laid down on the lawn by a pond. A few people ambled about, carefree visitors who hadn't lost their most precious possession, their only link to a father who had abandoned them decades ago. She rolled to her side. It would require a Herculean feat to make the trek back to the parking lot.

Suddenly, in the distance, Pomona spotted Parker, walking straight toward her, striding with purpose. She wobbled to her feet. Without a thought she hurried toward him, her life opening before her like a butterfly fluttering out of a dark cave.

Pomona looked to his hands, but he did not have the book. By now she was almost upon him. She searched his face, then stumbled back. The man wasn't Parker at all.

"Can I help you?" the confused person asked as she turned and ran toward the entrance gate.

If only I'd come earlier, Pomona fretted as she headed back up Allen Avenue. Parker might have come at ten when the Huntington first opened. Maybe he had to work, or maybe that little blonde tart forbade him from coming. She was definitely the jealous type. Probably tied him to the bed and hid the car keys.

Any of these scenarios seemed possible. Unless he just hadn't come. He didn't have the book, or just didn't care.

Stupid, you blew it. Should have gotten here sooner, sleeping til noon.

Nora would have laughed. She never chased men in an outward way. Her methods were much more devious and she stuck to those strategies even if they often backfired.

"Let him sweat," she would have said. "Let him think you didn't come. He'll only want you more."

Pomona wished she had the confidence to believe she could make a man search for her high and low, but she didn't and she also needed *Ramona* back. It was her only connection to Francisco who was now taking up more and more space in her brain.

When Pomona got home she took three aspirin and slouched on the sofa. She stared at the living room layered with months of dust. The closer she looked the more she realized spiders had taken over. Cobwebs were everywhere, draped along the walls. Hanging from the ceiling and spun across the doorways and windows.

"I should clean," she told Delilah. The idea was preposterous, the same as believing she could run a marathon when she could barely move a muscle. Delilah, for her part, stretched out her long body and gave a dubious stare.

"I'll go back tomorrow, Delilah," Pomona told the cat as she lay down and curled into a fetal position. "I'll get there early and wait under the palm."

Pomona willed herself off the couch at eight the next morning, and forced herself into the shower. She stuck a hat in her bag and after some deliberation, added a book from Nora's shelf. She pulled into the Huntington parking lot at 9:45 a.m. After buying another ticket she went directly to the palm garden and sat beneath the tree. Pulling *Ulysses* from her bag, she turned to page one:

STATELY, PLUMP BUCK MULLIGAN CAME FROM THE STAIRHEAD, bearing a bowl of lather on which a mirror and a razor lay crossed. A yellow dressing gown, ungirdled, was sustained gently behind him by the mild morning air.

Pomona turned to the sky. Clouds were forming. She had not thought to bring a sweater. She looked back to the page where words blurred together among a smattering of tiny black spots. She brought the book to her nose and sniffed. It reeked of mold. She should have brought *The Great Gatsby.* Its pages had more white space but she had worked hard to feel optimistic that morning. To believe that anything could happen. That she could read and understand *Ulysses* and that Parker would bring her *Ramona.*

Both ideas sprung from a delusional mind.

A light mist fell upon Pomona's bare shoulders. She shuddered. By 2 p.m. a steady drizzle made her cold and miserable. She closed *Ulysses,* having never moved beyond the first paragraph with Stately Plump Buck Mulligan and his bowl of lather, its mirror and razor. She imagined the razor, sharp and gleaming, and considered the ease in drawing such a razor across her wrists.

Pomona left *Ulysses* beneath the tree because she knew she would never read the book and she didn't want to think about the razor. It was a cheap paperback, anyway, something Nora had bought at a yard sale. The drizzle would dampen its thin pages and they would melt together. No one would ever read the book again.

She drove Pearl back at Nora's apartment. There the walls closed in. Pomona regretted not jumping from the bridge when she had the chance. Now she was stuck alone in a dirty apartment at the bottom of a well of sadness.

The next day, Friday, Pomona stayed in bed. Parker was by now a ghost and *Ramona* as good as gone. With the cat curled by her feet, she succumbed completely to a bitter, clawing loneliness. As she lay numb, staring at the ceiling, a single sentence commanded her mind:

"Read *Ramona,*" Nora had said.

Why? What message did the book contain? That true love is worth pursuing your entire life even if you fall over dead, alone, with nothing to show for your efforts?

"No, it's better I lost the book," she told Delilah. "What does it matter that it was daddy's mother's book. I only met my grandmother once, when I was three. Why chase a memory that will only break my heart even more?"

Three hours later Pomona woke up in a panic, her entire body drenched in sweat. She could feel Francisco all around her like an afternoon heat.

"I need my book," she cried to Delilah as she rolled from the bed. She needed the book like a ship captain needs the North Star, not just to break a curse, but to her find her way back to the little bit of family she ever had and to make peace with them.

"I need the book," she repeated as she drove Pearl through the streets of San Marino, back into the Huntington parking lot. When she opened her wallet at the ticket booth she saw that she had no more money so she loitered around the coffee cart until a tour group gathered. As a docent checked tickets she kept her head low and shuffled around the chattering people. It shouldn't have worked but it did. She wandered in with the group, splitting off and moving toward the palms as the others headed toward the Library.

She sank to the ground, to the exact spot where she had been sitting when Parker had burst into her life two days earlier. She noticed that *Ulysses* was gone. Probably a soggy mess in a garbage can.

She sat for a spell. Then, as she rose to go, Pomona noticed something stuck to the palm at eye level.

She looked more closely: a scrap of paper was stuck into the tree trunk with a bent paper clip.

She pulled out the clip and unfolded the paper. Her heart raced as she read the words:

POMONA: MEET HERE SATURDAY @ 3 p.m. I HAVE YOUR BOOK. PARKER.

The letters were big and blocky, strong and sure.

Oh god, was it Saturday or Sunday or already Monday? Pomona couldn't remember. She jumped to her feet and ran down the pathway bordering the garden.

"Hello, hello," she called to a man and woman walking hand in hand. "What day is it? What time?"

"It's Saturday," said the man, glancing at his wristwatch. "Almost two." He peered at Pomona who had covered her face with trembling hands. "Are you okay? Do you need help?"

"I'm fine." She laughed. "If it's Saturday then I'm great."

Chapter Ten
The Original Orange Grove

Standing on the pathway, Pomona hardly knew which way to turn. Should she remain in the palm garden?

She had an hour and needed every second to prepare. What was she wearing? She glanced down to see the floating red cherries of her favorite dress. The dress she was wearing the day she had met Parker.

Had she slept in it last night? She paused to think.

No, thankfully she had taken it off, only because it had been so hot. But clearly at some point she had put it back on. The dress had a frayed hemline and a smattering of tiny gray spots on its skirt.

"Never keep anything stained," Nora always said. "If it's stained it's got to go. And never try to scrub out stains – that only makes you look more poor."

She could rush home and change. But what if she had a flat tire? Anyway she didn't have money for admission and might not be so lucky to sneak in again.

Pomona hurried up the path to the entrance pavilion and found the bathroom. She pushed through and took a hard look at herself in the mirror, scrutinizing her reflection. Thankfully (miraculously!) she had taken a shower that morning. Her hair was clean.

Pomona rifled through her purse and found a hairbrush and lipstick at the bottom, next to Nora's canister. She could improve things, but who was she kidding? Virginia would already look flawless with styled hair, perfect makeup, and manicured hands. Parker's girlfriend would never leave the house with a frayed hemline and stained skirt. She would never sleep on the couch in her clothes.

It didn't matter. Girlfriend or not, Parker had come. Had left a note. At least she could get back Francisco's book.

Still, her entire body ached with desire and longing for this beautiful man who was looking for her! No one had looked for Pomona her entire life.

She began brushing her hair as women moved around her, stepping up to the sink, washing hands, and leaving. She brushed and brushed until it cascaded down her back to her waist. She reapplied her lipstick. Revlon's Rum Raisin, her mainstay since high school, not too burgundy, not too brown.

Had she shaved her armpits? Pomona lifted arms to see black stubble. She caught a whiff of sweat. Pulling paper towels from the dispenser, she wet them and wiped her armpits and the nape of her neck. She wet more towels and laid them against her forehead.

"What time is it?" she asked the woman beside her.

The woman glanced at her watch. "2:40."

Time to return to the palms.

Sitting beneath the tree, Pomona was a firecracker about to explode.

You don't have to think of anything witty to say. Just be yourself.

As if that had ever worked out.

Pomona sat with her legs curled to one side and arms resting in her lap. Her belly flippity-flopped. A few moments later she moved her legs to the other side and rested her arms by her side. Maybe sitting was all wrong. Too casual. Too desperate. As if she had been waiting for hours. She should hide in the desert garden behind a cactus and when Parker arrived make him wait five minutes before nonchalantly strolling over.

Oh, yeah, I just happened to come today and saw your note. That's so nice of you to remember my book...I kind of wondered where it went....

But then, before she had a chance to move a muscle, let alone make a decision, it happened. The sky opened and the clouds shifted and Parker was walking toward her, striding purposefully across the grass. He was a vision of blue: navy blue jeans, periwinkle button-down shirt, and sky-blue eyes. All around him birds chirped songs of joy. Pomona could hear their happy songs as he approached.

Or was it her heart?

No, it was Parker, whistling as he moved across the grass until he was standing right before her, looking down and smiling.

"Hello," he said in a voice husky and sure. "I've finally found you, Pomona of the Orchards."

The moment was as huge as a harvest moon.

"Hello."

"You found my note."

"Just an hour ago. I was looking for my book."

Perspiration was building in Pomona's armpits and dripping down her sides, rivulets running to her waist. An inner heat was building and exploding. Cheeks reddening, she lowered her gaze.

Actually, I have both your books," Parker continued. "I assume you left this, too?" He held up *Ulysses*.

Pomona almost laughed with joy to know he had come the day before and yesterday, too. "I was reading when it started to drizzle and I guess I forgot it beneath the tree."

"You have intriguing reading tastes. I wonder what you'll leave behind next."

But Parker made no move to give her the books. He knelt down so they were on the same level. He looked at her with his curious blue eyes framed with lashes long and brown.

Staring back Pomona could not form words.

"Have you ever been to Kansas?" Parker finally asked.

"No."

"Can I see your hands?"

Pomona didn't question the strange request, just held them out.

As if handling porcelain, Parker carefully wrapped his fingers around hers. He turned them over to look at her palms "Good planting hands," Parker concluded. "I would love to plant with you someday. Corn in the spring. Sunflowers in the summer,"

Was he babbling? Was he nervous too? Pomona had the distinct sensation of melting into the grass.

Parker reached an arm into the khaki bag that hung from his wide shoulder, pulled out *Ulysses,* and laid it before her. Then he took out *Ramona.*

Relief flooded Pomona. "Thank you. I need that book. I promised someone I would read it." As she took the book from Parker's hand, their fingers brushed. She felt sparks shoot into the air.

"Let's walk," Parker said into the stretch of silence. Pomona nodded and, books in hand, she stood. They headed out, past the desert garden, an otherworldly wonder-scape of exotic agave, cacti and succulents, past the lily ponds where neon koi shimmered among flotillas of lily pads and lotus flowers. From there they traversed a wide lawn and entered the subtropical Jungle Garden. They ambled along an upward hillside path until they encountered a wide-branched thick-trunked tree.

"An Ombu tree," Parker said, stopping. "Native to the grassy Pampas of Argentina. They were called lighthouses of the Pampas because gauchos used them for shelter while traveling. The tree naturally repels insects."

Pomona read the placard at the base of the specimen:

On the grassy pampas of Argentina, Ombu trees are usually scattered many miles apart and are often the only trees to be seen. The native cowboys (gauchos) have long used them as shelter. This Ombu tree was planted in 1914.

Parker took her hand and pulled her beneath the tree. They sat within its wide, low branches as if in their own fort, and looked south across a wide expanse of lawn. To one side a rushing waterfall splashed into a pond where Pomona noticed a turtle sunning itself upon a rock.

After some moments, Parker said, "I hope you don't mind that I peeked at your book, *Ramona*. The greatest story of California ever told. I want to know that story. I never learned about the Missions and rancheros that once covered California. Not at my school in Kansas. We learned about the Louisiana Purchase and Jayhawkers."

"It's actually my father's book," Pomona said shyly. "Stupid of me to have left it that day."

Suddenly, Pomona wanted to ask Parker a thousand questions: Why did he come back? Where was Virginia? Why did he climb up palm trees? But most important, could he ever love a girl like her, a mixed up eccentric girl with stains on her dress who two days earlier had almost jumped from a bridge?

But before she could open her mouth, Parker took her hand and squeezed it tight. He looked into her eyes and smiled. In that moment the need for words disappeared.

They sat beneath the Ombu tree and gazed at the grassy slope rolling into a distant forest of trees. The soft fabric of Parker's periwinkle shirt brushed against her shoulder. The sensation of his hand in hers warmed her entire body as if candles had been lit in her heart.

The silence between them grew more comfortable the longer it stretched and it was twenty minutes later that Parker began talking in a low voice. At first Pomona could barely hear him through the enormous excitement of sitting so close to this man she desired. She thought he might be speaking a foreign language until she recognized the name "Henry Huntington" in his tumble of words.

"Do you think Henry and Arabella Huntington ever sat beneath this tree when they lived here?" Parker asked. "They had the entire estate to themselves and could roam as they pleased, could lie beneath the stars in the desert garden, in the shadow of a Saguaro. Or, have brandy in the Japanese Garden, naked if they wanted. Who would see them except maybe a servant?"

"I can't imagine Arabella Huntington naked," Pomona said. "I've seen her portrait in the art gallery. She was rather matronly and proper, wearing a dowdy black dress."

"Wearing Widow's Weeds for her first husband, Collis, who was actually Mr. Huntington's uncle. I read a book about them, about their love for collecting books and art and plants." Parker gazed into Pomona's lovely eyes and wanted to tell her all about the book.

"It's called *The Huntington Botanical Gardens 1905-1945*. It was written by a man named William Hertrich. A German immigrant who was Henry Huntington's first gardener and superintendent of grounds. The palm garden was among the first of many he planted at the San Marino Ranch in 1905." Parker loved the book so much he had never returned it to the University of Kansas library.

"The Huntingtons were in their sixties when they got married," Parker added, suddenly shy and grasping for something to say.

"Ancient," Pomona murmured.

Parker laughed. "Mr. Huntington always with his hat and cane. Maybe they weren't the type for midnight skinny-dipping in the ponds, but you never know. He was the master of his universe."

As Parker spoke he saw from the corner of his eye how she gazed at him with an expression of absolute rapture. He wondered if she was mesmerized by the story of the Huntingtons or if maybe she liked him as much as he liked her. He wanted to kiss her hard on the mouth. Push her to the ground by the strength of his lips, but he didn't dare set himself up for rejection. He wasn't ready. So he kept talking.

"In like 1910 Mr. Huntington built a rose garden and Japanese garden. He created those gardens out of love for Arabella. She had first married his uncle, but after he died she married Henry. Might seem a little weird but they kept the fortune in the family and that money fed their passion for gathering beauty around them. Look at all the beauty their love built."

Parker turned toward her, his gaze lingering on her lips.

Pomona thought he might suddenly kiss her, imagined them passionately kissing beneath the Ombu tree, his lips crushed against hers. His strong arms engulfing her body and their legs entangled like two more limbs on the tree.

"He made his fortune in the railroad."

Pomona focused on Parker's words. He was talking, not kissing.

"Here's something really crazy. Huntington was a railroad man so he built railway tracks right up to his house so a freight car could deliver entire libraries he'd bought on the East Coast right to the door of his library. When he first bought his ranch it was six hundred acres of open land. But over the years he sold off parcels so he could buy more art and rare books and manuscripts."

Pomona suddenly realized Parker was talking out of nervousness. He didn't know what to do either. Was it possible that he liked her?

"Another great California story, just like your book *Ramona*," Parker continued. "How many great California stories there must be. But surely many have been lost." He looked at her, wistful. "Do you know where Henry and Arabella are buried?"

She shook her head. Maybe talking was fine. What more could they do under the Ombu tree?

"Right here, on the estate, in the mausoleum over by the old orange grove." Parker sat up. "We could go see them." His eyes brightened. "The mausoleum is beautiful. Imagine two people who've shared a life of such beauty and passion now buried together forever."

But before Pomona could respond a guard peeked his head beneath the branches.

"We're closing now folks. Time to head for the exits," he said with raised eyebrows. Parker climbed from under the tree and flashed the guard an easy smile. He took Pomona's hand and helped her out. Standing, she brushed dirt from her skirt, avoiding the security guard's curious stare.

As Parker and Pomona walked toward the exit, the security guard turned and headed in another direction.

Parker grabbed her elbow and pulled her close. "We can do it if we hurry," he whispered in her ear.

"Do what?" She giggled with giddiness.

"Go see the mausoleum. Keep your head down and we'll dodge the guards and get a peek."

Before she uttered another word Parker took her hand (so soft, he thought, as if he had taken a handful of flower petals) and pulled her along. He picked up his gait until they were almost running across the lawn. They passed a long row of stone statues, ancient Roman gods and goddesses that had been standing in formation for a hundred years.

"Go, go, faster," they seemed to chant. Pomona threw back her head as a burst of laughter erupted from some deep crevice within. She never thought she would ever laugh again, not such a loud from-the-belly laugh. She stumbled, losing grip of Parker's hand, then, in a moment of impulse, slipped off her sandals and scooped them into her arms.

She ran as if going barefoot was the funniest thing in the world. Pomona wondered if Virginia would take off her shoes and run through the grass with such a snorting laugh.

You don't have to think about her. She doesn't matter—he's here with you, not her, she thought.

"I'm not much of a runner," Pomona gasped as they came upon a large round stone fountain where water gurgled from the mouths of bronze fish. Parker took her hand and pulled her along, past a conservatory, a building, and hedge.

"Almost there," he said slowing down. "We're in the original orange grove. Hardly anyone comes back here. We're safe for now."

They walked along holding hands, through rows of orange trees heavy with golden globes. Parker picked one and held it to her nose. She took in its fragrant citrus perfume, laughed and nodded. "Best smell in the world. I came here once with my father." She saw herself, small and happy, walking along with Francisco, who was singing a song in Spanish and teaching her the words.

"Really? Here? What did you do?"

"He put me on his shoulders and I touched the branches. I picked an orange and we ate it together."

"So sweet. Then you know orange groves are another great California story. Mr. Huntington planted these trees in the early 1900s when citrus barons were rushing to California for the second Gold Rush. Groves of oranges, lemons, and grapefruit were everywhere as far as the eye could see. I wish I could have seen that."

"My father said the first orange grove was planted in the garden of the San Gabriel Mission, which isn't far from here."

They came to an intersecting pathway and turned a corner. Before them, on a grassy knoll, rose a white marble dome overlooking the orange grove, an exquisite double-colonnaded Greek temple. Its stately beauty stopped them in their tracks.

"Mr. and Mrs. Huntington are buried beneath this temple dedicated to eternal love," Parker said with reverence. "The architect John Russell Pope later used a similar design for the Jefferson Memorial in D.C."

They approached the domed temple, climbed its stairs and laid their hands against its cool white marble. A memory flashed through Pomona of Nora, dead in her bed. Beautiful vivacious Nora died with no true love at her side. Why did some women have men build them Greek temples of e ternal love while others died alone?

"We'd better go," Pomona said.

Parker detected the sadness in her voice, and without a word, they turned and headed back toward the parking lot. The sun was dipping and the shadows lengthening.

Just a few cars remained in the stalls. Parker followed her to Pearl. Pomona took out her key and looked at Parker, aware of the expectation of expectations and ready to accept disappointment.

But Parker did not disappoint.

"Now that I've found you, Pomona of the Orchards, I can't lose you again. I won't." He touched her cheek. "How will I reach you?"

Chapter Eleven
A Mexican Fan of Rare and Unequaled Beauty

After a dinner of black beans and tangerines, Parker sat on the front porch and sipped a beer. When darkness came, he prepared himself for the night. He filled his thermos with coffee and laced his boots. He took his worn leather jacket from the back of the kitchen chair. The phone rang again, the third time that hour.

This time, though, the ringing continued until the message machine clicked. Christ, he thought, standing frozen in the kitchen. She's going to leave a message.

Parker knew Virginia well enough to know that leaving a message, for her, was an act of aggression. The last time Virginia had phoned was the night he had left for Los Angeles. He had not picked up the phone then either. He had not had time then and he had not wanted her to know he was leaving. Once he'd left he'd vowed he would never return.

I should have known she would track me down, he conceded to himself. I really should have known.

Parker moved toward the door. He did not want to hear her message. She had probably already killed a bottle of wine and it would get ugly.

No one's ever going to love you like I do, Parker. That's why I'm telling you, go back. There are things you don't know and it's the only way you can clear up this mess so that we can have the life we are meant to have . Anyway, that Mexican worker is still in jail where he belongs. You've got to go back to claim what's rightfully yours.

That's what she'd said in her room at the Chateau Marmont. He knew "rightfully ours" meant money and power.

"What things do I not know?" he'd asked, his heart clenching at the thought of Incencio in prison. He wanted to tell her Incencio was Salvadoran, not Mexican, but such a distinction meant nothing to her. All the while he was aware of the bad stink rising from his body, the stink of his cowardice and guilt.

Parker suddenly realized that Virginia could well be just around the corner, parked on a side street and calling from her car. He grabbed his backpack and keys and hurried outside into the cool night, locking the door behind.

Thunder and lightning roiled his brain. Virginia was the storm while Pomona was that rare peace he'd found among the palms. In her presence he believed that for once he could stop looking over his shoulder.

Parker climbed into his truck parked alongside the curb and started the engine. He would drive. The night air would clear his head. He shifted into gear and moved through the residential streets of Elysian Park until he hit Riverside Drive and headed north. Riverside Drive skirted along the 5 Freeway, crossed over Los Feliz Boulevard and took him into Griffith Park, the largest park in all of Los Angeles. Parker rolled down his window and caught a strong whiff of distant skunk, the delicious mix of sulfur, burning tires, musk, and really good weed.

Did Pomona love skunks? Parker rolled through a stop sign.

There were no guarantees but he bet that she did.

He glanced over at the empty passenger seat, now covered with his gear, backpack and jacket. There had never been room for anyone before, except Manuel. For Pomona, he would clear space.

Leaving the park, he zoomed up the Forest Lawn freeway onramp and headed west. The 134 was fairly empty as it merged into the Hollywood Freeway that took him westward through Studio City, Sherman Oak, and Tarzana. Thirty minutes later he exited at Kanaan

Road and headed south, through the Santa Monica Mountains, winding for ten miles along the two-lane road bisecting the dry scrubby landscape. Now, it was not skunk, but the sweet smell of sage that filled his senses.

Looking through his dirt-streaked windshield into the black night he saw her everywhere. Pomona of the Orchards, sitting beneath the Ombu tree, running barefoot through the orange grove, her black hair streaming across her laughing face as she stumbled toward the mausoleum, the final resting place of Henry and Arabella Huntington – one of the great California love stories.

Could he and Pomona create their own great love story? He would build her gardens and temples, just as Henry had for Arabella.

No one's going to love you like I can, Parker. No one knows you like I do. We're not like other people and you're a fool if you pretend otherwise.

He winced at Virginia's words. She had saved him in the past, had brought him home when he had been flailing in New York two years earlier. Maybe his relationship with Virginia was a foregone conclusion. He remembered those miserable years after college, when he was more angry than lost. He had tried to make another life, as an artist in New York City. When that hadn't work out, he had became an adventurer on an Alaska fishing boat. It lasted barely a year before he had headed home to Virginia. Always back to Virginia. That time he'd made a decision he thought he could live with. He would return to the family business, but would start at the bottom, in the slaughterhouse, and work his way up.

No way would Parker play the role of entitled son with a spacious office, indulging in steaks and scotch with clients, making small talk about their wives and kids. Not like Caleb. His younger brother was already working overtime to emulate Amos' natural zeal for buying and selling, outwitting other men, living by maneuver. But soft-hearted Caleb was too flat-footed to achieve any real success. As earnest as a Boy Scout, he actually cared if a client's kid made the all-star team or got into a good college. He was soft as Velveeta cheese.

Amos Wilson, on the other hand, was hard. And he was furious that his rebellious older son, by starting at the bottom, was spitting in his face. "You're smarter than that," he had shouted at Parker. "You've got an audacity that could work in your favor, if you only had discipline."

Amos Wilson's face appeared like a goblin before Parker's windshield. He stepped on the gas and drove even faster, sailing and swerving along the canyon road.

Two years earlier Parker had first reported to the kill floor as a liver hanger. For ten hours each day, he stood in the thirty-four degree cooler and took freshly eviscerated calf livers off an overhead line and hung them on carts to be chilled for packing. It was difficult work for which he was paid nine dollars an hour. After a month, his supervisor promoted him to a quality-control position, a job in which he worked as an intermediary between the USDA federal meat inspectors and the kill floor managers.

Parker turned on his radio and found the classical station. He didn't want to think about those days. Kanaan Road led him to Pacific Coast Highway at the north end of Malibu, a few miles up from the enclaves where celebrities lived. As a violin wailed, he turned right and headed north, past the white sands of Zuma Beach and onward. The beaches became more rugged, remote, with access only available by hiking down narrow hillside paths lined with scrubby coastal sagewort and blue lupine.

Parker knew where he was going. He drove faster, the wind blowing through the open window. His anxiety lifted as strains of Beethoven swirled through the cab.

Ten minutes later Parker pulled into the small parking lot on the bluff overlooking El Matador State Beach. He opened the truck door and slid out. With his backpack of gear in hand, he walked along the bluff overlooking the ocean. The sandy beach below was strewn with big rocks. A short walk along the bluff led him straight to the palm he had dreamed of for months. Just the sight of it made his breath catch.

A Mexican Fan of rare and unequaled beauty rose over 120 feet into the sky, standing tall and proud as it had for decades, head and shoulder above the other nearby *Washingtonia robusta*. The grand old dame was leaning south, as palm trees do, into the sun and partially hanging over the cliff that dropped one hundred feet to the shoreline and an outcrop of rocks and boulders.

The view from the top had to be spectacular. A full moon glowed in a black satin sky. Parker had been waiting so long to climb this palm, almost a year, thinking it was beyond his skill, but now with the adrenaline of new love pumping through his veins, he was ready.

In the past the tree's skyscraper height and precarious lean over the rocks had given him pause. So had the patches of old, dried fronds that lay against its slender trunk. They formed a dense, brown, shaggy petticoat below the living, bright green, fan-shaped fronds that held their own danger.

Parker knew that when fronds first wither and die they initially remain fastened to the palm's trunk. As time passes, however, the fronds rot off at the trunk although they remain intertwined. When an inexperienced person climbs up a tree and cuts loose the lowest fronds, the whole skirt can slip down the trunk and can pin him beneath. The weight can smother him to death. Parker had seen this firsthand.

The new cardinal rule of palm maintenance dictated that trimmers use a cherry picker and trim from the top down. He would have to climb through this thick upper skirt to reach the top. He had done that before, but with a crew, in the day, never alone, at night, and so high over crashing surf and rocks. Between his anguish over Virginia and his desire for Pomona, Parker's muscles strained with a new strength.

His body began to move, instinctively preparing. His legs bent into squats, his arms circled. He reached his fingers to the sky and then bent and touched his toes. He eased into Tai Chi moves: Straight spine, pushing hands, deep breathing, gathering all his energy that would take him to the summit. He began yelling and yipping, jumping foot to foot and clawing at the sky as he connected to some unseen force.

He opened his backpack, took out his spurs and attached them to his boots. He peeled off his flannel shirt and tied it around his waist. He put on his safety harness and attached his safety rope around the tree's trunk. He slipped his buck knife into his belt and adjusted his headlamp on his forehead. Climbing the palm alone in the gusty night and trimming dead fronds over the crashing surf was dangerous. Other trimmers would excoriate his risky behavior. They abhorred stupid trimmers, who chanced their lives and gave them all a bad rap.

But that was the rush. He knew he could do it. Would do it. The moon was full and the night was magic. Parker was crazy for palms, for their power and beauty. Now he was crazy for something else: a nocturnal mermaid with a Mona Lisa smile who could rebuild his heart. Pomona's midnight hair blowing about her face, red lips curled in a cryptic smile. As beautiful as the palm before him. A fiery-hot passion for both smoldered through his body.

Parker circled his arms around the slender palm and drew himself close. He brushed his lips against the rough trunk and took his first step. He drove his left spur into the trunk's side and then drove in the right. He pulled out the first and took a step upward. Up Parker walked, one foot after the other, hugging the palm, bringing it to his will. Slowly he inched skyward, his chest pressed against the tree. Ecstasy.

He wasn't even halfway up when it came. A voice began shouting, taunting him, calling him a coward, a loser, a murderer. With Virginia's arrival, the terrors he thought he'd escaped had returned.

He tried to shake it off. Kept climbing. Pushed through. Before him was a dense thicket of dead fronds. Parker pulled the knife from his belt, knowing his loner approach was reckless. Nonetheless he reached up and with his knife and cut through a thick frond. When the frond severed from the tree, he jumped to one side, out of its way. With a burst of strength, he yanked the frond and sent it crashing to the ground. One down. He needed to trim only four more fronds to clear a path to the top. Wild waves pounded shore. A gust hit him from the side. Parker gripped the palm trunk and continued to work, cutting through another frond, moving out of its path, and yanking it from the tree. As every frond fell, he inched higher and closer to the tree's crown.

A startled bat appeared from within the foliage and brushed past his head, so close that Parker looked into its eyes. It was a good omen, he decided.

California's beauty had seduced him on that initial trip when he was only fourteen. He had begged to return every summer. When applying to college, Parker wanted to go to UCLA or Pepperdine, a place near the ocean with palms. But every generation of Wilsons had attended the University of Kansas. His father would never pay for an education taught by liberals and hippies.

"We need you here, on the ranch, Parker, not cavorting on the California beach like some good-for-nothing surfer," Amos Wilson had said with a dismissive hand as he'd leaned back in his chair and rested his boots upon the desk.

Parker recalled staring at the soles of Amos Wilson's custom-made Wheeler crocodile boots. A new crack in his heart filled with hate for the man who spent five hundred dollars on a pair of boots, but would not waste a second on his oldest son's dreams.

Anger flared through his chest. If only his father had allowed him to leave, Caleb might still be alive. Like a drowning man clinging to and submerging his rescuer, Parker's desperation had killed his brother. Parker stabbed his buck knife into the tree, then pulled it out.

No. That was the old Parker. He had found his way back to the palms. Into their accepting fronds.

He had never wanted to share this precious love with anyone, certainly not with Virginia. But Pomona? Maybe he would let Pomona glimpse his secret life. Would she understand his need to climb a hundred feet into the sky? Could his life hold both palms and Pomona?

He had ascended hundred feet up into the green fronds. He was at the crown. This was it, everything he lived for, this breathtaking, life-affirming moment alone with the palm. His heart raced with his love for it all. With his love for Pomona. He settled into position, leaned back into his safety belt. With his feet lodged against the tree, he slipped into a hypnotic state and regarded the ocean and the moon floating in a sea of black.

He closed his eyes and began drifting away. The waves crashed in and retreated with the same rhythm as his breath. His connection to this source of light and love was complete.

Suddenly without warning the nightmare broke through. A jagged breath caught in his throat. Before his brain could send out a reflex and shut down the past, there was Incencio in the black sky, dancing around the dusty yard behind the slaughterhouse, jabbing at the air with clenched fists. Everyone understood their Friday night fights were just for fun, blowing off steam after five long days of carnage. The workers took to the fights as naturally as horse sweat to a harness. They wanted to fight. The systematic violence of killing animals all day fueled their pent-up aggression. But other factors fed their frustration too, such as not making enough money to pay all their bills and send something back to their families in Mexico and Central America. Money was always the match to their tinder. Parker's frustration as the bosses' son on the kill floor was flaring too so those Friday night fights worked for everyone.

A boisterous wind almost toppled Parker from his spot. He clung to the tree. The fronds rustled and swished with unusual aggression.

The fights started with the men creating a makeshift boxing ring— thick white chalk lines on the cement ground—and placing their bets.

In the first fight Parker knocked Incencio to the ground in the second round. The knocker lay on his back and hooted, "You got me, rich boy. Let's go again and see how your luck holds." His open laughing mouth revealed sepia teeth, a snaggletooth.

Parker kept a poker face but was frankly astonished by his win. Incencio was six inches shorter than him but had the burly muscled arms of, well, a prizefighter, and the fancy footwork of a talented salsa dancer.

Incencio beat him the next time and the time after that, but it didn't matter because from then on he regarded Parker with a new respect. Or if not exactly respect, then an acknowledgement of his willingness to be humiliated so as to break the barrier between himself and the other workers.

One day soon after, Incencio motioned Parker over to smoke a cigarette with him, and gave him advice on holding the carving knives, along with tips for surviving the day-to-day misery of such a soul-crushing job.

It all played out well for several months until that hot May night a year ago.

"Who am I gonna fight now?" Incencio had shouted, his brawny arms flexed. He had already fought many kill floor men and even some guys from other slaughterhouses who heard about the Friday night fights and came to see for themselves the glorious mayhem.

The moment had arrived, Parker knew, to arrange the fight he had fantasized about for some weeks. The first time he had considered presenting this contender, even he had to admit it was beyond outrageousness. But the more he thought about it, the more perfect it became.

"Someone special, my friend," Parker had promised. "You won't believe who, but trust me, tonight's gonna be really fun."

Now hanging onto the palm as the wind whipped, Parker wondered how setting up his brother in a fight he had no chance of winning could ever be considered fun. He knew that of course Caleb had no chance against Incencio who would pummel him in five minutes. He must have really hated Caleb to set him up to die

Chapter Twelve
Rally at the South Central Farm

" You can't throw a stone in this town and not hit a Mexican Fan, the common house cat of palms," Parker told Pomona, who was sitting across from him in a flowing red dress, her black hair woven into a loose braid and her planting hands cradling a steaming latte.

"Palm trees are everywhere, yet hardly anyone seems to notice them." Parker stopped talking and eyed Pomona suspiciously. "You really want to hear this?"

Pomona nodded. She didn't care if he talked about palm trees or corporate tax law. He was so adorable with a lock of brown hair falling across his forehead and one-day stubble on his chin. Was that a leaf sticking out from his hair?

Sitting in the cafe across from Parker, Pomona felt, against all odds, pretty. She had spent half the night looking for the right outfit and despairing that she had only the cherry-print dress, when from the back of the closet, she pulled out a red dress of a gauzy gypsy-peasant style with a flounce around its hem, a forgotten Christmas present from Nora.

"But what about you, Pomona of the Orchards. How do you fill your time besides reading and losing books of classic literature in beautiful gardens?" Parker flashed his easy smile, his blue eyes crinkling around the edges. He had just finished his cup of black coffee. His fingers danced across the table as if playing piano scales.

"I guess you could say I'm between jobs," she began, not sure how much to reveal. "I had a job at the library, but I left it a little while ago. I wasn't an actual librarian, just worked the checkout counter and shelved books. Nothing as interesting as palm trimming." She bit her tongue. Would he think her an unemployed sloth? Didn't men want women with good jobs?

"Working in the library sounds great. Don't undersell yourself."

Pomona studied Parker's earnest face for a hint of mockery, but there wasn't any. "I suppose," she said, remembering how she loved organizing books into their exact location using the Dewey Decimal system. The clear order of that classification delivered a sense of happiness. Pomona knew a book's subject by its Dewey Decimal number: 100 was Philosophy and Psychology; 200, Religion; 300, Social Sciences. She took pride in never misclassifying a book and fixing the occasional mistakes made by other shelvers.

"I'm working on next steps to my life as it stands now," she said, cringing at her awkward words. "But you're right. Palms are everywhere and I never think about them. Didn't know there were so many types."

Parker jumped to his feet. "Come with me."

Pomona drained her latte and followed Parker out of the café, along the sidewalk and next door into the bookshop. She followed as he made a beeline through the tall shelves of Current Fiction, Non Fiction, into Travel, through Home and Cooking into Gardening and, finally, Nature and Trees, an area nestled in a back corner. The bookstore had just opened and was still fairly empty.

Parker scanned book titles. *Bamboo*, *Fruit-bearing Trees*, *Native Trees*, *Natural Landscapes*. His finger buzzed back and forth along the spines. Standing behind him Pomona noticed several twigs and leaves as well as grass poking out from his shirt. Had he been lying in a field? She inched closer and took a deep breath. He smelled of salt and sweat and even seaweed. Sand stuck to his neck. Had he camped at the beach last night? In fact, he smelled divine. The earthly smells aroused her, as did the way his torso filled his blue T-shirt. His chest and arms were strong yet his skin looked so soft. She longed to caress it, to reach her arms around Parker's waist and draw him into her so they would merge as one.

Parker remained focused on the books, making his way through orchids and finally arriving at palms. The bookstore had several great books about palms that he could show Pomona, which was perfect because she loved books and he loved palms. She was standing so close, her warm breath tickled his neck. In that breath lay his destiny.

Overwhelmed by her soft body pressing against his, Parker turned and wrapped her in his arms. Together, intertwining vines, they stood within the narrow wall lodged between Nature and Trees and Environmental Studies.

"You are beautiful," he murmured, touching his nose to her neck. Parker ached to put his lips to hers and kiss her, but the anticipation was so delicious, the slow heat before the full fire, that he resisted with every ounce of willpower he could muster.

"Didn't you want to show me a book," said Pomona, breathless.

It was impossible for Pomona to know how long they stood intertwined by the wall because in those moments her entire life flashed before her. The thirty years that she had managed to live without Parker, without knowing that her body could ache with such intense want, for anything, let alone a man. Every second of those years surged through her body. No wonder Nora had chased this euphoria at the expense of everything, including her daughter, her work, even her sanity.

Pomona sensed a presence. She opened her eyes to see an elderly woman reaching for a book on a high shelf in the adjacent Roses section. The woman was attempting to ignore them as she strained on tippy toes.

"We should leave," Pomona whispered. She wanted to slink away with her head down, but Parker greeted the woman.

"Let me help you," he said, reaching his hand. "Is it this, *Southern California in Full Bloom?*" He smiled with gracious ease and the woman actually giggled.

Did he realize his undeniable effect on women?

"Let's go," Parker whispered, pulling Pomona close with a firm grip. "I don't need to show you a book."

Holding hands, Parker led Pomona out onto the sidewalk, where the sun shone bright.

"What are your plans today?" Parker asked. "I could show you a great stand of fan palms in Venice Beach or we could lay on the lawn at the Hollywood Forever Cemetery and take in the palm skyline there. We could even drive to Palm Springs and visit the Palm Oasis." He worried that he sounded ridiculous. Imagine Leonardo da Vinci attempting to explain the Sistine Chapel or Ansel Adams describing a snowy night on Half Dome in Yosemite. What's the point in using mere words to describe the indescribable?

"Oh, shoot." Parker smacked his hand against his forehead and gave Pomona a rueful smile. "I just remembered I promised my friend Manuel I would attend a rally at the South Central Farm."

Pomona's cheeks reddened with embarrassment at her eagerness to follow Parker anywhere. "Don't worry about me," she said with forced nonchalance. "Got stuff to do at home."

Like crying with my cat, she thought.

"You want to come? I understand if you're busy but I think you'd love the Farm."

"A farm? In South Central?"

"Do you know about what's going on at the South Central Farm? Been in the news a lot. It's a huge community garden on Alameda Street that's in trouble. People been farming there at least a decade, probably longer, and now a developer is trying to kick them all out so he can build warehouses or something."

"I haven't heard."

"I'm sure the farmers will win in the end. Would be tragic for everyone if a single developer could close down the largest community garden in the country. My friend Manuel has a plot there and he grows chilies, corn, tomatoes, herbs, flowers. "

Pomona nodded. "Okay."

Parker's eager smile relaxed into relief. "Really?" He hadn't thought she would agree so easily.

"But I have to feed my cat."

"The cat, of course. We can stop by your place on the way and you can feed the cat and leave your car."

Pomona paused. She wasn't ready yet for Parker to come into Nora's apartment, that den of despair, but she could ask him to wait in the truck while she ran upstairs. Surely he wouldn't push the point.

Pomona pulled Pearl against the curb and waved. "Be right back," she called as she walk-jogged toward the building, not giving Parker time to try to tag along. She raced upstairs into the apartment where Delilah greeted her with an accusatory meow.

"Where've you been? The nerve of you leaving this morning without feeding me," she seemed to say, swishing her tail.

"I'm sorry, Delilah." Pomona leaned against the kitchen counter, nerves and excitement in her belly. "I'm going to spend the day with Parker. He seems to really like me. If he wanted Virginia, he'd take her, but he asked me. That's a good sign, don't you think?" She picked up the cat and peered into its green eyes.

Delilah squirmed from her clutch and jumped to a chair with a complaining yowl. Pomona over-filled Delilah's food bowl and set it on the floor. "Listen, I'm sorry to leave so soon, but I'll be back later, so be a good kitty. Eat a big lunch and take a long nap." She reached to stroke the cat's head but Delilah slinked away, not ready to forgive.

She was being crummy to the cat but Parker was waiting.

"I'm sorry, but I'm pretty sure if you met a hottie tom-cat you'd do the same," Pomona muttered.

The cat then hovered beneath the window and unleashed a pained meow. Delilah wanted to sit in the open window but Pomona worried that if it was opened, the cat would jump outside and not come back. On the other hand, if she didn't open the window, the cat would be stuck inside alone, crying for hours. Pomona's guilt won out. "Fine, but come back before dark." She opened the window and the cat disappeared in a flash.

Pomona grabbed a sunhat and locked the door behind.

Downstairs Parker was waiting in his old red Ford truck that was covered with dents and rust. He leaned against the cracked leather seat, a baseball cap pulled low on his head and his arm draped across the seat-back. As Pomona climbed in, he pushed back his cap and gave her a lazy wink.

"I hope your kitty is fine."

Tufts of foam oozed from gashes in the seat that smelled strong as horses. Parker pulled the truck away from the curb. Pomona noticed bits of grass stuck to his sleeve. He really must have spent the night sleeping in a field.

Chapter Thirteen
The Farm is Not for Sale

The crazy day had started when he had climbed that spectacular Mexican Fan at the beach. Hanging over the cliff in the full moon was pure rapture. With the waves crashing below, the salt in his nose, he had never felt so alive, so free and happy. When he met Pomona at the cafe, his bliss soared higher. She had given him strength to climb the Mexican Fan in the first place. He glanced over to see her leaning against the seat, a tiny smile teasing her lips as the wind blew in through her open window, blew through her thick dark hair. What was her story that she seemingly had no job, friends, or family competing for her time?

As Parker drove Pomona tried to imagine this place he spoke of with such enthusiasm—the Farm. She envisioned a red barn with goats, pigs, and cows. Fields of crops, stalks of corn, and rows of golden wheat. She knew this was ridiculous and wondered where he was taking her. South Los Angeles was not a place of pastoral farmlands, at least not anymore. It was marked by stretches of industrial buildings and poor neighborhoods, and immigrants.

She knew the basic history: In the 1980s, South-Central was famous for violence between the Crips and Bloods gang members. Back then white people avoided South Central. Then came the 1992 riots – five days of rioting and looting that erupted after a jury acquitted four LAPD officers for using excessive force in the arrest and beating of Rodney King.

She said, "I remember watching the L.A. riots on television by myself. Mom was out on a date when this terrible video came on."

"Did you see the actual riots?"

She shook her head. It was difficult explaining the riots to someone who didn't experience the hopelessness that engulfed the city. Even from their Pasadena apartment, Nora and Pomona could see smoke rising from the fires burning all around. The U.S. Military and the National Guard patrolled the streets, but people still shot and assaulted each other. She remembered the date: April 29, 1992, the night before her sixteenth birthday. She always had bad luck with her birthdays.

"My understanding is that afterwards the city gave the land to the neighborhood so that they could create a community garden," Parker said. "Plant seeds of hope. You can ask Manuel or one of the other farmers about the history. Listen, if you don't like it, we can make a quick getaway. I just told Manuel that I would come for the rally. The Farm means so much to him and he means so much to me."

"Sure."

Parker headed east along Vernon Street until he approached Alameda Street. He turned left and followed Alameda south, away from downtown.

All the while Pomona's gaze was drawn to Parker's right hand gripping the steering wheel. His hands were gloriously seductive. She shifted her focus and followed the entire length of his arm. She wanted to run her fingers along it, stroke his neck and the curl of hair at the base of his neck. She imagined his skin hot to the touch. She studied his profile. His strong nose, straight but slightly knobbed at the end, reminded her of a painting; she immediately knew which one because she had lingered over it at the Norton Simon Museum during lunch breaks from the library. It was Peter Paul Rubens' "David Slaying Goliath." She remembered how David held his sword over his head with his own strong arms while his foot balanced on the head of the giant Goliath. He too had brown curls and that determined, fierce expression.

With a reflex that was fast becoming habit, Pomona reached into her bag and brushed her fingers against Nora's tin of ashes and Francisco's book. How strange that both her parents were gone but she felt more attuned to them than ever.

"Almost there," Parker murmured and Pomona waited for her first glimpse of this strange notion, a farm in South L.A. She could not imagine plants growing and thriving in this vast stretch of warehouses and factories. A stench of diesel exhaust from a truck barreling past blew through her open window.

Parker pointed to a chain-link fence that rose at the corner of 41st and Alameda Streets and ran all the way down the long block. Beyond the metal fence was a view to dense greenery; trees and plants as far as her eye could see. Along the fence bordering this field, a crowd moved along the sidewalk, people young and old, brown, black, and white, groups of teenagers, couples holding hands, families with kids and babies in strollers. They all traveled in one direction along the chain-link fence, with hats and backpacks and protest signs. A row of red-painted cardboard letters hung from the fence. The letters read:

SAVE THE FARM

Just beyond the sign Parker backed the truck into a curbside parking spot. "We've arrived."

"It's huge." Pomona exclaimed.

"Fourteen acres. About twelve football fields put together."

As soon as Parker and Pomona stepped onto the sidewalk they were swept into the stream of people moving toward the Farm's main gate. They passed through an open dirt area that was encircled by a seemingly endless landscape of trees, plants, and crops that rose beyond the fences and gates. Sitting at folding tables were several people who greeted them.

A young woman wore a T-shirt that read: The South Central Farm Feeds Families. "Welcome to the Farm," she said. "Have you been here before?"

Pomona shook her head. "I haven't, but he has."

Parker smiled. "We're here for the rally."

"It's set to start between four and five but you're welcome to take a look around. Meet the farmers and sample their produce. Help make protest signs. If you haven't already, please sign our petition."

"What for?" Pomona asked.

The woman gave her a quizzical look. "To stop the eviction. To get the City to keep its promise to find a way to let the community keep the land. The petitions will be presented to the City Council next week."

"Glad to do so," Pomona said quickly, not wanting to admit that she had never before heard of the Farm.

Parker and Pomona walked along a wide dirt path that stretched north and south. They headed towards the center. As they walked Parker noticed her red sundress clinging to her voluptuous body. Thank god she was not one of those skinny girls with no ass or boobs. She had both and looked fantastic.

Pomona noticed the air was fresh and much cooler than in the surrounding city where cars and trains, concrete and asphalt drove up temperatures. She felt the freshness the minute she had entered the farm. Destroying this thriving ecosystem would be criminal.

The path through the garden intersected other pathways, which were identified by hand-made cardboard signs: They ambled across Granada Street, Quayaba North, and Izote South. They passed row upon row of garden plots, all laid out in a grid-like fashion, each bounded by its own chain-link fence. The sizable plots were bursting with plants, bushes, and trees. Peeking through fences Pomona saw that each was in some stage of cultivation. Some with plants low to the ground and others with towering stalks stretching to the sky. Some plots were covered with flowers and clusters of cactus, rows of vegetables. In most every one people were working the land. One woman, a baby strapped to her back, planted seeds while children with plastic buckets dug the dirt with sticks. In another plot an elderly couple weeded side by side in unison. The pathway ended at a clearing anchored by a magnificent tree, its triumphant limbs reaching far into the sky.

"Listen…what a ruckus," Parker laughed, and Pomona tuned into a cacophony of trills and tweets and caws coming from within the branches. She spied a crow and mourning doves.

"This walnut tree is literally the garden's beating heart," Parker said.

At its base stood a plaster statue of the Virgin of Guadalupe, her hands pressed together in prayer, an angel peeking from beneath the hem of her fuchsia robe. She was surrounded by vases of calla lilies, sunflowers, and snapdragons.

Pomona bent down and greeted the Virgin. "You're watching over a paradise," she murmured.

Beneath the tree groups of people congregated. Women rocking babies. Pretty young girls nuzzling their boyfriends. A man strummed melodies on a guitar.

"A magic garden hidden right in the middle of the city," Pomona said as they both stood beneath the walnut tree. "I had no idea."

Parker smiled wistfully. "It would sure be another sad California story if we lost this all. Let's find Manuel and see what's going on in his garden."

They found Manuel deep in a north-east section of the garden, within his fenced plot. Together with two women he was turning soil in a raised bed.

"Mis amigos," Parker exclaimed as they approached. "Manuel, this is my friend, Pomona. Pomona of the Orchards, who has the most beautiful planting hands."

Pomona blushed and attempted to slide her hands into her pockets before realizing her dress didn't have any. Manuel stepped from the raised bed onto the firm ground and wiped his hands on a rag before taking Pomona's hand into his. "Mucho gusto," he said with a small but formal bow. A baseball cap with "South Central Farmers" embroidered along the front shaded his craggy face. "These are my friends, Irma and Josefina."

The two women, standing in the raised bed, were both small and lithe as sparrows. Irma, in baggy trousers and a floral shirt, had short-cropped silver hair. Josefina, in a loose dress, wore a long gray braid that fell to her hips. Both wore pink gingham half-aprons with oversized pockets. Nodding their heads they spoke to Manuel in rapid Spanish.

"They say our garden is your garden," Manuel told Pomona. "They invite you to join us for lunch."

"We were just saying we could sure use more help so it's a good thing you came," Irma said with a wink.

The women dragged over a metal bucket and poured its contents into the soil. "We are making compost," Manuel said. "We throw in old food, leaves, cut grass, all in a pile, then water keeps it wet as we turn it over and over every day for weeks. It becomes the best food for the dirt."

"Nutritious," murmured Josefina.

Soothed by their friendliness, Pomona knelt beside Manuel. She placed her palms on the soil that filled the raised bed. "It's so squishy," she laughed.

Manuel held out a spade. "Use this."

"Oh, no, I'll just watch. I don't know anything about gardening," she protested, wiping her hands together, embarrassed by his presumption.

He continued offering the spade. "But Parker says you have good planting hands."

"He's joking." She turned to him with raised eyebrows.

"I'm not." Parker said.

"Pomona, no one here judges anyone," Josefina said as she took the spade from Manuel and placed it in her hand. "We are all here to honor our Mother earth who returns us many blessings. Caring for the land is traditional medicine and anyway, we need your help, believe me. "

For a moment Pomona wanted to leave. She hated feeling put on the spot and she had never gardened before, except for picking fruit with Francisco. But she didn't want to be a spoil sport so she stuck the spade into the planter and gave a shy smile.

Manuel, Irma, Josefina, and Pomona spent the next hour turning compost into the soil. When Pomona jumped at the sight of a worm, the women patted her arm and smiled.

"Worms are amigos," Manuel said. "They do much work for us."

Parker, meanwhile, nailed together a dilapidated vegetable planter bed that Irma had found. "We can use it for tomatoes," Irma said with happy excitement.

Finally, Manuel declared the soil ready and Irma and Josefina brought forth little scraps of folded paper from their aprons. Everyone gathered round as they carefully unfolded the papers like secret messages.

"Pimienta, cebolla verde, frijoles, lechuga, rabano," Manuel said as the women opened each paper that contained a pinch of seeds.

"Peppers, green onions, beans, lettuce, radishes," Parker translated.

After the group pushed the seeds into the rich soil, Irma and Josefina took a metal pot from beneath a small wood table and set it upon a camp stove. Fifteen minutes later they pulled out foil-wrapped bundles that, when opened, revealed plump tamales and chili rellenos. The group sat on metal folding chairs and ate their lunch with corn tortillas, chopped onions, and sliced avocados.

"Tell us how the Farm began," Parker said. "It was around 1994?"

Manuel nodded. "I wasn't here yet. I came in 2000, but Irma told me the land was dirty, nothing but trash, old tires, broken refrigerators, rotten chairs, and graffiti."

Irma nodded and pointed across the plots with animated gestures. "Just an abandoned field where people dumped trash for years. My son Rudy asked me to help. He was a student at East L.A. College, studying political science. One day, he explained, the city of Los Angeles had put the Regional Food Bank in charge of working with the locals to build a community garden. They needed people to do the work. I thought, wow, a garden! It had been two years since the riots."

Josefina had finished eating and was now mending a shirt she had pulled from her bag. Pomona wondered if her hands were ever idle. She said, "The neighborhood was still suffering, buildings burned out, businesses gone, people without jobs. Politicians talked about rebuilding, presented big plans, but nothing much happened. This idea of a garden was a little seed of hope."

Irma stood rigid with folded arms. "So many markets had been destroyed. Burned down. Even then they didn't have much fresh food. Better for people to grow their own food than depend on handouts from the food banks. Most of that stuff is processed junk from big corporations anyway."

The group sat silent while around them bees buzzed and crows cawed. Josefina's face darkened with a flush of annoyance. "I know some people complain that it's mostly Latinos here now, and that so many other people live in this neighborhood," she said. "We do have black and Asian families here. But many Mexicans and Central Americans showed up to work. Because we come from farming pueblos. It's what we know."

With an aggressive swipe Irma swatted at a fly. "Every day we worked like donkeys moving the trash," she continued, her voice defiant, as if someone had challenged her. "The dirt was bad, poisoned by chemicals and oil.

"Vermin infested and tire fires," interjected Josefina. "When you'd dig you'd hit the foundations from old warehouses."

"The Food Bank trucked in dirt," said Manuel. "We had to bring in a lot of dirt so that we could garden."

Irma added: "At first we didn't know if the land could become healthy again after being so sick. Now ..." She looked around at the garden. "Three hundred families and so much food." She raised her hands and ticked off her fingers: "Avocado, banana, beans, jimsonweed, wild yam, pennyroyal, spinach, sapodile, seepweed, wormseed, yerba mora, walnut, sugarcane. Seeds passed from one farmer to another. Children come every day with their families. They don't have yards where they live."

"This is their yard, their home, and for years we had the best meals together. The best time. The best music," said Josefina.

"If more people came we just added water to the pot of beans," said Irma. "Everyone was happy. Where it used to be bad violence. contamination."

"We started poco a poco," said Manuel. "So many native people who live here now work the garden. I know guys Mixtec, Tojolobal, Triqui, Tzeltal, Yaqui, Zapotec. It gives us a piece of what we left behind. The land we cared for and loved. To us, the city is scary. We feel safe here."

Pomona was confused. "If the community was given the land by the City of Los Angeles, and people worked so hard building it, how can anyone take it away now?"

"My understanding is that after the farmers had the land for twelve years, the former owner, his name is Horowitz, said the City had taken it away unfairly through eminent domain," Parker said. "He sued to get it back several times. The courts always ruled against him. Then one day, for reasons no one understands, the City sold it back to him for way below market value, five million dollars. Basically what they paid him for it years earlier."

"The worst was that no one knew anything," said Irma. "No one warned us or told us anything. That horrible day we arrived at the garden to find everyone upset, crying. The Food Bank had posted a single page notice, in English for crying out loud, on the front gate saying that the City had sold the land back to Ralph Horowitz. And never a word to us."

"No one had any idea this was even happening," muttered. Josefina. "We were thanked for our work but the program had ended."

Irma and Josefina both stood and began gathering the lunch dishes with quick, irate movements. "Can you believe that shit," Irma muttered under her breath.

Manuel shook his head.

Parker busied himself at the camp stove. "What we need is some strong coffee," he announced.

Irma addressed the group with hands on hips. "Listen, I understand that we're invisible people. The City doesn't care about us. They call us illegals, wetbacks, dirty Mexicans."

"I'm Guatemalan so speak for yourself," Josefina said with a laugh.

"Stealing your jobs and all that," Irma continued. "Even though we take care of your kids, mow your lawns and wash your cars. Clean your houses. But this was making the whole community better. We thought surely someone would listen. Maybe the city council lady for this area. Why does she have that job if she doesn't care about the people who live here?"

"It's what always happens," Manuel said. "You take workers when you need them, then you toss them out when you don't."

"I never heard about the Farm until today," Pomona said, instantly sorry for her justification. Why had she felt the need to explain her own ignorance?

"Yeah, I know. We're another world down here," said Irma with a hint of sarcasm.

Pomona winced at her implication, that she was a rich girl who didn't need to care about a group of poor people trying to save a piece of land in South Central from a developer. Or did Irma not like her for some other reason? Was her usual insecurity just coming through?

After everyone drank coffee, Parker pulled Pomona aside. "We've been here a while and the rally hasn't started. We can leave if you want."

"I want to stay," Pomona blurted out. She really did. Not just to show Irma that she was a serious person, but because she did care. Anyone with half a brain could see the Farm was worth saving. And to be honest, it was a real relief to spend a few hours thinking about more than her own problems.

At 4 p.m. Parker and Pomona retraced their steps to the center of the Farm. More people now surrounded the walnut tree. A cluster of lit candles flickered around the Virgin of Guadalupe. Handmade signs surrounded the tree:

The Farm is Not For Sale
We are Not Starving for Warehouses but for Good Food
We are Still Here
Cesar Chavez Would Have Fought for the Farm

A man strummed a guitar and a young woman sang a languid ballad in Spanish. An elderly man circled about playing a flute. Several young men beat upon drums. Suddenly, the growing crowd parted and a dancer wearing a feather headdress made his way to the center of the crowd. He danced in twirls and high steps while pressing his lips upon a large pink conch shell. The low tone resonated through Pomona.

"Aztec dancer," someone whispered in Pomona's ear. She turned to see that Manuel, Irma, and Josefina had joined them. A wizened old man now moved among the dancer and musicians, the tree and the people, with a smoldering bundle of sage that he waved across their hearts and over their heads. The sweet scent of sage perfumed the air. The rhythmic drumming grew stronger.

"To go to the spirits the shamans need some kind of transportation," said Irma. "The most powerful transportation is the drum. The drum is like the horse. It can take you anywhere."

Pomona turned from her spot to see more people approaching the clearing.

"So many people are here for the rally," she whispered to Parker.

He gave her hand a gentle squeeze. "Manuel just said there's a rumor going around that Mr. Horowitz has decided to sell to the farmers.

There's talk that we may hear a big announcement. May be good news tonight."

A young woman with long brown hair and a stout man with broad cheeks, came to the base of the tree and addressed the crowd.

The woman scanned the crowd with fierce determination. "Listen, compadres, as you know, we are not people used to speaking out because we know police brutality and migra raids," she said. "Throughout this country, our people know what it's like to live without legal recognition or political representation. Many campesinos are forced to migrate from Mexico and Central America because mega corporations stole our natural resources. Took away our livelihood gifted by our ancestors. Still we persist."

The crowd clapped and whistled in agreement. The woman's voice grew more forceful.

"You are brave to step from the shadows to fight for this land, knowing you could lose everything – your ability to stay here, to take care of your families, to earn a living."

The man stepped to the microphone. "Two years ago Mr. Horowitz issued a notice saying we all had to leave. Without any warning we had to find a way to fight back. That's when we found our lawyer and followed every rule and instruction asked of us – we attended city council meetings and courtroom proceedings, wrote letters, had protests so the rest of the community could be made aware of what they stood to lose, too. Now we have some news to share."

The crowd stood still and silent with anticipation.

The man said, "I took up this fight with you all because I know without the land we are nothing. History is made by the people in the streets; it's made by the farmers, the workers, the working class people. Yes, our lawyer Mr. Dan Stormer has a big announcement. It's true, Ralph Horowitz has made us an offer."

The crowd erupted in whoops and cheers as a man in a rumpled suit and tie with a graying beard and shaggy brown hair came to stand at the microphone. He stared out over the sea of exuberant faces without a smile.

"This fight was always predicated on our belief that there's something really problematic in the transfer of the property title and that the developer doesn't have a right to this land," he said. "But as you know, after many court decisions against him this court decision has now sided with Mr. Horowitz and he has started the eviction process for the South Central Farm. But Mr. Horowitz has just told us he is willing to sell this land that you have been cultivating with your hard work for the last twelve years."

The crowd erupted in uproarious jubilation. Parker gave Manuel a high five and Irma and Josefina hugged and kissed cheeks. They hugged every person they encountered as they turned and twirled and jumped. Relief washed through Pomona. She just could not take anymore bad news. But Dan Stormer held up his hand. "Don't get too excited yet," he cautioned.

"Why not?" someone shouted. "We've been begging him to sell us the land for years. This is the best news ever."

"Yes, Ralph Horowitz is willing to sell the land," Mr. Stormer said with a grave nod. "But his asking price is $16 million dollars, and his deadline to accept this offer and pay the money is in three weeks."

Chapter Fourteen
Virginia

It was seven when they left the Farm and headed to Elysian Park. Despite the terrible news that had ripped through the farmers and their supporters, Parker was determined not to let his perfect day with Pomona be ruined. He could have predicted that Ralph Horowitz would not give the South Central Farmers any consideration. Whether the man thought the land was worth $16 million on the open market or whether that's what he believed he could gain from this particular situation, for him, business was business and what real people and the community stood to lose meant nothing.

Parker knew Ralph Horowitz because he knew Amos Wilson. Just thinking about his father brought on anger, so he shifted his attention back to the moment at hand. A balmy breeze wafted through the open truck windows.

"This is one of the steepest streets in L.A.," Parker said as they ascended Baxter Street that rose toward his house as if rising toward the moon. Once home, Parker planned to change out of his dusty clothes and take Pomona to a quiet spot for dinner (Italian for sure) where they could bask in the glow of candlelight and sip wine. As the street crested he slowed and pointed south to the view of downtown and its silhouette of skyscrapers and buildings. Even though he was the L.A. transplant and Pomona a true native, he felt proud of his neighborhood, its natural beauty and sweeping views.

"Gorgeous isn't it..." But even before Parker finished his sentence his smile was replaced by a grimace.

"What is it?" Pomona asked, startled by the change in mood.

Parker forced a weak smile. "Nothing at all. Now it's my turn to run in. You wait here and I'll be right back." He pulled the truck to the curb and killed the engine.

But his abrupt shift in demeanor jolted Pomona and she instantly knew; they had been together almost all day and now Parker just wanted to go inside and be left alone. She had seen this scenario before.

"Listen..." she began.

"Just wait. Don't go anywhere, no matter what happens." His tone bordered on pleading. "I'll be back, soon as I can."

Pomona shot him a quizzical look. Did he think she would, for no reason, start walking back to Pasadena?

But Parker was already off and running toward an adorable little house complete with a white picket fence. He ran up the front walkway and bounded the three stairs that led to the porch.

Pomona's stomach knotted. It was too much too soon. Parker was freaking out. That's what men do. How many times had she watched some guy run away from Nora. One date, a real prince, the potential for true love with Nora humming a tune in the kitchen. Then, wham, the guy disappears and Nora's catatonic, sitting at her bedroom vanity, staring blankly into the mirror, downing glass upon glass of red wine. As much as Pomona played nursemaid to Nora, she could remain despondent for weeks, even months.

Disappointment swelled into Pomona's throat so that she could scarcely get a breath. She had been blindsided, believing her own fantasy, believing Parker would be different from other men and love her without complication. She wondered how long he would leave her sitting in the truck before returning to say he had a work emergency or his dog was sick. Nora had heard them all.

Pomona knew she should have cut it short after the bookstore. You don't let a guy think you have all day to follow him around like a lonely puppy, especially a guy like Parker. Entire books were written about the advantages women gained from playing hard to get. Nora had read them all. Pomona used to laugh at her mother's dating "rules" although clearly Pomona did not know the first thing about dating a man.

It's got to be something else, Pomona told herself. Get a grip.

She knew he was also upset about the South Central Farm and this Horowitz guy, but would he really dump her after an otherwise remarkable day?

Or was Nora right? Were they really cursed in love? If only she had read *Ramona* maybe this would not have happened. She reached into her bag to find the book. She could start now and read until he returned. She pulled out *Ramona* and her fingers grazed Nora's tin of ashes.

I know mom, I'm supposed to take you to the Colorado Street Bridge and shake you into the Arroyo, but I haven't had time.

That sounded crummy.

I mean, I need you close now. I think you'd like this guy.

Slightly better and true, actually. Unless Parker didn't come back. Then she wouldn't like him at all.

Pomona lifted her gaze and stared toward Parker's house. His door remained shut. As downtown's buildings moved into shadow, she opened her book and began reading.

Parker ran toward the house, blinded to all except the silver Cadillac parked on the street.

He knew that car well with its 275-hp, 4.6-liter V-8 engine. He had driven that car just last week, had sex in that car. Why the hell was it parked on his street?

Virginia couldn't possibly be inside. He had locked the door last night. The windows were secure. He stood on the front porch and grabbed the doorknob, but then yanked his hand away as if scalded.

What was he doing? He couldn't go in and confront her now. Not with Pomona waiting in the truck. He was ashamed at how terrified he was of seeing Virginia, or was it how terrified he was of Virginia seeing him with Pomona? No. What was he thinking? He couldn't risk losing Pomona. He needed her rooted love.

Parker turned away from his house and headed back. But just as he started down the porch stairs his front door clicked open. He jumped as if a shotgun had fired.

"Parker." The voice was perfectly chilled, dry white wine on ice. "Where the hell you been? Back up in one of your palm trees?" Virginia stood in the doorway wearing nothing but black lace panties cut high on her thigh and a plunging bra. Her straight blonde hair, swept to one side, draped over a sloping shoulder. "I thought I heard your truck pull up," she purred, hand cocked on her slender hip. "I've been waiting since last night. I'm famished. You'd better take me to dinner."

Parker leapt to the doorway and blocked Virginia's body with his own. "How the hell did you get in my house," he seethed, pressing against her to block Pomona's view.

Virginia took this as an invitation to step in closer. Parker reached around Virginia and, hugging her close, pushed her back into the house. At the same time he grabbed the doorknob and slammed the door shut.

"You think it was hard getting into this shack? Spare me the shock." Firmly pressed against Virginia, Parker had an urge to throttle her with his bare hands, to grab and shake her shoulders.

But Virginia was caressing his back with her hands. "Where have you been all night, Parker? What's going on?" She rested her head on his chest. She nuzzled closer and an undeniable warmth spread through Parker's groin.

"No," he said, pushing away.

"What do you mean, no," she said, taking his hands and placing them on her breasts. "I'm feeling a big hot yes."

"Listen, I've been working all day and Manuel's waiting in the truck. I gotta take him home. You wait here and I'll be back in an hour." His shame on full display, he knew he was still the same messed up guy, a lying son of a bitch who didn't deserve Pomona. He and Virginia came from the same pile of trash. Trash knows trash.

She eyed him with suspicion. "I don't know why but I smell a rat." She narrowed her eyes. "I actually came here to tell you the news you keep avoiding. If only you'd let me talk sooner and not ditched me at the stupid garden it wouldn't have come to this." She moved his hands from her breasts to her hips.

Parker leaned against the door, dizzy from his lack of sleep and his own arousal. He fondled her hip and longed to pull her toward him, to merge with her flesh. At the same time he wanted to run from the house back to Pomona. He shut his eyes and sighed, instantly realizing his blunder. Virginia was in high alert and smelled his resignation, like a hound picking up the scent of prey.

"Let him take the bus. That's what he usually does," she said.

"What? No. Why are you here?"

Parker's blunt words came out with such a force Virginia teetered in her high heels. Parker instinctively reached out to grab her arm. He could already see a smear of her blood on the white paint. But Virginia caught her balance in an excellent save. Her breasts shuddered against the black lace of her bra. Her green eyes hardened. For a long moment Virginia stared at Parker with such a murderous scowl he thought she might hit him. Instead she laughed. "You wanna play rough? We always had our fun when it came to fighting."

Parker put his hand on the doorknob and considered Virginia's lingerie and stilettos. When it came to speed, he had the advantage. He could slip out, sprint to the truck, and take off with Pomona before Virginia could stagger to the curb. But Virginia was sizing up the situation as well. She moved her body to block the door.

Quicksand filled Parker's lungs. He struggled for a breath. How long had Pomona been sitting in the truck? Five minutes? Eight? Surely she was getting antsy, perhaps even curious enough to come looking for him. She could knock on the door any second.

Or she might just leave and be gone when he finally returned.

Just as his brain finished these calculations, Virginia took her other hand and laid it on his crotch. Parker opened his mouth and was surprised to hear words surface through the quicksand.

"Listen, Virginia," he began, trying to ignore her hips. "The problem isn't just Manuel waiting in the truck…"

The problem was she could hurt Pomona. Physically. Verbally. Virginia would hold back nothing in her attack. Pomona would flee. She would never speak to him again.

Virginia lifted her head and sniffed. "With all the horse shit I smell there must be a horse around here somewhere. Wait, is this about that the fat girl from that garden?"

His expression must have been a dead giveaway because Virginia lifted her foot and attempted to stab Parker's leg with her stiletto heel. She almost got him right in his groin but he fell to the floor. He reached up to grab her arm but he missed it by inches and instead watched aghast as she flung open and ran through the door.

Chapter Fifteen

You Can't Just Leave Your Past Behind

J UAN CANITO and Senor Felipe were not the only members of the Senora's family who were impatient for the sheep shearing. There was also Ramona. Ramona was, to the world at large, a far more important person than the Senora herself. The Senora was of the past; Ramona was of the present. For one eye that could see the significant, at times solemn, beauty of the Senora's pale and shadowed countenance, there were a hundred that flashed with eager pleasure at the barest glimpse of Ramona's face; the shepherds, the herdsmen, the maids, the babies, the dogs, the poultry, all loved the sight of Ramona; all loved her, except the Senora. The Senora loved her not; never had loved her, never could love her...

Pomona read this passage over and over, sitting in the truck, waiting, trying to understand why the Senora did not love Ramona. Was it a classic jealous stepmother scenario or had Ramona done something that made her guardian so emphatically detest her?

She laid the book aside. Why hadn't Parker taken her with him if he meant to be gone so long? He had been gone a long time. She could just as well have sat in his house. Pomona squirmed against the warm leather seats. She peeked at Parker's closed front door.

Open. Open. Please open.

With every passing second her disappointment swelled.

She wrapped her fingers around the door handle. "Get out and find him," she told herself. "Maybe something's happened."

Of course she should go to the door. Anyone with confidence would not think twice to knock on the door of a man with whom she had just spent the day and had invited her to dinner.

But a sinking feeling kept Pomona rooted to the seat. Glancing back at the door, she whispered, "Please open."

In that exact second, it did. The front door swung open.

It took Pomona several long moments to comprehend the blur of action that surged from the house. A small figure burst through the door and began running down the walkway. At first she just stared at the incomprehensible scene. Then her brain began registering details: a woman was running down the walkway. She was running in black stiletto heels. She was wearing nothing but a bathing suit. No, not a bathing suit, but rather a fancy low-cut bra and scanty panties. A house fire, Pomona thought. This poor woman had been dressing when a fire broke out. She needed to call 911, but she did not have a freaking cell phone! They were so expensive and who was going to call her anyway?

Then Pomona realized – the scantily clad lady was running not from just a house. It was Parker's house. By now the woman had reached the end of the walkway. She stopped running and stood still staring down the street. Pomona could see her eyes settle on the truck and in that exact moment she realized who the woman was.

"God help me," Pomona gasped.

Virginia, the size two, Kansas debutante with the silver spoon forever lodged between her unnatural pink lips, was running practically naked from Parker's house.

As Pomona gaped Virginia glared back and the two women locked eyes.

Only one word could describe Virginia.

Furious.

And her fury sent her charging down the street as if she was wearing not stiletto heels but track shoes. How could she run so fast in high heels without tripping and flying across the asphalt? I could never manage that, Pomona thought, as if nothing else could register.

Within seconds, Virginia was standing right before the truck, pounding her fists on the hood.

"What are you doing in Parker's truck?" she screamed. "Get out, get out now."

Panicked by the real possibility that this tiny woman could drag her from the truck and rip her to shreds, Pomona locked her door just as Virginia flew around to her side of the truck.

"Enough Virginia," a voice yelled.

Pomona, sweat dripping down every part of her body, watched as Parker grabbed Virginia and pinned down her arms. But Virginia broke free and pounded on the windows.

As Virginia's pink lips contorted outside her window, Pomona flashed to the time she had read Stephen King's novel about the rabid dog Cujo. She remembered how the crazed dog had thrust himself against the broken-down Pinto with the mom and boy trapped inside. Nora had laughed at the book, but Pomona had been heartsick for the characters.

Closing her eyes against the crazed pounding, Pomona bent over and buried her head in her lap.

"Get out of the truck," Virginia screamed.

Pomona crouched even lower in her seat.

I'm going to be trapped in this truck. Die of dehydration. No one can help me. I'll die of thirst.

In *Cujo* the little boy dies of dehydration because his mom can't escape the car to get water. The story had haunted Pomona for weeks, to be trapped in a hot car by a mad dog while you're dying of thirst.

Parker tackled Virginia and threw her over his shoulder. Several neighbors appeared on their porches. to enjoy the spectacle of a nearly nude woman having a profanity-laced meltdown. She cussed and shrieked as Parker carried her up his front steps and back into the house.

When he set her down she let loose: "You want that hideous fat girl when you could have me? I think you're the reason Caleb fought with that Mexican worker in the first place and then you ran away like a coward when your own brother got knocked out. You think your brother's dead but he came out of the coma six months ago and is now at home recovering and you're the one who's dead to your family. They think of YOU as dead. You killed yourself."

Parker's first instinct was to defend Pomona. She was not fat by any stretch of the imagination. She was perfect, voluptuous, and bountiful. She was probably also gone and he wanted to scream but when he opened his mouth only some sad, incomprehensible babble came out.

"Of course he's dead," he said. Virginia was a malicious liar determined to take him down. He had watched Caleb's head hit the low brick wall with a brutal force. No one survived such a blow. The doctor had said as much. Virginia was desperate and vindictive but her ploy to control him had backfired. "That's what the doctor told me at the hospital." He knew the truth, yet still felt his legs trembling in spasms.

Virginia by now was zipping up her mini skirt. "Maybe you wished Caleb dead. I don't know why you always gave him such a hard time. He never had your looks, definitely not your passion. Everyone was always so seduced by your passion, even me, but that doesn't make you a nice guy. You're a horrible person, selfish, and egotistical."

Parker shook his head and stretched out his arms. "You should have never come here. I don't want to know what happened after I left. When I crossed the Kansas state line I cut all ties to my life – that person doesn't exist anymore."

"You can't just leave your past behind."

"Yes I can. People do it all the time."

"Are you telling me you don't care that your mama sat by Caleb's bed every single day for six months and prayed? Prayed alone. Prayed with your daddy and the preacher and every damn person in Garden City. I went every week too because I've always liked Justine. 'God's going to bring my baby back,' she insisted. Of course, we all knew Caleb was a goner. His head was bashed bad. He was never a fighter. But here's the crazy punch-line – one day Caleb really did just open his eyes."

Virginia's words were a ball of fire. They roared from her flaming mouth and singed his hair, his eyelashes, and skin. They scorched him head to toe. He saw what he had hoped never to see again. What he had almost forgotten in this new life. He saw Incencio's left hook slam against Caleb's jaw. The terrible force knocked him back. So far back his body hurtled across the thick white chalk line marking the makeshift boxing ring. His head smacked on the low corner of the cinderblock wall.

"He's out!" someone had yelled into the erupting chaos.

"No! He's-"

The crowd scattered in two seconds flat. Only Parker stood there alone as Caleb's blood flowed from the deep gash on his head and pooled around his ear.

Chapter Sixteen
Never Bet Against People You Love

After several long moments of silence Pomona lifted her head. She unlocked the door and stepped from the truck into the empty street where just minutes earlier Virginia had threatened her life. As she clicked shut the truck door, her legs buckled. She slumped against the door's metal panel and slid to the ground. She heard a ripping sound and turned to see her dress flounce, stuck in the door, torn from the hem of her skirt.

"God damn, that just takes the cake."

Sitting on the street Pomona could not think of a single person she could ask to come get her. She had less than five dollars in her wallet. Where would she find a cab anyway, here at the top of Baxter Street, the steepest road in all of Los Angeles? Pomona pushed herself back to standing and grabbed her bag from the seat. She began walking down Baxter Street. Pomona set her sights on the purple San Gabriel Mountains that splayed before her like sleeping bears.

"As long as I keep walking toward the mountains I'll find my way home," she told herself reassuringly. It seemed strange to be walking, given that a boulder had just crushed her heart. "As long as I set one foot in front of the other I'll eventually make it home," she mumbled. As Pomona walked, she realized, no matter what, her route would take her across the Colorado Street Bridge. "That's great. A second chance. Now I only have to walk two hours to do what I should have done in the first place."

As Pomona trudged along through the neighborhood, she saw Nora hunched at the kitchen table with a tattered paperback copy of *The Rules*.

"The writing's terrible but I might agree with the book's thesis that women have a better chance of landing a husband if they make men pursue them," Nora had said. "The idea is that hunters don't hunt animals that chase them or wait for them. They hunt unique animals that are hard to find."

"Ridiculous," Pomona had replied. That was when Nora was still pursuing love. When she still thought she would meet a wonderful man, not be taken down by cancer to die alone in bed, or rather, with her daughter and cat by her side but without true love.

Pomona was halfway down Baxter Street when she heard a menacing roar and screeching tires. A car racing down the street. She ran for cover in the nearest yard and hurled herself behind a rosebush, where she curled into a ball. Everything she had managed to hold together inside was collapsing, imploding in that fragile area between her ribs and heart.

A blur of silver blazed past. Crouched in the dirt behind the bush, wheezing with fright, she was incredulous that she had escaped Virginia.

After several long moments, Pomona stood back up. Her knees and elbows were scraped and bloody from rose thorns. She stumbled back to the street and continued walking down the hill in the direction of the bridge. Worse than the stinging scrapes was the hot wave of shame that flushed over her chest. Shame that she had been so willing to follow Parker like a puppy. That she had believed he could love her. That she had been so stupid to think love could find her.

Nora was right. They were both cursed in love.

By cutting through Elysian Park that surrounded Dodger Stadium, Pomona could get to Figueroa Street, which ran north toward Eagle Rock. From there she would get onto Colorado Boulevard and take it to the bridge.

Her feet and back hurt. When her left eye began twitching with spasms, making it difficult to see, her impulse to jump faltered. All she wanted now was to go home, burrow in the bedcovers with Delilah, and cry. She was just about to enter Elysian park when an engine sputtered beside her and a frantic voice called out, "Dear Pomona, I am so sorry."

She picked up her pace. Damn. She had almost made it into the park. The truck rolled along beside her.

"Let me explain," Parker said leaning from the driver's window.

"Go to hell."

"I deserve that, but hear me out."

"What could you possibly say? I certainly don't want to know why that crazy woman wasn't wearing any clothes." Pomona hurried along the empty street. Her left eye twitched so hard she almost collided with a telephone pole.

"Truth is Virginia was my girlfriend, for a long time. But I left her a year ago. Not just her, my entire life in Kansas. She came to California and tracked me down. I don't know why she wasn't wearing any clothes."

"Blah, blah, blah. You think I care about your trashy drama? Leave me alone." Pomona broke into a clumsy jog. The soles of her feet were numb.

"I know I screwed up. But let me at least give you your book."

"What book?" Pomona turned to see wild-eyed Parker holding *Ramona*.

She had done it again. In the midst of the commotion she had left the book on the seat . "Give it here," she said, moving toward the truck. As she reached out her hand, Parker took her wrist.

"Let me go!"

"I can't, beautiful Pomona of the Orchards. I'm falling for you. Falling hard. Let me at least give you a ride home. It's eight miles to Pasadena. I may be unworthy but I can't leave you stranded."

Eight miles? She had estimated only four or five. The distance was too much to absorb with everything else – Nora's death. The book. Her father. The Farm. Nearly naked Virginia trying to kill her. The burning scrapes on her knees. Her brain catching fire.

Then there was the matter of Parker's declaration. A cheap ploy to make amends. If he really cared for her he would not have been so reckless with her life. Her heart.

"You also left this on the seat," Parker said, holding up the rusting tin.

Holy tomato, she had left Nora's ashes again? She really was losing her mind.

"I need that," she shrieked.

"What's in it?" Parker peered closely at the tin. "Drugs?"

Pomona pulled open the passenger door, slid onto the seat and grabbed for the tin but Parker held it overhead. "I'll give it back but let me take you home," he said.

She snatched it from his outstretched hand and grabbed *Ramona.* "Fine, take me home but never darken my doorstep again." She turned her head toward her window to hide her watery, twitching eyes, no doubt red and bloodshot, too.

"What's the story with the book?" Parker asked as the truck picked up speed. "Why do you keep leaving it behind?"

"None of your business," she seethed. "Don't you dare ask me about that book. Or the tin."

"Okay, but I'm the one who keeps bringing them back to you."

"You're the reason I keep losing them." She turned and glared with her twitching eye.

"Alright then, I won't ask any more questions."

Without another word, Parker drove onto the Two Freeway and headed north, then segued onto the 210 Freeway east toward Pasadena. But he did not exit at Lake Avenue and take the usual route to Nora's. He kept driving.

"You're passing my house."

That's when she saw the fierce David-slaying-Goliath expression on his face.

"I can't lose you."

"You can't kidnap me either. Take me home now or I'll report you to the police."

"Something special is happening. I know you feel it." He knew he was crossing a line, but he could simply not lose her.

"Where the hell are you taking me?" Pomona was crying now, tears plunging down her face. "This was one hell of a coffee date. A naked woman almost killed me, and now you're kidnapping me." Then it hit her. "You're going to kill me, aren't you? You really fooled me, taking me to meet those nice people at the Farm. Are they part of this? Are we going to the desert? People get murdered in the desert."

Parker veered across two lanes of traffic and took the next exit. "I wouldn't hurt you for anything," he said, sounding deeply hurt. "Listen, we're near Eaton Canyon. Let's sort this out there."

"There's nothing to sort out," Pomona shouted. "Everyone's chasing something that doesn't exist. Making themselves miserable for a fiction only found in corny romance novels." She held up *Ramona*. "Love stories are made up by writers. That's why people read this trash — to live through sweet virtuous Ramona and noble heroic Alessandro and their amazing, fantastic passionate love. But it's hogwash. I would throw this book out the window if it didn't have sentimental value."

Parker stepped on the gas and pushed his old truck up Altadena Drive. He pulled into the Eaton Canyon Nature Center parking lot and cut the engine. Only then did he turn and look at Pomona, her face shiny with angry tears. He knew he was dangerously close to spinning out of control, what with the lack of sleep, the long day at the Farm, and now the elation of having intoxicating Pomona by his side. That he had told Virginia to go to hell had freed his heart now to love Pomona with everything he had. He jumped from the truck, ran to the passenger side, and opened the door.

"You say that love is not real but I'll prove it is. I don't know how I know because I've never been in love. But the feeling I have when I climb into a palm, it's a kind of love. I feel that for you." He took her chin in his hand and turned her face toward his. "Don't you feel this magic?"

"Because you love a tree and feel something for me, you think that's real love?"

"Yes, I think so."

Pomona sighed, suddenly overwhelmed by exhaustion. "Listen, I need to tell you something. I should have already. Then you'll know why I'm so on edge."

"What?"

"My mother died."

"She did? When?"

"Last week. I still can't believe it. I can't catch my breath."

"But we met last week. Wait, are those...?"

Pomona nodded. "Her ashes. I'm supposed to throw them over the Colorado Street Bridge." She began coughing and wheezing. "I can't. I really mean I can't catch my breath." She clutched her thighs with her hands and leaned forward.

His instinct told him she needed fresh air. He took her hand and pulled her from the truck into the cool night. "Let's walk slowly to get your circulation moving."

She didn't resist and together slowly they walked down a trail that snaked along the canyon, over a dry creek bed, and through a scrubby terrain of Coastal live Oak and Sycamore. They came to a small bridge that took them over a stream and into a cluster of mighty oak trees. In a clearing, Pomona dropped to the ground. "I'm so tired and hungry, I can't go any farther."

Parker shook his backpack off his shoulders and pulled out a small pouch. "Apples and tamales from the Farm."

They ate ravenously there in the dirt beneath the oaks in Eaton Canyon. They drank thirstily from Parker's water bottle. When they finished Parker asked, "What happened to your mother?"

Pomona was too exhausted to wonder how much to reveal. But what difference did it make? After this night she would probably never see Parker again. "Have you ever taken care of someone who's so sick they can't walk to the toilet so somehow, by yourself, you have to move them off the bed into a wheelchair because they refuse to let anyone else in the house? And even though they're skin and bones you drop them while trying to move them onto the toilet and they're lying on the bathroom floor crying, urinating, and you want to run away, but you can't because it's your mother?"

Pomona could see Nora lying on the yellow bathroom linoleum, her nightgown wet and twisted around her scrawny body, sobbing as Pomona tried to prop her up, tried to calm her and all the while she was screaming inside. "You get so tired from the day-to-day of the feeding, cleaning, of loving someone who's dying, you wish they would go to sleep and never wake up. But you're so terrified as they sleep that they've died and they'll leave you all alone."

Pomona's eyelids drooped and her head nodded forward. "I've never been so exhausted in my entire life," she mumbled as she slumped to the ground.

"Lie down. Get some rest and then I'll take you home." Parker slid his backpack beneath her head. He draped his jacket over her shoulders.

Within seconds Pomona was fast asleep. Parker listened to her breath deepen. When it was clear she would probably not awaken for a while, he let himself climb into the oak that she slept beneath.

From the oak's top branches Parker studied the sleeping form nestled on earth. Pomona's lush black hair draped across the makeshift pillow. She was curled up like a baby, her face obscured by his jacket. The soft earth was the best place for her to lie. Her body would naturally release its pain and the ground would swallow it up, transmute it. Mother Earth absorbed the great pain of humanity. All the suffering and misery, loss and death, whether from wars between countries or wars inside one person, all this pain was deposited into the earth and soaked into the roots of trees.

Sitting alone in the tree he listened closely to the night. An owl hooted; a coyote howled. The distant 210 Freeway traffic hummed like ocean waves. Had only twenty-four hours passed since his momentous climb into the Mexican Fan at El Matador beach? Parker loved when a huge wave of life washed through a single day.

And it had.

He only wanted to be with the palms and this singular woman sleeping beneath the canyon oak. But Parker shuddered because he knew, for all his justifications, he still had blood on his hands. He had bet against Caleb. Gonzales, collecting the money that night, had been incredulous. "$100 on Incencio? You mean Caleb, right?

No, $100 on Incencio.

"I don't get it man. You're not betting on your brother? But you brought him to fight."

"How many guys bet on Caleb, Gonzales?"

Five. Five of thirteen guys. But they weren't so much betting on Caleb as betting Incencio would go easy, give him a break, given that he was fighting not the boss's tough, rebellious son but the softer one who was really second-in-command to the entire slaughterhouse operation.

"Caleb knows what he's doing, Parker? You sure he really wants to fight Incencio?" Gonzales looked leery as he clutched a stack of twenty dollar bills.

"Yeah, yeah, he wants to. Shut up and take my money."

Crouched in the limbs of this Live Oak in the ghost quiet night Parker understood he should never have bet against the people he loved. You should always believe they are winners. Just believing gives them power. Now, he would spend the rest of his life wondering what would have happened had he placed his bet on Caleb.

Parker looked down at his sleeping beauty and felt safer knowing she was there. She was mad now but he would find a way to convince her his love was true. She could keep him anchored to the earth. Yes, he loved the palms, was thrilled by how they gave him a way to float up into the sky, away from his guilt and self-loathing, but Pomona could give him something he needed just as much. An anchoring to the earth.

They would be good for each other in just the right way.

Chapter Seventeen
Poor on Purpose

The next afternoon Pomona was napping on the couch in Nora's apartment when the knock came.

"Pamela, are you there? It's Stacey."

Pomona jumped up at the sound of the voice. "What? Who are you looking for?"

"It's Stacey, I need to talk to you."

Pomona opened the door to find the super's wife wearing her usual yoga pants.

"Pamela, my dear, how are you holding up?"

"Pamela? I'm sorry, my name is Pomona."

Stacey looked perplexed by this news. "Listen, I am heartbroken about your mother. So much personality. So much fun. We were all a little in love with Nora. You're staying until the end of the month, right? Three weeks? Slightly less I think. If you need more time, another month, we can talk."

With an aggressive push against the door, Stacey poked her head into the apartment and took a quick survey.

"I see you've got your work cut out to clear this place. Nora collected a lot of stuff, the books alone, good grief. I could maybe give you another month but then we need to ready the apartment for new tenants."

Pomona wasn't on the lease and Stacey wanted her out. Nora had lived in the apartment for almost twenty years and her rent was under market. A little paint and the unit could rent for $300, even $400 more each month easy. Completely out of Pomona's budget, which at that point was zero. She considered logistics she had not yet dared to think about, such as how she would get $600 to pay an extra month's rent and where she would go once she left. She was about to be homeless.

"We're poor on purpose," Nora used to say when Pomona was small, to explain their bare-bone bohemian existence, the reason she didn't try to find a good-paying full-time job.

Poor on purpose let Nora justify her decision to teach only three English composition and literature classes at Pasadena City College each semester instead of the six needed to make a living. But teaching only three meant that she had more time to live a free-spirited life focused on literature, ideas, and beauty as well as dating and travel. Poor on purpose meant Nora could openly disdain her well-to-do parents and their Cincinnati Colonial-style mansion. She could denounce their crass pursuit of the almighty dollar. Nora never felt poor on the inside. She had grown up with comfort and security. Her father was a judge with a good income and solid social standing, and she chose to cast it off. First, she had married the man she loved, an immigrant without a solid profession. Then to indulge in her bohemian ideals. Being poor for Nora was romantic while it filled Pomona with panic and shame.

Slowly she shut the door, giving Stacey the hint to pull her head back away from the door and out of her space. Pomona would have to sell the books and sell them quick. She could try to raise funds from Nora's hodgepodge of antiques and vintage finds though Stacey would never let her hold a yard sale in front of the building. "I'll let you know in a couple of days whether I'll stay longer," she said. "Thanks for coming by."

"Hold on," Stacey said. "There's also the problem with the cat."

"What problem?"

"Mrs. Fassbinder saw it sitting under the mailboxes yesterday and pointed out our strict no pet policy. I let your mother have the cat because, well, it was your mother and she could charm anyone. In hindsight we should have said no. The cat has to go, of course. I can't let other tenants think I'm playing favorites."

Delilah had been mewing under the mailboxes when Pomona finally returned home after midnight. She was so relieved to see Delilah, she didn't consider that her foolhardy decision to let her out would lead to more problems. "Well, hopefully we'll both be gone in three more weeks."

Pomona tried again to shut the door, this time with more firmness, but Stacey stuck her pink athletic shoe between it and the jam. "You can stay, honey, but not the cat. Has to be gone by tomorrow."

Stacey could not have said more plainly that Pomona was not fun and charming like Nora. To Stacey she wasn't even Pomona. She was some Pamela, some nondescript person living in her apartment that Stacey could be renting for a lot more money.

Chapter Eighteen
Nighttime Palm Tree Climbs

After working all day, then showering and dressing in his nicest slacks, Parker drove to Nora's apartment to take Pomona to the dinner they had missed the night before. He had insisted during their drive back from Eaton Canyon (at midnight after Pomona had slept for two hours) to take her to Palermo's Italian restaurant on Vermont Street in the Los Feliz neighborhood where he would order calamari and eggplant parmesan, garlic bread, and Chianti.

She didn't refuse and he sensed a softening in her composure.

When Parker stepped into Nora's apartment the weight of the place crashed around his head. The odor was overpowering, discordant strains of heavy perfume, clove cigarettes, and cleaning products mixed in with cat litter and a moldy undertone. The air had ceased circulating long ago.

He glanced around as Pomona disappeared into the bedroom. The small living room had the classic features of 1920s Spanish architecture with dark wood floors, thick plaster walls, arched doorways, and high ceilings. The apartment could have been handsome were it not overstuffed with too many shelves crammed with books. Parker had actually never seen so many books outside of a store or library. Old brass lamps and porcelain figurines – Chinese women with parasols, Spanish dancers with fans – crowded together on side-tables and cabinets. But it was not just the clutter and stagnant air that made Parker uneasy. It was the whiff of death that he knew so well from the slaughterhouse.

No wonder Pomona had tried to escape. Nora permeated the place.

"I know it's a mess," Pomona said as, carrying a cat, she returned to the room. "She liked flea markets. All this stuff…for her, each piece told a story." Pomona sat on the sofa and hugged the cat to her chest. "My mom rescued Delilah from the SPCA. The landlord's wife told me today I have to get rid of her by tomorrow. I'm sorry to take her back to the shelter." The cat swished its tail and meowed. "Oh, dear, does she know what I'm saying?"

"You can't take that cat to the shelter. She could be euthanized."

"But who would want this cat?"

"Bring her to my house."

"What?"

"My landlord is cool."

Pomona stayed quiet as she digested his proposal, sure there was a catch or a good reason it would never work out. "She'll freak out in a new place all alone," she finally said.

"Then you come, too."

"Excuse me?"

"Stay for a few days until the cat gets situated. Maybe it's not such a bad idea for you to have a change of scenery as well. I mean, a lot has happened in this apartment." Parker tried to keep his expression neutral though he couldn't believe the words coming from his mouth.

Pomona, for her part, composed a thoughtful expression, as if she were deciding whether to order soup or salad. Inside her heart roiled with the prospect of being inside Parker's house. "Probably a bad idea," she finally said. "Last time I went near your house my life was threatened."

Just the thought of Virginia made her blood boil. In high school mean girls like that looked right through her. Still though, she couldn't deny her attraction to Parker. Her body tingled whenever he came near.

"I understand why you'd never dare come near my house, but I promise, she won't bother you. I won't let her. She won't come back. Believe me."

"Are you sure?"

"Absolutely." He wasn't, but if necessary he would build a ten-foot barricade around his house to keep Virginia out.

The entire drive home Parker was amazed by what he had done. He had never wanted anyone in his house before. He never wanted anyone to see his night ritual – moving in rhythm with the moon, lacing up his work boots after dinner and restlessly waiting as darkness descended to venture out and find that one special palm for the night. Searching for those alluring, beckoning palms along the coast, from Malibu all the way to Laguna. His entire time in California had been organized around his secret nights out. They brought him the calm he craved to get through another day.

Bringing Pomona into his life could end all that. At the same time, the idea of having her close thrilled him. By inviting her in, he had let down his defenses. He understood he was the one who had made the case for love. He was sure this was the right thing. This would make him stronger. And he had to believe she wouldn't have come if she didn't like him too.

Delilah meowed the entire car ride and commandeered their attention from the moment they entered Parker's house. Pomona checked and double-checked every door and window before allowing Parker to open the cat carrier door and release the frantic cat. Once he did, Delilah was gone in a flash, into the bedroom and under the bed, meowing and bellowing with righteous indignation.

"She doesn't like being displaced," Pomona said. "Maybe I shouldn't have brought her."

"Give her three days and she'll never want to leave."

Pomona wondered if she would feel the same. Now in Parker's orbit, she was pulled toward him like the moon to the earth.

Parker showed Pomona around his small, old, sparsely furnished home. The small kitchen with its gold-flecked linoleum and pine cabinets.

The pink-and-black tiled bathroom with a chipped claw-foot tub. Pomona noted the arts and craft styled wood rocker and a wicker chair with tropical print cushions. A futon couch.

"These were all curbside treasures found on late night drives," Parker said. " People in L.A. throw out the nicest things." A river-rock fireplace graced the living room. The rooms were lit by a mix of floor lamps.

They sat at the red Formica kitchen table and shared the roasted chicken, hummus, and bread that Parker had picked up on the way home. The way Parker ate with gusto made her stomach churn with desire, his open pleasure so attractive. Their quiet meal was punctuated by the clacking tic-tock of an old clock hanging on the wall. Even Delilah had become silent.

"I'll only stay a few days until I figure out what to do with the cat," she said. "Maybe two. Three at the most." She had no idea why she chose those numbers since she had zero prospects for finding the cat a home.

With the cat now hunkered under the bed, Parker considered that Pomona could go back home. He would happily feed the cat, but he did not want her to leave.

After dinner Parker showed Pomona his bedroom and said that it was hers. That the mint green sheets were freshly laundered. He emptied the top drawer of his dresser for her things by throwing the contents onto the floor of his closet. Then he stood in the doorway and shoved his hands in his pockets as they stared at one another. He cleared his throat. "I want so badly to kiss you."

Pomona swooned. One touch and she would go down like a redwood tree. But she wasn't ready to lose herself this way. She went to the doorway.

"Good night," she whispered as she took the doorknob and pulled the door shut. It took all her strength not to fall into his arms as he stood there looking into her eyes with a smoldering lust.

Chapter Nineteen
City of Second Chances

At 6 a.m., as Parker tiptoed into his bedroom for his forgotten belt, a sheen of light filled the room, just enough to illuminate Pomona's black hair spilling across the pillow, the nocturnal mermaid, her midnight hair floating across a bed of sea moss.

It took everything he had not to go over and lay beside her, to smell her hair and touch her skin.

He went to the kitchen and filled his metal thermos with black coffee. He loved the deep stillness of the early morning, how the anticipation of a day among the palms moved him through the solitary chore of organizing his work paraphernalia. A serious palm trimmer knows the importance of having good solid work boots and spikes and ropes with no frays or tears. He sat at the kitchen table and laced up his boots. He liked the way his toes and heels perfectly filled the shoe. He paid good money for his boots because a palm-trimmer's feet are critical, like a surgeon's hands, foundational to the work.

At 7 a.m. Parker pulled his truck to the curb at the corner of Los Feliz and Glendale boulevards. Manuel opened the door and stepped into the truck. He was holding a coffee from a nearby donut shop.

"Buenos dias, jefe," he said. His brown face, etched with a thousand wrinkles, always reminded Parker of the parched desert ground. As they drove through the quiet streets Parker flashed back to the black hair spread across his pillow. He liked the way her lush body filled his bed. He hoped she was still sleeping, soothed by the morning silence.

Parker looked over to see Manuel slumped against the seat with downcast eyes. "Things are tough at the garden I imagine," he said, contrite that he had not asked sooner about what had happened since the lawyer had announced the developer wanted $16 million for the land.

Manuel crossed his arms. "Farm leaders tell the campesinos not to give up, that we have to believe we can raise $16 million, but it seems to me a foolish dream. I've seen this before. Anyway, I just want to plant my garden and be left alone. I have sweet peas sprouted from seed to get in the ground and you know, Parker, sure as the sun rises, I have to pay my rent. Send money to Dolores."

Parker took most every trimming job that came their way. He was always driven primarily by his hunger to discover new palms, though he needed to earn money too. But Parker's ambition in building a business was mainly motivated by his need to provide Manuel with steady work and pay. Afterall, it had been him who'd convinced Manuel to leave the crew and become his partner. And that decision had been predicated on the unfortunate incident he witnessed just months after joining the crew.

It was an early morning in Venice Beach and the trimmer was young, nineteen or so. Parker remembered watching him chop at the fronds of a Mexican Fan with a reckless abandon that made his knees weak. The boy was actually singing as he whacked, belting out a tune in full force Spanish as his arms swung around like propellers. Parker couldn't bear to see the kid making so many mistakes, so he turned away. He was still the new guy and it was not his place to tell other trimmers what to do.

A few moments later Parker realized the singing had stopped. He looked over to see that the boy had pulled the wrong frond, releasing a thick ring of fronds that had plunged down on top of the boy.

What the boy didn't know and would never have the chance to learn was that dead fronds, which can appear to be attached to the tree, are actually only attached to other fronds. When the dead fronds are pulled loose, the whole weave collapses. It pinned the boy from Salcido to the tree. Gulping its dust he had battled to breathe but it weighed too much.

The other trimmers couldn't get to him quickly enough. The boy was asphyxiated.

After they took away the boy's limp body, Parker turned to Manuel and said, "Well, I never want to see that again." He sized up the older Mexican man who, despite his age, was the best palm trimmer he'd ever met. "Listen, I'm going to leave the crew and work for myself. If you come along we will be equal partners. We can make more money. Choose jobs we want. Don't have to watch bad trimmers butcher trees. I've been moonlighting for a few people so we already have a couple of clients." Parker held his breath, realizing how much he hoped Manuel would say yes. Unsure why the man would put his trust in him. But knowing Manuel would be key to making the venture a success.

When Manuel nodded yes, Parker promised himself he would make sure his new partner never regretted this decision.

Jobs came entirely through word of mouth and grew steadily because Parker and Manuel always arrived on time, never left behind a mess. Careful and efficient, they only left behind beautifully trimmed palms. Parker also knew that some clients liked the fact that he was a white guy who spoke English without an accent. He noticed how some clients never even looked at Manuel or spoke to him directly. He was invisible to them. The undocumented Mexicans and Central Americans who worked in Los Angeles trimming trees, mowing lawns, washing cars, cleaning houses, and caring for children lived in a parallel universe divided from white culture, just as in Kansas.

The dead boy had come from Refugio Salcido, a Durango ranching village that had started making inroads into the California tree trimming business in the 1980s. For years decades, since World War II, tree trimming in California had been dominated by Japanese Americans. But as the Japanese gardeners aged, and their children went to college instead of joining the business, the Japanese old guard took on Mexicans and Central Americans as their helpers.

Accidents increased, Parker knew, because some people did not care who trimmed their palms, as long as they got a good price. They often did not care if trimmers had insurance or any kind of certification. They did not care that these trimmers used chainsaws, though that's the quickest way to spread deadly fungi. Novice tree trimmers were the first to die in falls after mistakenly cutting through their security belts with chainsaws. They accidentally cut their arms and toes. Trees fell on them. They were electrocuted and mangled in grinders.

The body of the young man from Refugio Salcido was sent back to Mexico for his burial. Gardeners from his village donated the money to fly him home. Parker had thrown $65 into the pot, all the money he had made from that job.

That morning Parker and Manuel first tackled two palms in the front yard of a 1950s ranch-style house in Glendale. Then, after a quick lunch, they drove through Silverlake toward the upscale Los Feliz neighborhood. From Vermont Street they turned onto Edgemont and bee-lined to an estate at the top that abutted Griffith Park, a 1920s Spanish Revival castle on an acre. The house itself was painted as pink as a tropical sunset. The surrounding property was landscaped to perfection with blankets of bougainvillea and oleander, numerous jacarandas, a small orchard of pomegranate, avocado and olive trees. Around the pool towered an exquisite collection of Mexican Fans.

A butler ran down the driveway, opened the security gate, and with a smile waved Parker and Manuel through. "Parker, my friend, good to see you. We've got one hundred coming for cocktails at six so tackle the five palms to the north of the pool," he called through Parker's open window.

A pop star owned the estate. The last time Parker had come, two months earlier, he had watched her drive her silver convertible Mercedes down the curved driveway, platinum hair draped seductively across one eye. His heart quickened at the sight of her, not because she was beautiful and famous, but because her red lips were parted in a sly, knowing smile, as if she were letting him in on the big joke: "Hey, I'm a working-class girl from Arizona and look at me now." Yes, anything was possible in the City of Second Chances. If a girl from suburban Tucson could become a glamorous pop star, maybe a misfit from Kansas could find true love and salvation.

Chapter Twenty
First Day of the Rest of My Life

Pomona woke up and stared at a white wall.

Where was she?

She blinked and waited for some idea of reality to float back into her consciousness. She took a long breath and rolled away from the wall. A patch of soft light came through the single bedroom window, but she could not tell if it was morning or afternoon. She pushed herself to sitting. The room was small and bare with just the bed, a simple wood nightstand and dresser.

Parker's bedroom.

Pomona ran her hands along the mint-hued sheets. He had slept in these sheets, not last night, but in his life before her.

Had Virginia slept in these sheets as well? Falling back against the pillow, Pomona could not picture Virginia in this modest room with its old furniture and threadbare cotton sheets. Parker had promised she would not return and Pomona had to trust that he wouldn't knowingly put her life in jeopardy.

Anyway she was starting to feel right again, like a real person. Someone who could take care of herself. Pomona lifted her purse from the floor and pulled out *Ramona* and Nora's ashes. Having Francisco and Nora close by gave her confidence and strength. She slipped the book and Nora's ashes beneath her pillow and patted it down. They would be safe there for now. Pomona slipped out of bed and went to the kitchen.

She gaped at the ever-clacking kitchen clock. It was one in the afternoon. She had not slept so well in months. Parker had left out the coffee press and coffee beans. She filled the teakettle with water, inhaling the strong Guatemalan grounds. He drank his coffee black, she remembered.

After making coffee, Pomona looked for and found Delilah still under the bed. "I'm sorry, kitty, come out," she coaxed. After a few minutes of Delilah's snubbing, Pomona gave up. Throwing on her robe, she wandered the rooms, sipping the pungent brew. Curious to see Parker's possessions, she opened his bedroom closet. Just a few clothes hung from wire hangers. A couple of flannel shirts, a blue dress shirt, a brown wool jacket.

In the living room a fantastic nature collection covered the fireplace mantel: a scattering of stones and an assortment of bird's nests. She picked up an exquisite hummingbird's nest still attached to a thin branch and imagined Parker finding it abandoned on his trimming jobs.

To one side of the mantle lay a small stack of books. Pomona's interest perked. What books did Parker own? She picked up the first title: *The Huntington Botanical Gardens, 1905-1949: Personal Recollections of William Hertrich.* Ah, the book he had mentioned under the Ombu tree. She picked up another volume: *The Wild Muir: Twenty-two of John Muir's Greatest Adventures.* That made sense. *The Big Sleep*, by Raymond Chandler. Hmmm, interesting.

Inspiration hit and she went to the bedroom and fetched *Ramona* and Nora's tin from beneath the pillow and brought them to the mantle. "Stay here until we leave Parker's place," she whispered, laying the book at the other end of the mantle and resting the tin on top. Then she noticed a single book that looked brand new. *Chavez Ravine, 1949: A Los Angeles Story* was printed along its pristine hardback spine.

Pomona did not know this story of Los Angeles. She picked up the book and studied the cover photograph. A solitary man, his back to the camera, walked up a winding hillside dirt path toward a cluster of small simple houses that looked much like Parker's. The man's suspenders crisscrossed his white shirt and a brimmed hat covered his head. He was clearly of another time.

Pomona went into the kitchen, took an orange from a bowl, and went out to the front porch where she sat upon an old metal glider facing the street. She looked at the book. A sentence edging the cover read: "Photographs and text by Don Normark."

Inside the pages, black and white photographs depicted a rural neighborhood of yesteryear spread out in the shadow of downtown Los Angeles. The people in the photos looked mostly Latino. They all wore a style of clothing suggesting the 1930s or 1940s. They were engaged in daily tasks that make up a life. In one photo a cluster of children played ball. In others, a woman arranged flowers in a vase; a young girl in a frilly white dress brushed her long black hair; a small boy held his baby sister; an old woman swept a flight of steps. The dirt streets within this hilly community were populated with goats and chickens, dogs and cats.

After perusing the photos, Pomona returned to the book's introduction and read:

On a rare clear day in November, 1948, I was looking for a high point to get a postcard view of Los Angeles. I didn't find that view but when I looked over the other side of the hill I was standing on, I saw a village I never knew was there. Hiking down into it, I began to think I had found a poor man's Shangri-la. It was mostly Mexican and certainly poor, but I sensed a unity to the place, and it was peacefully remote. The people seemed like refugees – people superior to the circumstances they were living in. I liked them and stayed to photograph. I didn't know it at the time, but I was in Chavez Ravine.

Pomona closed the book. The day was bright and warm. A couple of kids, a small boy and girl with the same shiny black hair, were playing ball on the sidewalk across the street. She thought of crows in flight and wondered why they were not in school. This Chavez Ravine had been right here, just down the hill from where Dodger Stadium now stood. Where had all those people gone? How had they all disappeared?

It had been just over a week since Pomona met Parker. Since her impulse to jump from the Colorado Street Bridge had dissolved. Since her birthday. Since she found *Ramona* and Francisco's ghost returned. Since Nora died and she discovered the South Central Farm. It was early May and spring was in the air. Suddenly Pomona realized she could feel the edges in her life. The strangling numbness and stifling sadness that had kept her down for so long was beginning to lift, just slightly but enough for Pomona to know that she had been crushed by life for years.

She had gone down a rabbit hole and would have never emerged had she not turned left instead of right and gone into the palm garden instead of the Japanese garden.

She had been given a second chance.

Pomona pushed herself from the glider and walked out to the road. The playing children turned and waved. She waved back and the simple exchange filled her with optimism.

She remembered a phrase that Nora liked to say on special days that she marked as somehow significant. It was an old hippie saying splashed across t-shirts and posters from the 1970s.

"Today is the first day of the rest of my life," Nora would announce in those moments. Pomona knew that Nora meant she had learned a lesson. Taken a risk. Released a fear. Or maybe had even forgiven someone she thought had done her wrong.

It seemed those moments would never run out, back when time stretched into eternity, but suddenly Nora had no more first days of the rest of her life. No time left to learn from her mistakes. Which perhaps for Nora included never having read *Ramona*.

"But I do," Pomona whispered. In a second a life could shift from despair into hope. Sadness into happiness. Based on what? A connection to another person? To herself? She turned and walked back to the house. There she took *Ramona* from the mantle and began to read.

At 3 p.m., as the telephone pole shadows began to lengthen across the street, a loud noise made Pomona drop *Ramona* and jump from her chair. It was the same menacing roar that she heard a few days earlier when she thrown herself behind a rose bush to escape crazed Virginia buzzing down the hill in her Cadillac. She still had those scratches on her legs.

Pomona ran inside and slammed shut the door. As she stood perfectly still she imagined Virginia knocking it down with an axe. She was now trapped in another Stephen King novel, *The Shining*, with Virginia as the mad protagonist, Jack Torrance, chopping down the bathroom door to get his wife. Nora had laughed when she had read that book too.

Should she lock the doors and call the police? And say what? That a Kansas debutante was trying to kill her for stealing her boyfriend?

Cursed in love. We are cursed in love, Pomona.

The car was now just outside the house. Pomona dropped to her knees and crawled to the window that faced the street. She peered over the windowsill with shaking hands.

The street was empty. Had she imagined the whole thing? No matter. Huddled on the floor beneath the window, Pomona knew she was not safe in Parker's house. How stupid to think she was. And if she wasn't safe, neither was the cat. On hands and knees Pomona crawled stealth-like to the bedroom and peered under the bed. She found Delilah crouched in the middle of a field of dust bunnies.

"Come on Delilah," Pomona said. "This was a bad idea. We gotta leave." If she could get down the hill with the cat carrier she could catch a northbound bus toward Pasadena. She reached for Delilah, but the cat scurried further away. "We've got to go home," she hissed, fed up with Delilah's ornery ways. At that moment Virginia could be sitting in her car loading bullets in a revolver. No doubt a girl like that knew how to use a gun. Pomona grabbed Delilah's tail and dragged her out from under the bed, pulling along a mound of dust bunnies as the cat howled bloody murder.

"It's for your own good," Pomona cried, feeling terrible as she squeezed howling Delilah back into the tiny cat carrier.

Pomona picked up the carrier and went into the kitchen where she peered through the curtains into the street. She didn't see Virginia's car. The coast seemed clear. She hurried out the front door, across the porch, and down its three steps onto the sidewalk. She then spied another car ascending the hill. A silver late model Honda pulled up before the house. The driver's door swung open and a young man stepped out.

"Hello ma'am," he said. "Is this 63 Baxter Street?"

Pomona shook her head. "I'm not sure."

"Is this the residence of Parker Wilson?"

"Why?"

The man's smile widened. "I have some business with him."

Pomona grimaced, suddenly unsure of the right course of action. Had she already given this stranger too much information? The man was wearing a sports coat over a white dress shirt and brown slacks. He looked professional but in a worn and clumsy way, like a struggling writer working a temp job.

"He's not here now," she said.

"He'll be back later? Good, then, can you give him this?" The man rushed toward Pomona and handed her an envelope. "Make sure you give it to him," he said, almost tripping over the cat carrier. "Is that a real cat in there?"

She nodded, just then aware of Delilah's pained meowing.

"Doesn't seem too happy. Off to the vet? I won't keep you." The man returned to the street and climbed into the car. As he drove away Pomona realized that she could have asked him for a ride down the hill. She considered running into the street and flagging him down but her feet remained frozen in place. He was gone.

She looked down at the envelope clutched in her hands. It was thick and yellow with Parker's name and address typed on the front.

Why hadn't the man simply mailed it?

Suddenly Pomona realized she had forgotten *Ramona* and the tin. What was wrong with her? She picked up the cat carrier and returned to the house. She was acting crazy. Virginia was nowhere in sight. Surely Parker would not have left her alone if he thought Virginia would come.

Or would he?

She opened the carrier door. "Change of plans. we're staying."

With a howl Delilah skedaddled out and ran back under the bed.

Laying the envelope on Parker's nightstand, Pomona went to take a bath. If Virginia came to shoot her dead there was nothing she could do.

Chapter Twenty-one
A Rare Flower in Bloom

Parker and Manuel trimmed the five palms surrounding the pop star's curved swimming pool. All the while the butler directed workers and caterers setting up tables on the veranda that stepped down from the house. An emerald lawn rolled lavishly from the house to the pool.

Parker wondered what Manuel thought of the ostentatious wealth they sometimes encountered in their work. The 10,000 square-foot houses for a family of four. The luxury cars that cost more than he could hope to make in three or four years. The house staff and drivers.

Manuel lived in a two-bedroom apartment with four other men who had left their wives and children in Mexico and Central America to come to California for work. Manuel shared a bedroom with a guy from El Salvador. They took turns in the bathroom and if someone brought over a guest, the other guy knew to sleep on the couch.

"Mi amigo," Parker called to Manuel below gathering and bundling the fronds. "Have dinner with me and Pomona tonight." He would feed his dear friend a delicious dinner and they would all laugh and Manuel would forget the Farm for an evening and cheer up.

By 5 p.m., when Parker and Manuel had finished trimming the palms and loading the fronds into a small trailer attached to his truck, a clutch of waiters in head-to-toe black had gathered around the pop star's sparkling aquamarine pool. Parker pictured all the beautiful people appearing and floating across the grounds in their expensive clothes, sipping Moet Chandon, and reminding one another of the singular talent that had brought them into this rarefied circle: the hit song, high-grossing movie, or popular TV show. They would congratulate each other's particular genius and creative brilliance. Hollywood people trafficked in the ethers of ideas, reputations, and allure, all of which was enough to get you noticed, even if none of it went anywhere. Parker knew how the winds of good fortune and success could blow your way one minute, then shift and disappear the next. He beamed, knowing these lucky fools would spend their swanky evening beneath a canopy of perfectly trimmed palms, artfully lit by garden lights.

He and Manuel had done a perfect job of removing all the browned, dead fronds and leaving the beautiful green ones. They never cut the green ones as that weakened a tree. Palms needed as many green fronds as possible to stay healthy and stand strong.

The butler hurried to Parker's truck and handed him an envelope.

"Thank you, my friend," he said.

"No, thank you." Parker tipped his head with gratitude. He was lucky to have clients like the pop star, who paid top dollar for the best trim jobs. This allowed him to do what he loved more than anything in the world. Tonight he was lucky to have Pomona waiting at home and Manuel as a dear friend.

After leaving the fronds at the Glendale dump and driving back along Los Feliz Boulevard, Parker whistled a happy tune. How did you measure the worth of a day or consider time well spent? For his father, time well spent was measured by fortunes made through slaughtering and butchering livestock. Two hundred cattle slaughtered and butchered each hour put a lot of dough in Amos Wilson's pocket.

For Parker, a day well spent was measured by how many palms he might climb and how his heart sang each time he did. Today, having climbed and trimmed eight palms, and now on his way home to Pomona, his heart was as full and happy as it had ever been. Maybe today was the happiest day of his life.

In Echo Park, as Manuel waited in the truck, Parker ran into a grocery store and filled his basket with every delicacy that caught his eye. He knew he was filthy and dropping a trail of palm frond debris as he rushed around grabbing olives, a baguette, bars of chocolate, wine, eggplant, brie cheese, and salad. He spent more money than he should have but he did not care.

His luck was shifting. He was finally free of the past. Of the pain. Of his errors and sins. It was better that Virginia had ambushed him so that all cards were laid on the table. If Caleb really was alive then a miracle had occurred. He had never considered whether he loved Caleb. He didn't think he had previously knew what that meant. But as his love for Pomona grew it budded as well for the strangest people. Maybe to truly fall in love with a person meant you fall in love with everyone. With the whole world. Maybe for the first time he did feel love for his brother. But now he was going home to Pomona, to all that mattered.

As Parker drove onto Baxter Street he pounded the dash with his hand. "I love her, Manuel. This is the one."

"I believe you," Manuel laughed.

When Parker burst through the front door he found Pomona sitting on the couch in a simple yellow cotton dress. She looked even more sensual than he had remembered from that morning, lying in bed with her black hair swirled around her head. Her hair was now gathered in a long braid that trailed along her shoulder. After a moment of taking in her beauty he realized she was looking at the space behind his head.

"I hope you don't mind. I asked Manuel to join us." Parker turned to Manuel, standing in the doorway with the overflowing grocery bag. He bowed his head. "Buenos noches," he said with a formal bow.

For the next few minutes Parker rushed about, taking groceries, directing Manuel to sit beside Pomona on the couch, bringing them both a glass of red wine.

Manuel waved his hand. "No, Jefe, you sit with your beautiful lady. I will put the food away. I need to change my work clothes anyways."

Parker felt sheepish as Manuel went into the bedroom. "He's such a kind man, a great man. You will become close friends, I just know it."

As Pomona laughed all her afternoon fears fell away. She had taken a bath, washed her hair and carefully applied mascara and lipstick. Now, drinking wine with Parker, who was caressing her hand with his long fingers, she felt utterly adored.

After some time Pomona became aware of Manuel moving through the house, bumping familiarly around in the kitchen.

"I must stink," Parker suddenly exclaimed, jumping from the couch. "Manuel, sit with my Pomona while I shower and change."

When Manuel reappeared in the room he was holding and stroking Delilah, who was snuggling against him, purring. "This your cat? So nice," he said, settling on the couch. Pomona's mouth nearly dropped open as the cat sat peacefully on his lap.

"You have family in Mexico?" Manuel asked.

"My father was from Mexico. Tampico, on the Gulf Coast," Pomona said shyly. "His family is all gone. I've never been, but he said the beaches were fantastic, the water so warm."

Manuel smiled. "Tampico is famous for camarones, like Veracruz. Me, I'm from Chiapas in the south, almost to Guatemala. You know?"

Pomona shook her head. "Just been to Mexico once, with my mom. San Felipe, in Baja California. Not the main part of Mexico but still, everyone spoke Spanish."

"Sure, that's Mexico," he said, scratching Delilah's ears while she purred a storm. Watching the cat relax in Manuel's lap lifted a burden of guilt from Pomona. Coming had not been a mistake. As they sat together, she wondered how Manuel came to work with Parker. He was not young; he looked about sixty. Why had Parker chosen him as his helper?

"I know palms, like Parker," Manuel said, as if reading her mind. "We work together very good. You like palms?"

"To be honest, I never thought about them until I met Parker." The water pipes wheezed. Parker had finished his shower and would reappear in moments to fill their wine glasses and start dinner. Pomona lightly touched Manuel's arm. "I'm really sorry about what happened at the Farm the other day. Do you think there's any chance the developer might change his mind and lower the price? I know five million dollars seemed impossible, but to raise sixteen million...is that even legal for him to ask for so much?"

Manuel shook his head. "The campesinos are going to City Hall on Friday to talk to the politicians again. Me, I just want to plant my seeds, though maybe I am wasting time growing crops I won't harvest. For so many years we ate from el jardin and shared everything. If you wanted my maize, my cilantro or peppers, I would say, sure, go ahead." He gestured his arm towards Parker's living room as if it were filled with blossoming plants. "Sundays we prayed together under the walnut tree. A young couple who fell in love at the farm even got married under that tree." He sat up straight and put Delilah on the floor. "Sometimes too much hope is bad. It can take you down dead roads. We had many good times. Maybe better now to walk away."

Parker had watched her all through dinner, every move a graze to his heart, the way she cocked her head when Manuel spoke, leaning forward as she bit an olive in two. The gusto with which she sopped her bread in olive oil. The delight with which she threw back her head and laughed when he joked about the pop star's butler.

"He practically bowed before her as if she's the Queen of England. She's from suburban Tucson," Parker said, laughing along.

"Why are people so awed by celebrities?" Pomona said, sipping her wine with enjoyment, her dark eyes sparkling above the rim of her glass. She was backlit by the candelabra burning bright on the fireplace mantle. Her black hair had the shine of mink.

As Parker cooked, Manuel had set up a table beside the fireplace, added a tablecloth and dishware, all the while waving away Pomona's offers to help. He had even smudged the room with white sage that now intermingled with the aroma of Parker's eggplant Parmesan.

Sitting back in her chair, Pomona twirled her hair with her finger and focused her gaze on Manuel as she asked him questions about the Farm, Irma, and Josefina.

"What do you most like to grow?"

"Hierbas, you know, Epazote, Yerba Buena, oregano. I grow them for the yerberos."

What's that?

"Healers, like Josefina. They need so many hierbas, how you say, herbs, for their healing work."

"What does she heal?"

"When you are depressed, she helps to remove the stuck negative energy with a limpia, purification. With the crying babies she knows which herbs calms their spirit. Maybe someone gives you mal de ojo, a bad eye, when they look at you with jealousy or anger. This can give you a stomach ailment. She helps with that."

Pomona shuddered, remembering Virginia glaring at her through the truck window. She definitely gave her the evil eye that night.

As they ate, Parker wondered if Pomona had any awareness of the effect she had on people. When she wasn't hampered by her self-consciousness, she was charming. He could see how Manuel liked answering her unabashed questions. Virginia was so different from Pomona. Virginia would always calculate her exact effect on others, leveraging her beauty as a valued commodity, never leaving to chance what she could manipulate.

Pomona is so happy, Parker suddenly realized. This was undoubtedly the happiest he'd seen her in the week that they had known each another. Parker sat up straight and ran his hand through his hair. Yes, something within Pomona had opened; a rare flower in bloom. Once in National Geographic magazine he had seen a photo of the rare Queen of the Andes plant that blooms once every hundred years, its tall blossoming stalk a regal presence in the harsh desert landscape of Peru. Pomona was his Queen of the Andes.

Parker suddenly heard himself laughing along with Pomona and Manuel, at what, he didn't know. It didn't matter. We could laugh together forever. Why not, he thought.

Before Parker could even suggest coffee, Manuel was standing at the door bidding good night. It was late. Time to go as he needed to get to the garden early in the morning to water. He would return to Parker's by 8 a.m. so they could leave for work. No, he didn't need a ride. The night was beautiful and he wanted to walk. He would catch the bus.

Parker and Pomona were alone in the kitchen, laughing as they washed dishes, as if they'd done so a hundred times, he rinsing and she drying. He had known since dinner that tonight they would make love, in his room, on his bed, with the cat sleeping on the floor beneath them.

He handed her a plate and their fingers brushed. They both knew and neither needed to rush. It was almost fun to see how long they could stand apart when both their bodies were magnets. Every moment of the last week had conspired to bring them together here, in Parker's kitchen. She stood on her toes to place the wine glasses on a shelf. He leaned against her and placed his hands on her hips.

"Careful, don't break the glasses," she whispered.

He carried her from the kitchen to his bedroom and laid her on his bed. He leaned over, unlatched the window and pushed it open. The heavenly scent of Arabian jasmine filled their noses. Parker had planted the vine beneath his window precisely because it bloomed all year.

"I think I love you, Pomona," he said as he hovered above her. How naturally these words fell from his lips. Golden coins that she wanted to gather and keep forever next to her heart.

"How did this happen?" she asked.

"Don't ask questions." He unfastened the buttons that ran down her yellow gingham dress. His mind flashed to summer picnics beneath the ranch's regal oak, the long row of tables covered in gingham tablecloths shaded by the oak's leafy branches. He was as at home here with Pomona as he had been at the ranch during his boyhood when life there was still magical, before it had been derailed by his father's expectations and the horrible mess. His happiness soared with Pomona as it did at the top of any palm. Wasn't this what he'd been searching and praying for?

Did he deserve such happiness? Would he ruin it as he always did in the past? No, he would not let that happen. This time he would keep the bad luck away.

She arched her back and let him slip the dress over her shoulders and unhook her bra. It was her turn to un-zip his pants and in unison they peeled off the rest of their clothes. Finally they were lying together, limbs pressed upon limbs. Parker kissed Pomona so passionately she could only moan from a place so deep, a place so hungry and so ready that she was the glorious Queen of the Andes opening herself to the world.

"I won't hurt you," he said

She believed him.

I won't go home. I'll never go back, no matter what, Parker thought later as he drifted to sleep, his arms wrapped tight around Pomona.

Nora was wrong. I'm not cursed in love, Pomona thought as she lay wrapped in Parker's arms. If anything, I'm blessed. I really see no need to read that book now.

Chapter Twenty-two
The Letter

H e woke with a start as he always did at 6 a.m. She was curled languidly beside him. In that moment they were two rivers converging, waters flowing in a single current, running stronger together. Disoriented and spent but deliriously happy, he rolled to the edge of the bed and wondered about the cat. Besides leaving food and water, no one thought to check on Delilah last night and lo and behold, the cat was starting to grow on him.

Bending over the side of the mattress, his head grazing the floor, Parker peered beneath the bed. Green eyes glared back. He laughed. "Just wait, psycho kitty. You'll be eating out of my hands in no time."

From the corner of his eye, Parker spied something alongside the cat. He reached over and pulled back an envelope. It was probably a subscription appeal that had fallen from a magazine. He laid his head back on the pillow and stared at the typewritten address. It was addressed to Mr. Parker Wilson. The return address was the Garden City Public Defenders Office. As he stared the letters began to spin off the page. At the same time a terrible pounding erupted within his chest. He laid his hand over his heart but he could not muffle the pounding so loud that it would surely wake Pomona. He remained still for several long moments, keenly aware of the woman breathing beside him. The cat fuming beneath the bed. Before his brain could interfere, he peeled open the envelope and pulled out a single sheet of white paper. He unfolded and read the note's handwritten words:

Mr. Parker Wilson:

I am Isabella Salviederra, Incencio's wife. I came to Garden City from San Salvador six months ago. I came to help Incencio who has been in jail since the fight with your brother because we could never pay $200,000 bail, even though many workers have generously donated money toward this cause. Since we no longer have the money Incencio made from his job, I have been working as a housekeeper while the public defender tries to settle this case. Mr. Moreno is very nice and helped me write this letter because my English is not good. When I arrived he told me that when Caleb finally died Incencio would be charged with manslaughter and sent to prison for a long time. This terrorized my heart every day. Already our daughters have not seen their father for two years. Now they live with my sister while I am away. I pray every night to my Lady of Guadalupe. She heard my prayers because the biggest miracle happened. Caleb woke from the coma! We have new hope. Incencio says you know the fight was an accident and Mr. Moreno says that only your testimony can save him. Your father does not want him released from jail NO MATTER WHAT He has hired a powerful lawyer. Mr. Wilson, I don't know why you left so fast that terrible night. Incencio said you were friends. Maybe friend means something different in Kansas than in El Salvador.

Mr. Wilson, maybe you don't know Incencio. He is a good man. He made a dangerous journey to escape gangs. To build a better life. To send us money so we can survive. He has not seen his daughters for two years That is a kind of torture. Do you know the sadness of little girls who don't know their father?

I beg you to come to the Courthouse June 14 at 8 a.m. and speak at Incencio's hearing. People told me not to waste time looking for you. That you already showed your true face. But miracles are all around. We pray every day for justice, for Incencio's freedom, for Caleb's recovery. We pray you will help.

Sincerely,

Isabella Salviederra

Isabella's words exploded in his head. Parker's eyes focused on the address for the hearing printed at the bottom of the letter:

Finney County Courthouse
425 N 8th Street
Garden City, Kansas

Parker had last been to the courthouse to pay a speeding ticket. That had been years ago, lifetimes, and he had paid the fine from a wad of twenty-dollar bills pulled from his jeans pocket. Virginia had been with him, the old Virginia who was always fun and carefree. They had laughed and kissed in the courthouse hallways as if going to court was a lark and there wasn't a problem that couldn't be solved with a stack of cash.

So his brother really was alive. His friend Incencio now had a chance to get out of jail and reunite with his family. Except his father wanted Incencio locked up for the rest of his life.

Parker's breath caught in his throat. God damn it. He did not want these facts complicating his happiness. He had left to be free of this excruciating drama. A wave of nausea overwhelmed him. Isabella had wasted her time. He would not return to Kansas for anything. He had shown his true face. Not just to Isabella, but himself as well. He was not the guy to do the right thing. No way would he throw himself into that black hole. Even if he was the only person who could help set Incencio free. Parker turned toward Pomona, still sleeping like a kitten. "How did this letter get under the bed," he finally said in a strangled voice.

Pomona stirred.

Parker lay a hand on her shoulder. "Do you know anything about this letter? I found it under the bed."

She sat up, alarmed by Parker's tone. "Oh, I meant to tell you."

"Tell me what?"

"A man came yesterday afternoon and asked that I give it to you. I left it on the nightstand but it must have fallen off."

"What did the man look like? What did he say? How did he know I live here because no one knows except for you and Manuel and…."

Virginia knew. The walls closed in and Parker could scarcely breathe. The urge to box his way out began overtaking his muscles. His leg began to spasm. His arms trembled.

Jumping from the bed, he grabbed his pants from the floor and slipped them on along with a rumpled shirt from the bedpost. Running into the living room, the letter sizzling in his hand like a burning coal, he ripped it into little pieces and threw it into the fireplace. Parker grabbed his safety belt from the chair and ran out the front door.

The cool morning air slapped his face as he sprinted in bare feet down the street. He entered Elysian Park panting, near delirious, and gazing upward toward the crown of his favorite palm. Only by climbing a palm could he calm down enough to process the contents of the letter. That Isabella was living in Garden City, working with a lawyer to try to free Incencio who could still be prosecuted for assault. That Incencio had considered him a friend.

He tripped over a tree root and went airborne, soaring through space before breaking the fall with his hands. Parker sprawled across the hard dirt as searing pain shot through his entire body.

Wednesday, June 14, 8 a.m. Three weeks away.

Parker scrambled to his feet and wiped his hands on his pants, leaving a smear of dirt and blood. He continued toward his California Fan, the one he had climbed a hundred times and within whose fronds he had found often refuge and solace. He attached his safety belt and began ascending the palm, heel to toe, upward along the trunk. Pain shot through his scraped hands and feet as he inched higher and higher into the sky.

Pomona threw back the bed covers as the front door slammed shut. She jumped from the bed and hurried through the house, pushing open the door just in time to see Parker running down the street, his arms and legs pumping so fast he was quickly gone from view. She stood in the doorway shocked and surprised. She started to run after him but realized she was completely naked, save for a bed sheet draped over her shoulders.

She had been an idiot to forget to tell him about the letter but was its message so terrible? Why when things finally went well did everything crash down? Pomona stood frozen in the doorway, thoughts tumbling through her head, when something soft brushed against her bare legs. Startled, she jumped out of the doorframe just as a flash of black fled across the threshold.

"Delilah," she shouted, running into the yard, the bed sheet flailing behind. But the black cat was faster. The cat dashed across the yard and out into the street, then took off in the direction opposite of Parker.

Chapter Twenty-three
A Violent Blow

Parker had never had such trouble climbing a palm. It was slow going from the moment he hoisted himself onto the trunk. For starters, he had never climbed with bare feet before and the rough bark scratched like cheese against a grater. Every move upward sent fresh pain searing through his scraped and bloodied hands. Prickles of agony ran through his arms.

He was desperate to be among the peaceful fronds. The adrenaline pumping through his body was exhausting, not invigorating, and halfway up he was forced to stop. The morning was coming into focus with streaks of soft light. From his midway perch he noticed a couple of small tents set up within a circle of Manzanita.

Before he could reach the top of the palm, that night returned to him. The emergency room doctor had come at them like the Grim Reaper in the fluorescent-lit corridor of Garden City General Hospital. His prognosis was a litany of disturbing words: "Severe head injury. Skull fracture. Acute brain swelling. Hematoma. Coma. Unlikely that he'll survive until morning."

Those were the only words that Parker heard. In the chaos of his mother's hideous sobs and his father's gruff commands to everyone in sight (Call my lawyer! Get some coffee!), Parker had simply turned and left. He needed seven minutes to drive the two miles from the hospital to his apartment, to run upstairs and throw a few clothes into his knapsack.

He stuffed what money he had (seven hundred dollars in large bills) between the pages of the one book he grabbed, *The Huntington Botanical Gardens*.

He was zipping his backpack when the phone rang. He paused only long enough to hear the first few words of Virginia's message recorded by his answering machine.

"Hey, I just heard what happened…"

He was gone before she said anything more. He already knew that he would go to California, to the Huntington Gardens, to the palms. He would find his own paradise, forget this nightmare forever. That's all he ever wanted from the time he was fourteen, to return to the palms. The decision was finally forced upon him and he would be a fool not to run.

Pomona, now dressed, was standing in the middle of Baxter Street calling Delilah when Manuel trudged up the hill at 7 a.m. to meet Parker for work.

"He's not here," Pomona said as Manuel approached. "A letter came, bad news I guess, and he ran down the street toward the park." She pointed listlessly. The beautiful night had turned horribly rotten. She was mad at Parker. Mad at the cat. Mad at Nora for dying in the first place. Because if Nora had not died she wouldn't be looking for freaked-out Delilah in an unfamiliar neighborhood. Pomona wished she could be mad at Manuel as he trudged down the street toward the park but she could not think of a single reason why.

After several moments of deep breathing among the fronds Parker returned to himself. The palms yet again had restored his strength. He knew now he needed to go home and explain to Pomona. He had no idea what to say. He had made a spectacle jumping from bed and running out the door.

Inching down the palm, his bare feet numb with pain, he unhooked his safety belt too early and, for the first time ever, he lost his footing and fell from the tree. Parker hit the ground with a thud that tore through his right arm. The hit dislodged the seething from deep within that he had buried that night a year ago when he had hitch-hiked out of Garden City and rode to Denver with a trucker.

"Jesus," he cried as he lay on the ground, his right arm searing. His lungs bursting. The tree had tossed him to the ground as if shrugging off an invasive creature. He did not want to know about Isabella and Incencio's children. Suddenly Incencio's raspy voice filled his head. "Hey, White Boy, tell your daddy to pay me more so I can buy me a truck. Man, I'm tired of taking the bus." He had been standing with Incencio in the dusty yard, drinking coffee, smoking cigarettes, laughing, when Incencio made this request.

He lay motionless beneath the palm

"Hey, man, you okay?"

Parker opened his eyes to a concerned face staring inches from his.

"You took a nasty fall." He was a young guy with greasy hair tucked behind his ears. The sour smell wafting from his body told Parker he had probably come over from the tent encampment. Holding out his hand he said, "I'm Adam. We watch you climb that palm all the time. You're amazing. If I could climb like that I'd sit in a palm tree all day, too."

After the men shook hands Adam pulled a cigarette from his pocket and sat on the ground next to Parker's head. "Got a light? I'll share this cigarette with you."

Parker was smoking with Adam when Manuel appeared.

"You okay, Jefe? I never have seen you smoke before."

"May have broke my arm but otherwise I'll live," Parker said, lifting his head and squinting at Manuel. "This is Adam."

Manuel nodded with a guarded smile. "Mucho gusto, okay, but there's a problem. When I came to your house I found Pomona searching in the street for the cat. I like that cat. Now you might have a broken arm. Que mala suerte!"

"You got a missing cat?" Adam said excitedly. "I'll find your cat for $5 guaranteed."

When Manuel returned with Parker a half hour later Pomona instantly forgot she was mad at the sight of his sorry state. His pants were ripped and streaked with blood. His bare feet were dirty and scratched and he held his right arm at a peculiar angle.

"Slipped from the palm. Probably just a fracture, maybe just a bad sprain." Parker sat on the curb and looked into the street with a disoriented expression, his eyes never focusing on any one point. "What happened to Delilah?"

"Escaped out the door when I wasn't looking. Ran down the street that way," Pomona answered, alarmed by Parker's behavior. She wondered if he might have a concussion.

"I told you already I could find him," someone yelled. They all turned to see Adam coming upon them. "Tell me name and color. I'll find that cat for $5."

Parker tried to stand but his legs buckled and he sat back down hard. "Black cat named Delilah. I'll give you $10 if you bring her back."

Adam grinned and took off calling, "Here kitty, here Delancey."

"It's Delilah!" Pomona shouted as she took Parker's good arm to help him balance.

"It's my fault all this has happened," she said in a low voice. "Me being so careless with the letter. Then losing the cat." As Pomona watched Adam saunter down the street, calling Delancey, her throat tightened. She wanted to join Adam and scour the neighborhood. The cat was her responsibility. Now she was leaving her fate in the hands of a total stranger. A smelly one at that.

Parker was now lying back on the sidewalk, both hands shielding his eyes against a rising sun. "You need to see a doctor," Pomona said. "For your arm and your headache."

Manuel crouched between them. "She's right. Go see the doctor. I'll finish the trim job. No problem. Client knows me."

Driving Parker's truck, Pomona first dropped off Manuel at the job in Highland Park, then drove Parker to the emergency room at Pasadena's Huntington Hospital. They waited for two hours before a doctor diagnosed Parker's fractured arm and slight concussion. He applied a plaster cast and instructed that under no circumstances should Parker climb anything for at least three weeks.

"Stay out of trees," he admonished. "You know how many head injuries I see from people in your line of work? Lucky it wasn't worse."

When Parker and Pomona returned home they found Adam napping on the porch.

"I've been in every tree, down every street and alley and I'm telling you, that cat is gone," he said after they roused him, sitting up and rubbing his eyes.

Pomona's heart sank but she said nothing.

Parker gave him $5 for his troubles.

Chapter Twenty-four
Turn Around

In the late afternoon, Pomona drove Parker's truck back to the job site so Manuel could load all the work tools. Parker was by then sleeping, having taken both a painkiller and Ambien at Pomona's insistence. "Your body only heals while sleeping," she said.

He did not mention the letter again and she did not ask. It really wasn't her business, she told herself. Anyway she had her own secrets that she did not want him to know. Not yet anyway.

"You want a ride home?" Pomona asked Manuel when he had finished loading the truck. She had no idea where he lived.

"No, not home," he said. "Going to a protest at City Hall. Can you drop me at a bus stop? I just need five minutes to wash up at the hose and change into a clean shirt." He held up a shopping bag to prove the clean shirt existed. Manuel shook his head. "Really don't want to go. I've been to so many protests and marches in the last few years, but Irma and Josefina insist this one is important."

Pomona knew that now that Horowitz had named his price the Farm was gaining even more attention. The farmers and their supporters were fundraising with increased urgency, asking everyone they encountered to bear witness to the plight of the South Central Farmers. Surely a watching world would not let this pass.

"Can I go too?" Pomona blurted. "Parker's in a dead sleep. I don't think he'll wake up for a couple of hours." She did consider she should look for the cat, but Manuel looked so tired and defeated, she wanted to bring him comfort.

"Of course," Manuel replied.

They made the quick drive from Highland Park to the Los Angeles City Hall building downtown at First and Temple Streets. There a boisterous scene overtook the sidewalk at the west entrance of City Hall. At least a hundred people marched up and down the sidewalk, holding protest signs:

Save the Farm!

Si se Puede!

Food Not Warehouses!

We are not the Earth's Master; We are its Caretakers

Pomona stared mesmerized as the crowd chanted loudly:

"Land & Liberty – Long Live Zapata."

"When times get dark the eyes adjust – don't let the eyes adjust."

"Food Not Warehouses."

Some people ran into the crosswalk on a green light and shook their signs at the stopped cars. Drivers mostly honked and yelled from their windows in support.

All the while a girl in a green poncho with a charismatic presence strummed a guitar from the top of the City Hall steps. Along with another musician she chanted, "Todavía estamos aquí!"

The scene was pure street theater. Pomona had never been to a protest before and she was both a little embarrassed by the protestors' riotous manner and awestruck at their resolute passion and disregard for what passers-by might think.

Several television cameramen filmed the activity. Pomona suddenly worried that her face might be broadcast on the evening news. What if a former library coworker spotted her, or what would Stacy, the super's wife, think if she saw that, instead of mourning Nora or (more importantly) clearing out her underpriced apartment, Pomona was downtown protesting the closing of a community farm. Pomona decided it was probably better if she stand on the sidelines and watch. She wasn't officially a South Central Farmer anyway.

"What are you doing?" Irma cried in an accusatory tone when she came across Pomona sitting on the steps. She grabbed her hand and pulled her back to standing, then handed her a sign that said in bold black letters:

Food Not Warehouses: South Central Farm Feeds Families

"I thought I'd just watch," Pomona mumbled, letting the sign droop toward the sidewalk. Irma was starting to remind her of Nora, exhibiting with the same pushiness that made her want to crouch down and cover her head.

"Mija, right now you need to make yourself bigger, not smaller."

Making clear she had no intention of letting Pomona sit this out, Irma stayed by her side as they marched and chanted, "Aqui estamos y no nos vamos! We are here and we are not going." Pomona had to admit, the longer she marched the more powerful she felt, and the stronger her voice became. After twenty minutes a familiar-looking woman with waist-length chestnut hair stepped to a microphone stand perched atop the steps. She raised her hands and the protesters congregated near the microphone. Pomona saw fatigue burning in Manuel's eyes.

"He's been working all day and he's exhausted," Pomona whispered to Irma. "He should go home and rest."

Irma shrugged, tucking her South Central Farm T-shirt into her jeans with indifference. "He hates coming to these but when it comes to resisting an injustice no one cares if you are too tired to fight. In fact, your enemy counts on that to win. In this world, the more tired you are the harder you have to fight." She turned her fierce gaze to Manuel but the sight of him brought a softness to her face. "Okay, I know his jefe, your boyfriend, is injured and he has to work for two people so I will tell him to go. He doesn't live far and maybe Josefina can give him a ride. But don't think the revolution is fought and won by well-rested people."

The woman at the microphone began speaking:

"Compadres, I am , elected representative to the South Central Farmers. Today we ask the Los Angeles City Council, do the inner city conditions of extreme poverty, racism, lack of educational and employment opportunities, unsafe parks and widespread police abuse that were exposed worldwide during the 1992 Uprising no longer exist? Is that why the farmers' land is being taken away? We believe we have a right to land where we can continue to grow our own crops and feed our families fresh organic and affordable food."

The crowd clapped as stepped away and a young man stepped forward. His hair was dark and curly. His intense brown eyes resembled those of a nocturnal animal surveying a field. The reporters and television camera operators pushed in with great interest to capture his words.

"Who's that?" Pomona asked a guy beside her.

"A rapper, Zack de la Rocha, from the band Rage Against the Machine. He's a good friend to the Farm, and has spoken on the farmers' behalf many times already," he said.

Pomona nodded, not wanting to appear clueless. She had vaguely heard of Rage Against the Machine, an L.A. band, though she didn't know anything about their music. She imagined, with that kind of name, it was probably intensely political.

"Amidst a sea of hunger, Mr. Horowitz proposes to build a concrete warehouse from which no one living in our community will benefit." The rapper paused for dramatic effect. "As we approach the fourteenth anniversary of the L.A. Uprising I'm here to say that we must listen and learn what the South Central Farmers are teaching us about sensible, humane, and truly democratic forms of government in the city. The fate of the nation's largest urban farm must not lie in the hands of a greedy developer and a self-serving city council and backdoor midnight deals."

As the crowd clapped and cheered, a small, lean woman with short dark hair stepped to the microphone with joy radiating from her face.

Pomona leaned forward. Who was this self-possessed woman who looked like a young Isabella Rossellini?

The woman spoke as if answering Pomona directly:

"My name is Julia Butterfly Hill. I am most known for having lived in a Northern California fifteen-hundred year-old ancient redwood tree for over two years without my feet touching the ground to keep it from being turned into lumber."

Pomona pushed through the crowd, her heart racing. This woman lived in a redwood for two years? Without leaving the tree? How? Why?

"Perhaps you wonder, why is the poster-child of a tree hugger here?" Julia beamed as she scanned the crowd. "One thing I know, with six billion of us and growing on this planet, we must make our cities more livable."

Pomona stared at Julia, just a few feet away. She looked to be in her late twenties, maybe early thirties. Her own age. She had a wide smile and an accepting confidence shining from her eyes. She wore a green South Central Farm T-shirt. Gold hoop earrings dangled from her ears.

As Pomona regarded Julia, her heart burst with a strange sensation. She knew this woman. The Pasadena library had carried several copies of her memoir. Her librarian brain retrieved the book's title: *The Legacy of Luna*. Pomona had never read the book about her time spent living in the redwood. Now she wished she had. She needed to know everything about Julia—where was she born and who was her family. Why had she traveled to see the ancient redwood in the first place? What higher wisdom called to her? How did she know to climb into its branches and from where on Earth did she find the courage to stand up to a powerful lumber company?

She felt Julia held the answer to a question she couldn't yet form or articulate.

Julia continued: "When I was traveling through here last year with a sustainable tour I had representatives from the Farm come up on stage and speak and I said then if the eviction notice comes down I will come and stand in solidarity with you. Because the Farm and its people are as priceless and irreplaceable as the ancient redwoods, my comment for City Hall is a quote I heard while living in the tree; it's a good one for the politicians who made the choice to sell the farm. 'No matter how far you've gone down the wrong road, turn around.'

People started yelling, "Turn around! Turn around!"

"Thank you for your commitment to the Farm and to the planet," Julia finished. "It's an honor to stand in solidarity with you."

As the crowd cheered and clapped someone shouted Julia's words again: "No matter how far you've gone down the wrong road, Mr. Horowitz, turn around!"

"No matter how far you've gone down the wrong road, turn around," more voices echoed.

Leaving the stage Julia was swallowed up by a coterie of admirers and disappeared.

As the crowd dispersed Pomona stood still, absorbing the fact of this improbable, fearless woman who, in her early twenties, had climbed into an ancient redwood tree in Humboldt County and stayed in its branches for almost two years.

"Her life had been in jeopardy." Irma whispered in Pomona's ear. "She had been harassed by so many people when she was in the tree. I heard she had even received death threats.

"She must have really loved that tree, Luna," Irma continued. "They must have made a deep connection. Trees are alive with their own kind of intelligence and souls."

When Pomona returned home that evening Parker was still sleeping – the painkillers had really knocked him out – so she set out to search for Delilah once again. As she trudged along the hillside calling Delilah's name, she remembered the day Nora had brought the kitten home from the shelter. Barely three weeks old, she fed her by hand every two hours.

Pomona imagined the cat's distress to lose her beloved mistress and her only home. No wonder she ran away.

After an hour of fruitless searching Pomona returned and sat at Parker's kitchen table and worked on fliers to help find Delilah. It was only then that she realized she did not have a single photograph of the cat. She doubted Nora ever had one either. She wasn't sentimental that way. On a sheet of paper with a black marker Pomona wrote:

Lost: Black Cat
Small, female, green eyes and skittish disposition.

She added her name and Parker's phone number. Later, with a stack of copies made at a nearby print shop, Pomona tacked her sorry fliers onto neighborhood telephone poles. Poor Delilah. The fliers seemed beneath the cat's dignity but Pomona was increasingly convinced the point was moot. Everyone knew Los Angeles parks and foothills were filled with coyotes and that missing cats and even small dogs had most likely become coyote snacks. It was common knowledge that the healthy-looking coyotes that wandered through Elysian Park and its surrounding neighborhoods were fat from eating neighborhood pets.

Parker's arm throbbed as he lay in bed that night, listening to sleeping Pomona's shallow breath. He laid his finger upon her cheek while eyeing the bottle of prescription painkillers upon the bed side stand. He had taken the initial dose to appease Pomona. "Take them every four hours to stay ahead of your pain," she had advised.

Stay ahead of your pain. Could anyone run that fast? He had sprinted and it still caught him.

After Pomona left that afternoon to retrieve Manuel, Parker shook himself awake. For a long time he contemplated whether or not to make the call. When he finally punched in Virginia's number, he did not try to temper his fury. "You told Isabella I was in California and gave her my address," he seethed. "Why would I ever trust you again?"

"You never trusted me in the first place," she replied icily. "You left me behind with no explanation. I gave you ten years of my life. My twenties for God's sake. What a gift!"

Silence filled the phone line and Parker imagined Virginia retouching her lipstick or rearranging her hair. Whenever Virginia gazed into a mirror everything around her seemed to fall away as if she was presented with a great work of art. Or perhaps she had simply wandered away to refill a wine glass.

"How did you contact Isabella?" His tone was a sharp dagger.

"She found me. The poor lady was cleaning toilets at the Lavender and Sage café. I was just sitting there one day, drinking espresso with Marie, minding my own business, when she came to our table wringing her little cleaning rag."

"And? Did she know who you were?"

"She must have snooped around because she asked right away if I knew where you were and why you had vanished into thin air."

Parker swallowed hard. He had not once considered that Incencio's family would appear. That Incencio actually had people who cared for and loved him had never entered his mind.

Virginia continued: She's a regular Nancy Drew trying to get her husband out of jail. Incencio was the kill floor knocker so you know he's one tough guy, which makes me wonder why he's punching Caleb who we both know couldn't fight a Girl Scout. Look, I've always liked Caleb but he was something of a little twerp. No real gut or grit. I mean that in a good way. Never an asshole like you."

"I came here to be done with all that, with you. With them. So what do you know about what happened that night?"

Virginia spoke in a stage whisper, as if she had an eavesdropping audience. "Listen, there's something else you should know but I'll only tell you in person. Let's meet tomorrow."

"Can't tomorrow or the next day. Have to work. Some of us work." Parker knew he sounded childish but he really did have two days of trimming scheduled. Because of his arm, Manuel would do the work, so it was possible he could leave for a couple of hours but he needed time to prepare his head for a meeting with Virginia.

"Thursday. The bar at Dan Tana's. Wait, scratch that. Better not meet in public with you acting so crazy these days."

"This is a bad idea."

"For crying out loud, is Mercury in retrograde? Do you not understand anything I say? I am trying to help you save your life."

By the time they arranged to meet at the Beverly Center in three days time Parker's head was throbbing. He berated himself for his weakness. He knew he was betraying Pomona's trust, yet for all his misgivings he needed to know what Virginia knew about Incencio and Isabella. He knew it was his friend, Incencio, whom he had betrayed. Incencio was right all along not to trust a rich white boy. Parker had destroyed Incencio's life.

Chapter Twenty-five
Rose Parade Queen

The next morning, as Pomona brewed coffee, a news segment about the South Central Farm played on the radio. John Quigley, a local tree sitter and Farm advocate, told the interviewer: "You go half a block away, in the heat of the day, you feel that sun, the smog. As soon as you walk into this farm it's ten degrees cooler and there's this vibrancy of life and community. It's how our city should be. This is a working farm, not just a symbolic thing. It's about clean air and feeding families with good organic produce."

"We should go over," Parker said. "Check on Manuel and the others. I've heard it's become something of a three-ring circus with round-the-clock action as they try to raise money."

He needed to distract himself from his upcoming meeting with Virginia, especially since climbing a palm for escape was no longer an option.

Pomona had intended to go to Nora's and start cleaning out her mother's years of accumulated possessions, but she immediately agreed. She had risen early that morning and spent an hour looking for Delilah and taping more fliers onto telephone poles. Not a single person had called to report a sighting. Maybe a trip back to the Farm would ease her mounting despair that she'd ever see the cat again.

As Parker and Pomona approached the Farm's giant walnut tree they encountered a swell of people and television cameras looking up into the tree's strong branches. Pomona peered skyward too and saw the heads of several people, at least three, sitting on a tree-sitters platform.

"Who's in the tree?" she asked a woman beside her.

"John Quigley and Julia. Joan Baez is about to join them."

Pomona was already awed by the presence of Julia Butterfly Hill and John Quigley, but Joan Baez too? She took and squeezed Parker's hand with excitement. The famous folk singer was standing beneath the tree, answering a reporter's questions about why she had come.

As Pomona watched the hoopla, she imagined seeing the Farm through Joan Baez'a eyes. Was she impressed by the bountiful gardens and the dedicated people fighting for its future? Joan Baez had been to Woodstock and had protested the Vietnam War. Maybe one day she would write a song about the Los Angeles farm and its tenacious farmers.

"She's going to climb into the tree now," the woman said and the petite singer in faded blue jeans and a red bandana grabbed and ascended the tree's branches. The people beneath the tree whooped and clapped the higher Joan Baez climbed. The tree sitters above clapped and hollered.

Someone sang: "We shall overcome, we shall overcome, we shall overcome someday."

A chorus of voices sang these words over and over. Each time the refrain strengthened with conviction that justice would prevail.

When Parker and Pomona found Manuel, Irma, and Josefina, they filled them in on all the activity from the campesinos at 41st and Alameda. Every day more celebrities and politicians visited to help raise awareness and money, they said. On any given day one might see Martin Sheen, Danny Glover, Willie Nelson, and other well-known advocates walking along the garden paths and making statements of support from beneath the walnut tree. The Farm buzzed with activity as people came from far and wide to see this oasis in a concrete jungle, a cause célèbre that they read about in newspaper articles and heard about on the radio and television.

"They all say, 'We never knew about a farm in South Los Angeles,'" said Josefina. "They go home, tell their friends. Now we got crowds like Disneyland."

Besides famous and influential people, students came and musicians and artists, religious leaders and all kinds of regular folks. Hundreds of people came to stand in solidarity. Some stayed on to fight full-time so now even more camping tents squeezed into the Farm's pockets and corners. Now every day the beating rhythms of drum circles joined the clanging cacophony of passing trains. The farmers held nightly candlelight vigils in which hundreds of people gathered and walked the entire Farm perimeter holding lit candles, chanting, and singing songs.

"But the court says Mr. Horowitz bought a piece of land and he has the right to do with it what he wants," said Manuel. "Isn't that the American way?"

"We have to believe that we have a right to this land," Irma stressed. "Maybe we've only raised $490,000 so far, but so people now see its value. Something is going to come through. I feel it in my bones."

Parker was grateful for the distraction and for the spark it brought to Pomona. Her eyes shined with interest in every detail she learned about the case. Her enthusiasm relaxed his anxiety and he considered not going to see Virginia. What a stupid idea to play willingly into her manipulations.

Still, the pull persisted. What if she knew something. He had to hear but would remain adamant never to go back.

Under Manuel's direction the group spent several hours weeding, fertilizing, and planting the beds that Parker had fixed the week before. Pomona dug her hands into the dirt and helped plant forty tomato seedlings. When they finished Parker took her hands to see dirt wedged between all her fingernails. Crescent moons of soil. He smelled the garden that exuded from her pores, a scent loamy and earthy that made him crazy with desire.

Later that evening, back at home, they pieced together how they had missed each other by moments when returning to the Huntington the day after they'd met. They lay together in bed, teasing, reminiscing, and musing over incidents as if they had happened years earlier and not just weeks. They wove together memories as if establishing an origin story for their children. The story they'd recount year after year at family gatherings. "Tell us again, mummy, how you forgot the book beneath the tree and then daddy found it and you looked for each other for three days until you finally discovered the note dad had stuck to the tree!"

They both imagined these perfect children, the spitting replica of the other: A dark haired girl who read books; a blue-eyed boy who climbed trees.

The charade was charming but they both knew it didn't include certain details that neither wanted as part of the record. That Pomona planned to jump from a bridge at nightfall. That Parker had run to California from Kansas. That Pomona felt overshadowed and intimidated by Virginia's perfect beauty.

Parker locked the front door with the intention of keeping Pomona in and everyone else out. She had gathered bounty from the Farm – crimson beets, a cluster of broccoli, spinach, lettuce and kale – and she created a wondrous salad fortified with hard-boiled eggs and nuts.

As the evening slipped into night, they made love. (Parker a bit awkward with his cast but they laughed and it became funny.) At midnight they rose to eat a late supper. As they nibbled on bread, olives, and cheese, and sipped red wine, they marveled at how time had slowed to a crawl. By the time they drifted back to sleep at 1 a.m. it seemed an eternity had passed.

"When you stand in the present moment you are timeless," Parker whispered across the pillows. "Let's not think about the past or the future, Pomona. Let's just be here now."

They hardly bothered getting out of bed the next day, except to brew coffee and fetch fruit and yogurt. Dishes piled on the bedroom floor. "I should clean up," Pomona said as they lay close, holding hands and staring at the ceiling.

"This is heaven," Parker said. "My arm is hardly sore anymore and we're all alone with no one bothering us."

She rose from the bed and its tangle of sheets to stack dishes. She scooped clothes strewn across the floor and piled them in the closet. Pomona went into the bathroom and turned on the faucets, hoping the running water would drown out her sudden sobs.

A hand touched her shoulder.

"What's your story, morning glory?" Parker asked. He was sitting on the toilet seat wearing only his underwear and an expression of mournful tenderness.

"Maybe I'm crying because I am so happy here with you, but I miss my mother. I miss the cat." She did not say that she believed the cat was lost because she had brought it to Parker's house. Had she stayed at Nora's she would still have Delilah, but she didn't know if she would still have herself, at least not in one piece. She wouldn't have Parker.

She climbed into the steaming water and stretched back to wet her hair.

"You've never told me about your mother."

Pomona closed her eyes and allowed Nora to flood her senses. "She was drop dead gorgeous and vivacious, but she took up so much space. I spent my whole life trying to make myself smaller so Nora could fill the room. But she was so fun and made things special." Her body warmed as she remembered a typical Nora move. "We were poor when I was a kid, especially after my dad left. So we played badminton in the backyard in the summers when everybody else went to Catalina or Hawaii, and I thought we were the lucky ones. We decided we were badminton champions. We had uniforms and everything. My mom always said we were poor on purpose, like that was a fun thing. She liked living on the edge. She also had these crazy stunts and some of them embarrassed the hell out of me."

Parker moved to the side of the tub and squeezed a dollop of shampoo into Pomona's hair, the silky black hair that had attracted him in the Palm Garden. Using his good arm, he rubbed his fingers against her scalp in slow circles. Pomona melted further into the water.

"You've got to tell me."

"I can't."

"Just the most cringe-worthy."

"Well. She'd tell people she was once the Rose Parade queen just to get a free drink or a better table at a restaurant. She'd say, 'You can't make me sit by the kitchen; I'm a former Rose Parade queen.' I was mortified and terrified that one day we'd run into the real Rose Parade queen for 1970. I told her to say she was a princess. There were six so who's going to check. But no, she had to be the queen."

"Who was your mother robbing of her crown?"

Pomona looked into Parker's smiling eyes and laughed. "I checked the old Rose Parade programs in the library. Pamela Dee Tedesco, from Arcadia. I used to worry that one day Pamela would come into the library and hand me her library card and I'd just freeze."

"Your mom could have done worse things."

Pomona grew pensive. "I wasn't her ideal daughter. She wanted someone she could have fun with or maybe she needed a confidante, a therapist. I tried playing that role when I was younger, but as I grew older I resisted. Became angry. I didn't know how to take care of her. One year for my birthday we took a trip to Mexico and I blew a fuse because she was so immature and self–absorbed. She could be so cruel to my father for no reason. Suddenly when I was older I couldn't stand her. For three years we barely saw one another until she called to say she had cancer."

"That's rough. What about your father? What happened to him?"

Pomona was hit by a wave of shame that she was the kind of person abandoned by her father and without any family to speak of. The shame was compounded by the image of the book gathering dust on the fireplace mantle with Nora's tin of ashes.

She couldn't tell him. Not yet.

"There's not much to say. But what about you? Growing up on a cattle ranch must have been wonderful. Tell me about your boyhood."

"My boyhood…" Parker rinsed Pomona's hair with splashes of water, acutely aware of her tact at changing the subject. "What I remember most is the flat, wide-open space that stretched forever in every direction. Most every day I rode my horse for hours across the tall-grass prairie."

"You had a horse?"

"At least a dozen in the stables. My own stallion was named Blue Evening. Called him Blue."

"And your brother?"

"Did he have a horse?"

"No, silly, what is he like?"

Her question was innocent but it hit him hard but he couldn't answer. He remembered when they were boys Caleb would try to ride along with Parker on his own horse but Parker would gallop away, leaving his younger brother in the dust. What a mean way to treat a kid who just wanted his brother's companionship. Caleb, from the time he was small, rubbed him the wrong way. His younger brother was so easily wounded by Parker's inability to just get along. "Don't upset dad, just do what he wants," he'd repeat like a broken record.

Pomona turned in the bath to face Parker. She ran her hand through his brown hair. He hadn't bothered shaving over the past day that they had retreated into each other and a slight beard now covered his face.

"My dad was kind of like an artist," Pomona said, breaking the silence. She was overwhelmed by a deep sense of her father, Francisco. "He always found the beauty in things and liked working with his hands. He built chairs and tables in the basement. He was the hardest worker though he didn't always have the best jobs. When I was little, he repossessed cars for a while. He would break into garages or go to people's work and take their cars when they fell behind on payments."

"That's crazy work," Parker said, relieved that the moment had passed, thank God, and he would not tell her more about Caleb. At least not now.

"Mom would go with him late at night and read the Thomas Guide so that he could find the houses. She would drive our car home after leaving him in the middle of nowhere," Pomona continued. "I'd go too because I was so little. I remember lying in the backseat of our Ford Torino driving through the blackest nights. No city lights and so many stars. Dad smoking his Lucky Strikes. Mom using a flashlight to read the map, directing dad to the most god-forsaken places. Sometimes we'd get lost and end up in some strawberry patch or orange grove."

"You got to see the orange groves and strawberry fields?" Parker's voice was incredulous.

"My god, yes. I remember seeing orange groves as a kid. And the wonderful smell. Once daddy stopped the car and we got out and scooped fallen oranges off the ground. Mom said it wasn't stealing if we took them off the ground."

Pomona sunk deeper into the water and studied the flaking ceiling paint. She remembered the spongy ground beneath her tiny feet as she gathered oranges. Her joy sitting in the backseat peeling one and then another, sucking sweet citrus nectar as a wind through the open window, blew them along on their journey. She remembered her hands and face sticky. She remembered her parents bickering about getting lost and Francisco turning up the radio to drown out Nora's exasperated commands but how Nora eventually scooted to Francisco's side and laid her head on his shoulders as they both sang to songs on the radio. She remembered the tender way Francisco kissed Nora's head, letting his lips linger in her curls as he drew in a breath.

Her parents loved each other. She knew it even at four. What happened to make such a strong love disintegrate?

Submerged in Parker's bath Pomona even remembered the smell of skunk mingling with sweet orange to make the best scent in the world and how she finally laid herself down on the backseat and slept as her family glided along through the black night.

Chapter Twenty-six
Women's Collective Plot

T he next day Parker went to work with Manuel. The customer was new and Parker had to pretend to supervise Manuel to show he was the boss. People liked seeing authority.

Pomona forced herself to return to Nora's apartment to sort through her mother's possessions, her clothes and books and the mess she had left behind when she had hightailed with the cat for Parker's house. May 31 was looming in two weeks time, and if the apartment wasn't empty and clean she'd lose the security deposit and need to pay another months' rent and she could ill afford either.

Pomona didn't know where she would go. She didn't expect to stay at Parker's. She was so embarrassed by her lack of prospects, she decided not to think about anything but the moment before her.

A frenzy overtook Pomona as she stepped into the apartment. She spent the entire day attacking the dust and cobwebs in every corner, the moldy food in the refrigerator, the forgotten clothes piled on the floor, the stacks of newspapers and piles of mail overwhelming countertops. Pomona opened Nora's closet door and pulled out her size four Calvin Klein suits and St. John dresses that she would donate to a local women's shelter. Nora had scrimped and saved to buy her nice designer clothes from a San Marino consignment shop, feeling no shame in wearing the cast-off clothes from the San Marino monied set, the conservative Junior League moms with the cookie-cutter blonde highlights and Mercedes station wagons. Pomona always found it strange that Nora made ruthless fun of those mavens but didn't mind wearing their conservative second-hand clothes. Some part of Cincinnati still had hold of her.

She pulled from the closet a hot pink St. John knit suit with alabaster buttons and she suddenly saw Nora tugging at the pencil skirt in the powder room of the Orchid of Palm Court Restaurant in downtown Cincinnati. Pomona remembered her seven-year-old self, dressed in a blue velvet frock, perched upon an overstuffed gold sofa, her hair festooned by a ridiculous oversized pink bow.

"Little sister, don't tell your grandparents about daddy's job," Nora said as she retouched her lipstick, the soft almost nude mauve she always wore. "They only like doctors or lawyers. A banker might be okay. They would literally die if they knew he repossessed cars. Say nothing. Leave the talking to me."

Pomona already knew her grandparents did not like Francisco. He had not come with them on the trip.

"You didn't even come to my wedding," Nora had pouted after three martinis. (Even then Pomona knew to count drinks, to gauge when the drama might start.)

"A weekend in Las Vegas? That's a wedding?" Grandfather Donnelly had seethed.

Grandmother Donnelly had been more serene. "Darling, you have to understand your father just didn't know what kind of people you'd get mixed up with when you left for California. We were so proud that you'd been admitted to USC but you also got into Sarah Lawrence and that might have been the better choice."

That was the last time Pomona ever saw her Cincinnati grandparents. She wondered if they were still alive and should she tell them their only daughter had died. She remembered Grandmother Donnelly as a woman most everyone liked, always in a good mood and never a threat to anyone. She imagined the pain Nora must have caused. In a way it made sense that Nora called herself the Rose Parade Queen.

She was like the most beautiful rose with the sweetest fragrance. The one you desire to hold, to admire and smell, but with the sharpest of thorns that could prick and draw blood.

The next day Pomona could not muster any energy to return to Nora's apartment. While she had packed bags of clothes, she hadn't even made a dent in the kitchen's items and what about the books? There was still the bathroom and didn't Nora have some kind of storage space in the garage? What could she possibly have squirreled away in there? Pomona wondered if she dare start a small kitchen fire that could get out of hand and burn the place down. But she wasn't that ruthless so as she drove down Baxter with the full intention of going to Pasadena, she found herself turning right instead of left and soon Pearl was traveling along Alameda Street heading for the Farm.

She heard a steady drum of activity, clanking gates, shouted orders, ringing phones. She came in through the main gate to find a meeting space created from old office desks and chairs. Folding tables were crammed with fax machines and telephones so that Farm leaders could meet with reporters and politicians and celebrities and anyone who had any clout or platform or money. As Pomona passed through the gate she saw the Farm's two elected leaders, Tezo and Rufina, huddled there with the Farm's lawyer, Dan Stormer.

Pomona walked along the path toward the walnut tree and noticed even more tents pitched and squeezed in the encampment for the farmers and volunteers who now remained on site 24/7 in case the L.A. Sheriff began the eviction process.

Everyone was on high alert because at any moment the Sheriff could show up and demand that everyone leave.

Manuel was on a job with Parker, but Pomona wondered if Irma and Josefina were around. As she walked towards their plot she marveled how corn stalks were used as trellises for the beans and nasturtiums. Long rows of tall closely-planted cactus created a natural fence. She saw fruit trees bearing unfamiliar exotic specimens the color of candy with peeling bark and extravagant leaves. Despite uproar over the Farm's future, the plants did not stop growing, blooming, and bearing fruit.

"Pomona, over here!"

Pomona turned to see Irma waving from within a corner plot. She greeted her friend at the chain-link gate and then stepped into the most gorgeous, lush garden she had ever encountered, marked by numerous beds bursting with a riot of flowers, among them lilies and poppies, carnations and geraniums, oleander, sagebrush, California milkweed, sunflower, and crocus.

"Irma, my gosh, whose garden is this?"

"It's the women's collective plot. A special place for any woman tired of a husband or boyfriend or who just wants the company of other females and natural beauty. We all need that now and then, right? Come on, we're in the middle of bundling herbs just harvested."

Pomona trailed Irma, passing several expansive beds thick with fragrant herbs, rosemary, lavender, cilantro, and thyme. As they walked she feasted quietly on the delicious fragrances streaming past. Within a stand of fruit trees golden apricots gleamed and peaches glowed. The garden was pure enchantment and its fragrant air buzzed with bees, hummingbirds, and butterflies. In one corner of the garden they came upon a group of women and girls sitting in a circle, perched upon low camping chairs and overturned pails. Herbs filled the center of the circle, piles of lavender, sage, rosemary, and chocolate mint.

"Compadres, this is Pomona who works with me and Josefina and Manuel," Irma announced.

About fifteen faces, teenage to elderly, turned and smiled, including Josefina's. Pomona's instinct was to correct Irma's overstatement—she had only been to Manuel's plot a couple of times—but she knew Irma would find her modesty annoying.

Pomona took a seat within the circle on an available camping chair.

"We're discussing the Abundance Feast that happens in June," a woman said. "It's our tradition in Mexico to give thanks at the end of the growing season for the abundance of the land. Not everyone here is from Mexico, of course, but we've held the feast for the last ten years and it's our best party. Traditional dancers and musicians come and everyone brings the most delicious foods to share and we pray all night and make ofrendas at the altars decorated with flowers."

"We must decide if we should plan for the Abundance Feast this year as we don't know if we will we even be here at the end of June," another woman said.

"If we don't plan the feast we've already conceded defeat," said a third.

"But planning takes time away from our protests and political actions," another countered. "Rufina is busy coordinating everyday, locking the gates at night to keep our garden secure. Making sure people are patrolling our boundaries. Meetings with the lawyer and handling all the people who are now coming to see the Farm and help. She's on call day and night."

Pomona's head spun at this colorful scene of women surrounded by herbs and plants. How lucky that she had not gone to Nora's sad apartment.

Someone cleared her throat. The women fell silent and turned toward a trio of elderly women sitting on the ground, their legs folded beneath their long skirts. They wore glorious Guatemalan huipels, woven in electric rainbow colors of green, blue, yellow, red, pink, and gold. Their ancient faces were somber. One woman began speaking softly and everyone leaned in to hear. Her words didn't sound Spanish and Pomona knew, because Josefina had told her, that she was speaking an indigenous dialect. Many farmers spoke Zapotec and Mayan, having come from villages in Mexico and Guatemala. Spanish was not their first language. When she finished another woman translated her message.

"Madre Gloria reminds us that before anything else, we must honor our Mother, especially now when she is threatened, under attack, as usual, by the patriarchy."

"Same old story," someone called out.

"The feast is important to bring joy to all the families and children."

"Yes, we have a sacred obligation to care for nuestra Madre Tierra and show our gratitude," another chimed.

The elderly woman called Madre Gloria addressed the young girls within the circle and spoke at length. When she paused, Josefina translated. "Madre Gloria reminds us our duty as mothers, sisters, and aunts is to teach our daughters and sisters traditional medicine so that they too can heal with wild and cultivated plants. Plants hold intelligence of the universe. Not sharing this knowledge would be our greatest mistake. Especially now when many of our plants are under threat of extinction."

The woman spoke again for some moments. When she stopped Josefina said, "It's hard to translate, but Gloria said to have a radiant calm and balance of mind that we call equanimity is to be like the earth. All kinds of things are cast upon the earth, beautiful and ugly, scary and lovely, common and extraordinary. The earth receives it all and sustains its own integrity. It's a state of peace to accept things as they are."

Everyone nodded.

At that moment another of the women in huipels regarded Pomona with curiosity. Pomona turned beet red as she spoke and gestured in her direction. A woman with tinted pink hair sitting beside Pomona turned with a warm smile. "I'm Amparo. Juanita said she is glad you came to sit with us today. She's seen you around and wants to know who you are."

A slow flush spread over Pomona's cheeks. "I'm Pomona. I must say, I've never seen so many beautiful flowers growing in one place. My mother adored flowers."

"Your mother grows flowers?" Amparo leaned forward and a ray of light glinted off her small silver nose ring.

"No, my mother never grew a thing, not like my father. He would have loved this place." She looked at the expectant faces and grasped for something to say.

"Sometimes we got flowers from the cemetery. My mother figured out the groundskeepers at Forest Lawn every Tuesday gathered all the left over floral arrangements from services and discarded them in a gigantic pile on a hillside. Beautiful wreaths, bouquets, long stemmed roses." Nora had salvaged armfuls of roses, carnations, orchids, and peonies that she piled in Pearl's backseat. Pomona suddenly worried she sounded like a nut.

"We didn't take them from the graves," she hurriedly explained. "They were going to throw them away."

The women laughed. "You were liberating those flowers," someone said. "Giving them a second chance. Showing them some love."

"I wish I had thought of that. Your mother sounds so resourceful," another woman said.

"Whenever we see buildings being demolished, we go dig up the plants that will be killed in the rubble. It's the same thing," Amparo said. "Not many people realize plants have feelings too."

After the group dispersed, Irma and Josefina showed Pomona the beds thick with medicinal plants for the curanderas, especially yerba del venado. Butterfly plant with its bluish-purple, cone-shaped flowers was important and in high demand and they grew as much as possible to treat indigestion and colic, among other ailments. As they wandered around Josefina plucked a colorful assortment of blooms until her arms were heavy with hollyhock, sunflowers, cosmos, blue sage, sweet fennel, iris, and geraniums. She placed her elegant bouquet at the feet of a Virgin of Guadalupe who was presiding over an altar of candles within a small clearing by the tool shed.

"Goodbye Pomona. Come back anytime," the women said as Pomona turned to leave. "This is your plot too. Come grow your own flowers. This plot is for all women."

That night as Pomona slept Parker tried every trick he could think of to make himself stay in bed that night. He melted his bones into the mattress and counted stars in the vast black sky of his mind. He clung to the bedpost as if lost at sea in a violent storm. He curled up like a caterpillar and imagined himself shrouded in a cocoon.

The prospect of meeting the next day with Virginia was making him crazy. What if he couldn't resist her or wasn't strong enough to stand his ground? What if she actually had a trick up her sleeve that convinced him to change his mind and go back home? She had always known how to tear him down with her body and secrets. She was a master of manipulation like a Venus Flytrap. Those caught in her snare never realized until too late. He had to stand guard.

Climbing into a palm would level his head. He cursed Virginia and her conniving ways. He lamented Isabella's letter and the terrible information it delivered. He turned and stared at Pomona's back, momentarily mesmerized by her spine curving into her hips like a lazy river. He wanted to trace his fingers along this sensual curve and put his hand on her beautiful ass but he didn't dare wake her.

Instead, like a well-trained soldier, he rolled over the edge of the bed onto the floor and crawled from the room on his forearms. In the living room he stood still as a statue and waited for the sound of her feet padding upon the wood floor. Peering through the dark room, she would ask where he was going. He would say just getting water. But she never came and so he slid across the floor, opened the front door, and stepped into the night.

Was he a fool to believe Pomona alone was his salvation? He loved her. Needed her to ground him. But he still needed his fronds so he ran down the street with his backpack and almost cried at first glimpse of his California Fan.

There was the problem of the stupid cast. He never thought he needed one in the first place, had tolerated the whole medical procedure because of Pomona's concern. He stooped to the ground, opened his backpack and rifling through some tools, pulled out a mat knife. Using its sharp blade with careful precision he cut lengthwise along the heavy plaster. Then, with a pair of pliers and all the strength in his good hand, he broke the plaster cast off his arm.

Relief flooded his body as pieces of plaster fell to the ground and his arm emerged into the cool night air. He had only worn the cast for a week but he had always hated anything confining or binding.

With his safety belt in place, Parker ascended the palm with slow steps, careful to protect his aching arm. By the time he reached the summit his head was clear. His thoughts steadfast. He would never go back to Kansas. Never would he forsake his palms or Pomona. Not if his father died or Incencio spent his life in prison. Not if Caleb inherited the entire lucrative operation of killing animals and carving their bodies for money. Garden City, for him, had vanished from the face of the earth.

Two hours later he slipped back into bed and wrapped his arms around Pomona's beautiful back.

"Where were you?" she whispered, not an accusation, just a question.

Parker pulled her closer. "Needed some fresh air."

Chapter Twenty-seven
Caleb

Virginia was sashaying across Bloomingdale's shoe department in four-inch heels when Parker found her the next afternoon. She was jutting out her slender hipbone and staring at her pretty feet as they paraded across the marble floor with a supermodel's precision. He had naturally thought to look in the shoe department when she hadn't appeared at the agreed-upon-time in the department store café.

"There you are," she said without missing a beat, as if she had been waiting for him. "I wouldn't normally go for a Badgley Mischka. Too mother of the bride. But something about the styling on this classic pump accentuates my leg, don't you think?"

Parker threw himself into an overstuffed leather chair and folded his arms. At Pomona's insistence, he had conceded to wear a sling on his fractured arm. Virginia's legs did look great. They always did. He never had any problem with her legs.

Virginia looked at his face and laughed. "Don't worry. You won't be trapped here for long." She slipped off the shoes and handed them to a saleswoman. "A steal at $150. I'll take robin blue and Champagne."

Shopping bag in hand, Virginia and Parker left the store and wandered up the escalator to the third-floor café.

"What do you want to tell me?" Parker said after they had slid into a booth and ordered two iced coffees.

Virginia squinted at him a long moment before answering. "Damn, Parker. You look really good. Even with your arm in that sling you are seriously sexy. Don't tell me you fell out of a palm tree. Wow, it's really hot in here, or is it me?" She unbuttoned her light sweater and released it from her shoulders. With a sly wink she unbuttoned her shirt's top two buttons and leaned forward. "Sweltering in this cramped booth. Coffee is the last thing I want. My car is at valet. For all its problems, L.A.'s really got valet service down. It's ten minutes to my hotel. Come over and I'll make you my signature Old Fashion with Blanton's. I'll slip on a bikini and we can relax by the pool."

For a split second Parker wanted nothing more than to drink away the afternoon with Virginia. To melt into a lounge chair, stare into crystal clear water, float in a bottomless warm pool of amnesia. He gave her a wistful smile and settled into his relief. She was trying so hard. Losing the upper hand. He couldn't blame her for wanting to recapture the chemistry that had for so long held them together, their perfectly matched intensity for wild partying and sex. For ten years their hedonistic escapades had been one noisy and distracting sideshow. But he was no longer chained to its power.

"You wanted to tell me something," he said. "Let's stay focused." His tone was patronizing he knew.

Virginia leaned back against the booth. Her eyes flared. "Look, I didn't have to travel a thousand miles to tell you Caleb is still alive. No one knows why you split town after that worker beat him up but it doesn't look good. Caleb says he can't remember why he was fighting. Or doesn't want to remember."

She tapped five blood red fingernails upon the tabletop. Parker felt them tapping into his heart like nails. "The whole ordeal has taken a terrible toll on your daddy," she said. "Last time I saw him he looked fat and sweaty. May not be too long for this world. Here's what I think," she continued. "You have a narrow window that's closing fast but if you go home now and deal with this mess, you can still position yourself to get what's rightfully ours. Don't let Caleb make off with the family business because you're too busy rebelling. You're almost thirty; too old for that.

Once you get over your crush on that fat Spanish girl you will see how far you strayed and be glad I set you straight."

"What do you mean, 'what's rightfully ours?'"

"The ranch and slaughterhouse business, you nincompoop. We can have the life together we always planned. You're obviously not in your right mind so I'm thinking for you. The first step is that you tell the judge at Incencio's hearing that you know for a fact he wanted to kill Caleb. He told you he hated him. Talked shit about him all the time. No way that was an accident. You owe it to your father and Caleb to make sure Incencio stays in jail."

"What?"

"Even if he swears it was a Friday night brawl for fun, the knocker must know he can't fight with his superiors and not pay the price. He got what he deserves. Good riddance to that illegal worker."

Everything was moving fast but Parker was stuck on three of Virginia's assumptions: that he wanted her help so that they could return to Kansas and live an extravagant life off the slaughterhouse largess, and that Pomona was not significant to him. The third, however, was truly the worst. That Parker didn't care anything about Incencio and would sacrifice the Salvadoran's life for his personal gain. Heat surged through Parker's arms and chest.

"Virginia, did I make a promise to you I'm not keeping?"

Her lips twisted into a tight grimace and she bared her snow-white teeth. "You did this to me before. I rescued you in New York when you were going down and you cried big salty tears that I had saved your life. This isn't any different. Listen, I know your sensitive soul has suffered, that you are misunderstood by your daddy, but you can't just keep running away. Stop being so scared, Reclaim your manhood."

"What do you mean?"

"Maybe your father loved Caleb more, but he admired you most. Caleb was a weakling and an embarrassment. You, on the other hand, always stood up to your father."

Parker saw Caleb's soft, uncalloused hands gripping a beer can in the slaughterhouse yard, laughing nervously as Parker thumped him on his back, telling him not to worry, this was all for fun.

From across the table Parker took Virginia's arm. He drew her close and smelled her perfume, its strains of bergamot, mandarin, and gardenia, with undertones of sandalwood and musk. He'd inhaled her signature Fracas for years. It was the scent of their lustful youth but now it made him nauseous. His hand tightened on her wrist, the fragile bones he could snap with one twist.

"Let me go," she seethed, pulling her hand back. "You smell bad. Don't you ever take a shower?"

"Don't talk about my family," he spit back. "What I know is that you'll never be my Arabella. You and I will never create beauty together. Just ugliness."

"Who's Arabella? Another one of your sad fat girlfriends?"

"Stay out of my life, Virginia."

Chapter Twenty-eight
King of the World

Parker drove down Rexford Drive and when he hit Wilshire Boulevard, took a left and headed east, back toward downtown, gunning the truck, passing cars, sailing through yellow lights, like a horse galloping out of a burning barn. Trying to get the hell out of Beverly Hills as fast he could.

He hated Beverly Hills, its grotesque display of wealth. As if to prove his point he passed a young man with bright yellow hair driving a convertible 911 Porsche painted almost the same bright yellow. At a light the two vehicles stopped tire to tire. Parker glanced over at the punk driver, who didn't look any older than eighteen. When the light turned green Parker peeled out, to show the kid that a truck worth less than the sum of the Porsche's tires could leave the car in its dust.

Parker didn't begrudge anyone their due, but so many of these spoiled brats didn't earn what they had. They had never worked hard or sacrificed or knew the ache of hunger or wrenching disappointment. He knew spoiled brats because he had been one. But he had also been on the slaughterhouse kill floor with people who had to fight every single day to put food in their mouths. With Incencio who killed cows, all day long, for nine dollars an hour.

The Porsche disappeared in his rearview mirror as Parker drove too fast along Wilshire, reckless, swerving in and out of traffic, desperate to get the hell away from the Westside and its $15 cocktails and ubiquitous valet parking.

Mostly though, he wanted to escape Virginia. Was she insane? Did she not see how broken and destructive their "love" was?

Cars honked around him. His arm throbbed with the same intensity as when he first fell from the palm and hit the ground. At the next red light Parker reached into his glove compartment and flung out all its contents until he uncovered a bottle of aspirin. He opened it with his teeth, shook out four tablets and chewed them into a bitter paste.

His truck sailed over the intersections of Robertson, then La Cienega. Only after crossing Fairfax and passing the Los Angeles County Museum of Art did Parker start to relax as the distance between him and Virginia widened. He continued along Wilshire for five more miles until he could see a green expanse up ahead. Suddenly MacArthur Park popped into view with its shimmering lake and dozens of palms.

The neighborhood surrounding the lake was gritty, dense, and congested with traffic. Parker thought he would jump from his skin before he could maneuver the truck to the curb. He slid from the seat, slammed shut the door, and ran across the grass, straight toward the first palm he saw. On the wide-open lawn that sloped toward the lake he touched the rough trunk of a Mexican Fan. He hugged the palm tight, "My beautiful palm, thank you, thank you," he murmured. He laid his cheek upon his perennial friend.

"The righteous will flourish like a palm tree, they will grow like a cedar of Lebanon," Parker whispered. Psalm 92:12. How many times that psalm had saved him, grounded him when he was floating away.

"Hey man, you okay?"

Parker looked around and saw a group of young men gathered beneath the family of five trees to which the Mexican Fan belonged. They were passing a joint as one of them played the guitar badly.

"I'm in a lot of trouble," Parker responded.

"Smoke this and you'll feel better," a guy said, passing him the joint. The men were young, early twenties, in T-shirts and jeans. One bounced a hacky-sack woven ball with his gigantic foot.

Parker took the joint and inhaled. He filled his lungs as he focused on the words splashed across the man's T-shirt. He exhaled the smoke with a violent cough. He hadn't smoked pot for a long time. He leaned against the tree and waited. Within moments the worry in his head lightened and his arm stopped throbbing.

"I want to climb this palm more than anything in the world," he told the young men, his voice cracking with emotion.

"Go for it," one encouraged.

"I don't have my climbing equipment and my arm is weak and sore."

The guys all looked genuinely disappointed. "We'll give you a boost," one suggested.

Suddenly Parker realized it was possible; if he got a good start he could inch his way up the tree even with a bad arm and without his belt. He was strong. He had climbed a million palms. "Let's do it," he commanded. "But let me have another hit before we start. That stuff really makes my arm feel better." His whole body and soul for that matter.

The four men convened and after some back and forth it was decided that Parker should climb onto their backs. They surrounded the tree on hands and knees and Parker hoisted himself onto their backs and grabbed hold of the palm.

Parker found himself climbing the palm lickity split, like a monkey in the jungle. He imagined Manuel as a boy in Mexico climbing the palms all day with his friends and with his father. When Parker reached the top he looked down and whooped. He had climbed the damn palm with practically one arm.

"I'm king of the world," he shouted.

Not just with a weak arm and but without his safety harness or spikes. A delirious happiness filled him. The sun warmed his back, the birds chirped in his ears, and the insects buzzed about his head. As he peeked through the fluttering fronds he could see the entire city and across twenty-six miles of ocean clear out to Catalina Island. When a pod of dolphins and mermaids swam before his line of vision he knew that everything was going to be fine.

"I'm king of the world," he shouted again. He climbed even higher until he was nestled within the fronds. He studied his arm, the good one that had brought him all the way to the palm's crown, and saw a line of ants marching across his skin. Ants, he knew, were sentient creature that carried an entire universe within. He was thrilled to see them move across his skin. He also saw fluttering butterflies, purple and yellow, and red-crowned parrots squawking with delight. Suddenly, in the background he saw an electric yellow butterfly racing toward him. He rubbed his eyes. No, it was a bird, a canary maybe. But the canary grew larger until Parker realized it was the Porsche, zooming around the fronds with the yellow-haired punk laughing like a hyena. But wait, laughing along with him in the back were both Virginia and Pomona, holding hands and drinking cocktails.

"You turned down Blanton's Original Single Barrel Bourbon you asshole, but Pomona seems to like it," Virginia cackled.

With a curdling scream, Parker loosened his grip on the palm and spiraled to the ground.

He heard a strange knocking. Was someone at the door? He opened an eye and saw one of the guys throwing the hacky sack against his head.

"Hey, man, what are you doing?"

"Trying to wake you. I almost thought you were dead."

"Dead? I was at the top of the palm."

"Hey, we tried man, but you kept letting go. You might have gone five feet. When you fell down you passed out."

Parker glared. "What the hell was that pot we smoked?"

"No one said it was pot, man. Jerome's hash is good quality. Listen, we're taking off. You've been sleeping a couple of hours. A lady called on your phone and we told her she should come get you before dark. We'd hate to find you at the bottom of the lake tomorrow."

Parker pushed himself to sitting. Sleeping for a couple of hours? "What lady called?"

"Dunno but she's on her way."

Holy smokes, Virginia was coming and she would give him round two of bloody hell. He tried to stand but his legs wobbled. He fell back onto the dirt.

Then he saw her coming across the slope, arms pumping. But it wasn't Virginia. It was Pomona trotting across the grass, black hair flying. When she approached she fell to her knees and grabbed his shoulder.

"Are you okay? Did these guys hurt you?"

"What? No. I fell out of this palm."

"You fell out of another palm?"

"Apparently I only climbed five feet but it still was quite a fall."

"They said you were passed out for hours. And as I hung up that woman who wants to kill me called and said to tell you she's going to let Isabella know where you are anyway, so you'd better just go home. I said you'd have to call back. I hope you can explain."

Virginia called his place? How did she know his home number? Of course, she took it when she broke into his house. How had everything fallen apart so fast? The hacky sack guys were gathered round, watching the unfolding drama with rapt interest.

"I met with her because she wanted to talk to me about my brother and father," Parker admitted. "Big mistake. I should never have gone."

Pomona rose up and glowered "Does this concern the letter that came to your house?"

"Yes, but…It's no longer my business." He could not break through his defensiveness.

"You went to see Virginia." Pomona's eyes clouded with tears. "So you obviously still have business with her."

"I don't care about her. I love you."

Parker's words sounded forced. Hollow. Pomona knew she had been fooling herself. Love was terrible. She'd stupidly opened her heart. But she could never compete with Virginia. Guys were simply hardwired to lust for women like that. She had been Parker's convenient and easy diversion. Shame flooded her chest. "It's best that I go home and you go deal with your past."

Parker pulled himself up to stand and leaned against the tree. "I just explained my past no longer exists."

"It does and she's blonde and beautiful and wants to kill me."

With a foggy dragging brain, Parker tried to sort out his options. Maybe the right course was telling Pomona about Caleb.

"The letter was about my brother."

"He doesn't have a name?"

Parker sensed Pomona barricading herself within a wall. He tried to reach her anyway.

"Caleb. A year ago Caleb was in a fight with a worker at our father's slaughterhouse and got knocked out. It was a fight for fun that I set up. Not violent. But he hit his head. An accident. I thought Caleb was dead but I guess not. That's what Virginia said. Anyway the other guy...the knocker, on the kill floor...the guy who kills the cows...has been in jail since the incident. His wife came El Salvador to help free him. She wrote because she wants me to speak on his behalf at his hearing."

Parker closed his burning eyes. Bile filled his mouth. He had to puke, both from the effects of the hash and the pathetic details of his life. He turned around and retched into the grass. In his sad little heart he hoped his sorry state would soften Pomona. Instead she stood rigid, hands on hips, looking as if he'd confessed to stealing wallets from old ladies.

"Are you going to?"

"I don't know yet." Parker slumped back down and pressed fingertips to forehead. "Damn, my head hurts. My arm too. Maybe I shouldn't have taken off the cast."

Pomona grimaced. She said, "You arranged a fight that went bad and one guy's in jail and you don't even care whether or not your brother's dead or alive? Now I get it about you."

"Get what?"

Suddenly Pomona knew the aspect of Parker that both drew her in and repelled her. Nora.

"You're like my mother."

Parker's mouth dropped. "Your mother? Wait a minute. Maybe not everything is about your mother."

Pomona nodded vehemently. "It's true. Like her, you come from a good family. Have a college degree. Grew up on a ranch. Not too shabby. And you're white and a man so you can do almost anything you want. But you decide to live beneath yourself, trim palm trees, drive an old truck. Make friends with people who really do live on the edge. Tell them you care about their struggles, but when it comes down to it, you'll ride on your privilege and do whatever the hell you want. Because you can."

Dumbfounded by her tirade, Parker reached for Pomona's hand. She jerked it away. "Where is this coming from? I get that you're still grieving, but this isn't fair."

Pomona turned to the hacky sack guys, listening with curious faces. "That was my mother," she sputtered. "Poor on purpose. An apartment filled with cast-offs. But she threw out my dad when he didn't meet her standards. She returned in her head to her nice middle-class life whenever she wanted. La-di-da, bohemian on a whim. For all her posturing and pretending, she never left Cincinnati."

An unbelievable rage erupted within Pomona from a long dormant volcano. Her eyes locked on Parker. She felt nothing but contempt. "The reason I went to your house in the first place no longer exists. The cat is gone." The finality of it hit deep and hard. "I'm going to get my book and tin, go home, and never come back." She turned to the hacky sack guys. "Make sure he doesn't leave for at least twenty minutes. I need time to get my stuff."

Hot tears flooded Parker's eyes. "Seriously? After all we've been through you're going to throw this away? You love me and I love you. Fight for our love."

His words still vibrating in the air, Pomona turned and ran across the grass, back to Pearl.

"Wow man, you really fucked up," said the guy who'd passed him the joint. "I'd definitely wait more than twenty minutes before leaving. She'll kill you if she sees you again."

Chapter Twenty-nine
Uncle Tom's Cabin for Southern California

Two days later, when Pomona stepped through the gates at the South Central Farm, she saw Rufina and Tezo huddled with a group of people that included the Farm's lawyers and other professional types dressed in suits and ties. Something was brewing but she did not stop to ask questions. It wasn't her business. This wasn't her fight. Pomona continued to the women's plot, to the corner graced by the Virgin of Guadalupe altar. Someone had laid a fresh sunflowers at her feet amid a flicker of candles.

"I hope you don't mind if I join you," Pomona whispered as she unfolded a camping chair and sat beside the plaster icon.

The Virgin of Guadalupe ignored her question and gazed across the garden with infinite patience. Alone in the late afternoon, Pomona opened *Ramona* to the bookmark holding her place.

Here she was, finally reading *Ramona* because it was the only thing left to do. After two horrible days locked in Nora's apartment, scary days with disturbing thoughts and bone-crushing loneliness that descended the moment she closed the front door, she had enough sense to know that, instead of returning to the bridge, she had to punch her way out. The dying houseplants had really set her off. In her year at Nora's she had somehow managed a cursory weekly watering but now the forgotten bathroom fern and living room ficus were dried out and drooping, inches from death. She soaked the almost murdered plants in the bathtub and begged them for a second chance.

"Please don't die. I can't take anymore loss."

When the next day both plants had slightly improved, Pomona took this small encouragement to heart and decided she needed to stay alive for the houseplants, if nothing else. Clearly Parker had been a mistake, a wrong turn down a bad road. But she would begin again: read the book and then scatter Nora's ashes over the Colorado Street Bridge. Somehow she would find her footing. Now, alone in the sanctuary of the woman's garden, her jumbled mind quieted. The place truly emanated healing energy. She despaired to remember she had last read the novel in Parker's truck before Virginia tried to attack her. Now with determined focus in this enchanted space, she began to read.

The story of Ramona and Alessandro continued:

As if no time had passed, sweet Ramona, beloved by all at the Moreno Rancho, except for her cruel guardian, Senora Moreno, was still waiting for her soul-mate Alessandro to return from his visit to his Temecula Indian village. Alessandro had returned to his village to visit his elderly father. Before he goes he promises Ramona he will quickly return so they can elope. They are forced into this position because Senora Moreno has forbidden Ramona to marry an Indian, even though she is a half-breed herself. When Alessandro finally returns to the rancho several weeks later, he delivers dreadful news:

Dearest Senorita! I feel as if I should die when I tell you, -- I have no home; my father is dead; my people are driven out of their village."

American settlers had come to Alessandro's Temecula village with a court order stating the United States government had sold them the land and they were its legal owners. Alessandro's father was forcibly thrown out of his house, along with all his furniture. Alessandro had found his father lying in the sun, half mad, waiting for him.

They said it was the sun that had turned him crazy; but it was not. It was his heart breaking in his bosom."

Ramona then runs away with Alessandro, even though he warns her she will be a poor Indian as he no longer has a place for her to live because his village has been decimated by the white settlers claiming the land and homes as their own.

Pomona looked up from the page. What? The sentimental love story had taken a heart-wrenching turn. She wasn't sure she wanted to read a book filled with such tragedy, not with so much of her own heartbreak keeping her up at night.

A voice cut through the stillness and made her jump.

"Pomona, I don't mean to disturb you but I need to lock up our garden plot. I hate to kick you out, but with all the people coming to the Farm, we have to protect our medicinal plants. Some are extremely valuable."

Amparo stood before her with a backpack and a ring of keys in hand. She was dressed in back denim jeans and a khaki South Central Farm T-shirt, pink hair smoothed behind her ears.

"Oh, I'm sorry. Time to go?"

"Yes. We're getting ready for tonight's vigil. So many people are coming. More every day. What are you reading that's got your attention? Don't tell me you're a Harry Potter fan. Is that the *Half-Blood Prince?*"

Pomona held up the book. "Just an old-fashioned love story my mom wanted me to read. It just turned rather heavy though."

"You're reading *Ramona?*

"You know it?"

"Sure. Been called *Uncle Tom's Cabin* for Southern California."

Pomona frowned at this strange comparison. "But *Uncle Tom's Cabin* is a book about slavery."

"Helen Hunt Jackson wrote the book to show how badly the U.S. Government treated the Indians that were living in the missions and on the ranchos here so somehow it got that name."

"I always thought it was just a silly love story."

"Well, her message is sugar-coated as a love story. It's propaganda in the best sense of the word. But you probably know that."

"I'm embarrassed to say I didn't."

Amparo grabbed a nearby camping chair and plopped. She unfurled her arms and legs and let her head drop back. "First time I sat down all day. What were we talking about? Oh, yeah, I studied the book in a women's literature class at Pitzer College. I know it's a little fucked up because she portrays the missions and padres as sympathetic when they were brutalizing the Indians."

She rolled her eyes back in her head. "When you were a kid, did you have to build a model of a mission for your social studies class? Out of cardboard and popsicle sticks?"

"Made mine out of sugar cubes."

"That's our insane education system. Make kids build a mission but don't teach about the conquest and forced labor going on there. Wish I had a cigarette. You got one?"

Pomona shook her head. She couldn't believe Amparo knew about this book. "I wish I knew more about Helen Hunt Jackson."

"Get her biography. Someone must have written one. Read it for both of us. Right now saving the Farm is all I have time for."

Pomona remembered working at the library, all the books at her fingertips, how much she loved the quiet, precise work. She missed it so much. "I actually know where I can find one. So, do you come here every day?"

Amparo raised her eyebrows. "I never leave. I live here in a tent."

"Wow. You don't have to go to work?"

Amparo gave Pomona an impish grin. "Had a job but I quit. Work here now. Don't make any money but feel wealthier than I did before. Did you hear there might be news soon? It's possible our lawyer Dan Stormer got a message from Mr. Horowitz. Listen, when this is finally over, let's get a beer and hang. Talk about something besides the Farm and city politics. I'll bet we have a lot in common."

Amparo threw out this invitation with light nonchalance, as if forging new friendships was easy as pie.

"Sure, of course," Pomona responded with a flustered hand wave as her heart shouted, *yes, yes, a friend! I so desperately want you to be my friend.*

Pomona was leaving when she noticed a group of girls gathered around the picnic table by the front gate.

"Hello," one girl giggled as Pomona approached the table.

She noticed paint cans and cardboard. "Are you painting protest signs?"

They nodded. "We want to have extra signs to give people tomorrow who don't have one," a girl explained. She looked about twelve and seemed in charge of the three younger girls. "When the television camera people come, they'll see lots of signs that say why we want to save the Farm."

"That's a great idea," Pomona said. "Who told you to do this?"

The girl sat up straighter. "It's our idea. I heard you tell your story about getting the flowers from the cemetery, but I forgot your name."

"Pomona," she blushed. "Don't try that yourselves."

The girls smiled shyly. "My name is Desiree," said the lead girl. Long arms angled out from her thin body. "Those are my cousins Julieta and Beatriz. They are nine and ten. That's my little sister, Liliana. She's only seven."

"It's getting kind of late. Where are your parents?"

"They work as janitors in an office building so they are gone all night. We come here. Nicer than being in our apartment."

"Hot there," Marie said.

"And noisy," added Beatrice. "I hear loud televisions when I'm trying to sleep."

"You live close by?"

"Around the corner," Desiree said. "We don't want to lose the Farm. We've been coming here our whole life. There aren't any parks nearby and we couldn't go there at night anyway but our mom lets us come here with our aunt. She's at the vigil."

"I am going to make a sign that tells that man to let us stay at the Farm," Liliana said. "Maybe he has a house with a yard but we only have the Farm."

"Good point," Pomona said. "If Mr. Horowitz didn't have a house with his own yard and garden he would know how hard it is to live in an apartment without one."

Pomona sat with the girls and painted signs.

They covered one with a flurry of butterflies and ladybugs and wrote: "All God's Creatures Love the South Central Farm."

On another sign they wrote, "Plants Have Feelings Too."

"Will you come back tomorrow and help us again?" Desiree asked when, an hour later, Pomona stood to leave. "We'll come after school and make more."

"Yes, please come.," the girls chorused.

"I will try," Pomona said. She thought of the loneliness that would swallow her whole when she returned to Nora's apartment. She put her hand over her heart. "I will come tomorrow and help. I promise."

Chapter Thirty

You Can Cut all the Flowers But You Can't Stop Spring

S he did return the next day, in the afternoon, and headed back to the woman's plot to reclaim her space beside the Virgin of Guadalupe. At Nora's she dutifully watered the plants, and made half-hearted attempts to sort through more of her possessions, but by lunchtime a debilitating ennui set in. She was also tired of hiding from Stacey, who would certainly soon ask whether she planned to stay another month and if so, where was the rent. Strangely, Stacey had not yet come sniffing around.

"Did you miss me?" she asked the ever-patient Virgin. "I have something important I'd like to lay before you for a blessing." From her bag she pulled out Nora's tin and placed it in the dirt, among the candles and sunflowers.

"This is my mommy. We didn't always get along so well, but I miss her now. She was a queen. A lonely queen. A lonely and kooky queen."

Pomona then pulled *Ramona* from her bag and continued the story:

After Ramona and Alessandro secretly left the Moreno Ranch they traveled on horseback to San Diego and were married by the old priest Father Gaspara who lived there. After, they traveled through the Poway Valley until they arrived at San Pasqual Valley where they could live in peace among Temecula Indians there. Ramona and Alessandro built a house in the idyllic spot still unmolested by American settlers. Life unfolded and Ramona had a baby daughter christened "Eyes of the Sky" because her eyes were blue like her mother's. The little family finally finds happiness. Until one sad day word comes that white settlers have started knocking on doors and presenting government papers stating the land belongs to them. Alessandro is farming when a white settler comes and claims his land. He just got the papers from Washington last week and tells Alessandro to leave peaceably.

I know it does seem a little rough on fellows like you, that are industrious and have done some work on the land. But you see the land's in the market; I've paid my money for it…I've got my family from San Diego and I want to get them settled…we're from the States and she's been used to having everything comfortable…

Once again, Ramona, Alessandro and their baby are forced to leave their home and village, with nowhere to go.

A long afternoon shadow fell before Pomona and she jumped up from her seat.

"I didn't mean to startle you," a man said. "There's definitely a tension in the air that's put everyone on edge." He held out an elegant hand and looked truly sorry. Tall and slender, the gentleman, perhaps in his seventies, had a professional looking camera slung over his suit jacket. "You are such a lovely sight sitting in the garden with your book. Do you mind if I take your picture? This afternoon light is magic." He aimed his lens toward her.

"I'll go along but why are you taking my picture?"

He chuckled. "For the record books most likely, so one day we don't completely forget about this place." He held out his hand. "I'm Don. Been coming to photograph the farm over the past year. Was invited by the farm leaders. Don't move. It's the damn golden light."

Self-consciously Pomona looked back at her book but couldn't focus on reading as this Don guy clicked his camera. When the clicking stopped she looked up and regarded the man more closely.

"Sir, your name seems familiar and I wonder if we've met before?"

"Don't know. Think I would remember you. But I meet a lot of people in my line of work. I see you're reading *Ramona*. I never read it but saw the movie with Dolores del Rio."

"I don't know anything about the movie but this book is so sad. I always thought it was just a love story but it's really about the unjust treatment of the Indians. Imagine your family living for generations in a village and then one day a white guy shows up and tell you he owns your land and you have to clear out."

Don's lanky fingers opened the camera back and inserted a new film roll with rapid, practiced precision. "That is a sad California story but you know that book had an unintended effect the author could not have predicted," he said. "They say it brought droves of people from the rest of the country to our fair land. They read about the rolling hills, the endless sunshine and flowers, the good weather. Around the same time Southern Pacific Railroad's Southern California rail lines opened which also fed a tourism boom. If you've ever wondered by so many streets and avenues are called Ramona, now you know why." Don chuckled wryly. "Isn't it funny how you could try so hard to do one thing and something entirely different happens."

"Perhaps a miracle will occur."

"You never know. You think the arc of justice is on your side but power and money are brutal, especially in Los Angeles. Especially when it comes to land. I've seen it before. At this point in my life I'm less interested in politics than documenting the sheer grace of people living among plants."

An eerie feeling washed over Pomona. She narrowed her eyes. "Don Normark. I looked at your book, the photographs you took in Chavez Ravine when you were young, before the people living there were pushed out to build Dodger Stadium."

He looked pleased. "I was a young man then, lucky to stumble on such an incredible subject to photograph, but it's not true they were pushed out to build Dodger Stadium. Rather, the City Housing Authority decided the eyesore of a neighborhood – their words, not mine –was a prime location to build low-income housing. The residents were promised first dibs on a new house there if they left without complaint. It was only after everyone was forced out, including a few literally dragged screaming, that the mayor scrapped the project."

Pomona shook her head in bewilderment. "You spent time with those people, probably made friends with people who lost their homes."

"My dear, you can't turn bitter over the injustice in the world. Then you're useless to everyone around you. Try to find the hope and inspiration. I couldn't do my work otherwise. I always think of the Neruda quote. He said something along the lines, 'You can cut all the flowers but that won't stop Spring from coming.'"

Pomona regarded the man for a long moment. She then held *Ramona* close to her face with the cover facing out, the beautiful illustration of Ramona on horseback and Alessandro leading her down the mountain trail. "Take my photograph with this book, Mr. Normark. Maybe someday you will look at these photos and remember me reading this book in this garden that still blooms and thrives."

Don Normark laughed gamely. "Sure thing. Hold still."
Click.

Chapter Thirty-one
Helen Hunt Jackson

Motivated by Amparo's suggestion that she read a biography on Helen Hunt Jackson, Pomona the next day drove to the Pasadena Central Library. She sat in Pearl in the parking lot for twenty minutes, gathering her courage to walk up the library stairs as she had done a thousand times, and revisit a past she had tried to forget. Crossing the library transom into its stately main hall with its soaring ceiling, tiled floors, and handsome woodwork took her breath as always. The firm of Myron Hunt and H.C. Chambers had built the library in 1925 and it was listed on the National Register of Historic Places. It was a beautiful library and she had been lucky to work there.

Pomona searched the online card catalog and found a 2003 biography by Kate Phillips titled, *Helen Hunt Jackson: A Literary Life*. Locating the book in the basement biography section, she took it to a first-floor reading room and studied the cover photograph at a corner table. It showed a round-faced woman gazing out with a confident smile, bedecked in the high-collared dress attire of her time. Pomona opened the cover and read the jacket copy:

"Novelist, travel writer, and essayist Helen Hunt Jackson (1830–1885) was one of the most successful authors and most passionate intellects of her day. Today Jackson is best remembered for "Ramona," her romantic novel set in the rural Southern Californian Indian and California communities of her day. "Ramona" has become a cultural icon, but Jackson's prolific career left us with much more, notably her achievements as a prose writer and her work as an early activist on behalf of Native Americans."

Over the next few hours Pomona read about this long-ago author, her early East Coast life, friendships with Emily Dickinson and Harriet Beecher Stowe, two marriages and two children who did not live into adulthood.

Then came the pivotal life event, when she was in her fifties and already an established writer. In 1879 Jackson attended a presentation in Boston by Ponca Indian Chief Mantcunanjin, also known as Standing Bear, and other Indians on tour with the tragic story of the Ponca tribe and its attempts to avoid deportation from its original territories in Nebraska to a reservation in Oklahoma. Deeply moved by their pleas, Helen Hunt Jackson became fueled with a consuming indignation that directed her work.

She immersed herself in research, learning about government double-dealings toward Indian tribes that included the Utes, Cheyennes, Nez Perces, Delawares, Cherokees, Sioux, and Poncas. She collected and published these in her 1881 book, *Century of Dishonor.* Within its pages she examined the U.S. government's violations of treaties with American Indian tribes and documented corruption of Indian agents and the crimes of settlers who stole reserved Indian lands.

In 1883 President Chester Arthur appointed her a Commissioner of Indian Affairs with the assignment of reporting on the conditions of California Mission Indians. The results of the investigations appeared in 1883 as the "Report on the Condition and Needs of the Mission Indians of California." It recommended giving them extensive government relief. After a bill embodying her recommendations passed in the U.S. Senate but died in the House of Representatives, Jackson decided to write a love story that would spoon-feed the information as a romance. She took a story she had heard about a beautiful high-born daughter who falls in love with an Indian herder. This Jackson combined with a sad account from her own report of a young Cahuilla man killed for stealing a horse from a white rancher.

Ramona was born. It became a bestseller.

Pomona leaned back in her chair. A thrill ran down her spine. Helen Hunt Jackson was just one woman and look what she did. She wasn't just a romance writer. She was an activist.

Book in hand, Pomona went to the check-out counter where a clerk took her library card and exclaimed, "Pomona, my dear, I wondered what happened to you. The last we heard your mother was ill and you left to care for her. We sent a card to your apartment. Did you receive it? How's your mom?"

Pomona stared at her former coworker with fondness. "Daniel, thank you. My mom died, a few weeks ago. I'm okay. Listen, I don't know what was wrong with me. I was asleep in my life, but I think I'm waking up."

Daniel gave her a sympathetic smile. "Sorry to hear about your mom. But good morning to waking up. Hey, come back. We could sure use you."

As Pomona walked back out to her car, she remembered the life she'd lived before Nora's illness. Her job and studio apartment, the few friends she had let fall off. That life had held a simple sweetness she hadn't appreciated. It had been overshadowed by her ideas of self-worthlessness that she was beginning, for the first time ever, to comprehend.

Pomona had been avoiding Stacey, the super's wife, who seemed to do all his bidding while he stayed inside and watched sports on television. When she returned from the library she carelessly and literally ran smack into Stacey as she came around the building's corner.

"Shit, shoot I mean, Stacey, I've been meaning to talk to you," Pomona stammered.

Stacey looked resigned. "Turns out it's a good thing you're staying another month. The painters I lined up for a fresh coat before I advertise the place put me off for a few weeks so I might as well get another month's rent from you."

"I'm staying another month?"

"You don't remember? Your friend came and paid the rent. Said you were busy and wanted to be sure everything was squared away."

"My friend?"

"That tall drink of water in the red truck. Girl, I'm glad you're not letting your mom's death stop you from having some fun."

Chapter Thirty-two
The Farm is Saved

A journalist on a morning news show, reporting on site at the Farm, described how the good news shone upon the farmers like the bright sun after a heavy rainstorm. She said the farmers, with utter joy, had thrown down their rakes, hoes, and shovels and rushed to the walnut tree where they hugged their neighbors, hugged strangers, kissed children. They opened bottles of beer and wine and toasted Tezo and Rufina. Toasted Dan Stormer and all the lawyers. Raised their glasses to the hundreds of supporters and volunteers who had come every single day and donated money and believed they could win. They toasted the Trust for Public Land and the Annenberg Foundation that had stepped up to provide the farmers with the money they needed to buy the Farm.

Yes, a deal was reached to save the fourteen acres at 41st Street and Alameda in South L.A. The Annenberg Foundation has agreed to provide $10 million as a lead gift to buy the land and the Trust for Public Land would help to fund the rest.

"The monetary issue is now off the table," Dan Stormer said in the broadcast, setting off cheers among the farmers. While the farmers laughed and cheered they also cried with relief and unleashed their bone-deep exhaustion. They admitted that they had sowed seeds of doubts and disbelief they could ever win.

"Too many times, more often than not, the little guy doesn't win," a man told the reporter.

The reporter stated that the Annenberg Foundation was now reaching out to Ralph Horowitz and extending its offer even though it was several days past his stated deadline. He would, of course, take the money as he had promised, and the fight for the Farm that had dragged on for three long excruciating years would finally be over.

When Pomona heard the radio broadcast she grabbed her bag, jumped into Pearl and drove to the Farm. Her heart beat with the speed of a hummingbird's wings as she navigated the streets, through Eagle Rock, Highland Park, past Dodger Stadium where she trained her gaze ahead and tried not to think of Parker though, of course, she did.

He had gone to her apartment and paid her rent. He had saved her from more desperation. She imagined herself running through the Farm gates into a joyous celebration and falling into his arms. He would squeeze her tight and never let go. She would breathe in his earthy scent and relax into the strength of his shoulders, the lightness of his laugher, as he whispered how he loved her, missed her. He would be celebrating this moment with Manuel, Irma, and Josefina, this miracle that they had hoped and prayed for together. In her lowest moments Pomona had decided he had paid her rent to ensure that she would not show up at his door homeless. But in her hopeful moments she conceded that he still loved her.

When Pomona passed through the Farm's gates there was indeed a merry crowd surrounding the walnut tree and a celebration in full swing with music, dancing, and food. She scanned the revelers' faces but did not see Parker. She did not see Manuel, Irma, or Josefina either. She realized they were probably in the garden plot with Irma handing around shots of tequila and Josefina warming her special tamales. For a moment her heart seized when she considered that they had not included her. No one had called Nora's to insist she drive right over and join the party. They were, after all, becoming close friends. But in all fairness she did not know if they even knew her phone number.

Maybe they weren't so close after all.

By the time Pomona reached Manuel's plot her mind and emotions were in a whirl of possible scenarios and expectations. She hurried into the garden and her heart didn't just sink but plummeted when she saw it was empty. No one was there. Not a soul. Had they been at the walnut tree and she'd missed them?

Faraway shouts and whoops rang through the air but her ear attuned to a repetitive sound echoing from a corner. She followed the sound and spotted a person hitting the tip of a shovel against the ground. She walked over to find Manuel thrusting a shovel into the dirt, again and again with fierce focus. At first he didn't see her standing on the pathway and his obliviousness gave Pomona time to study the strong planes of his face, his high cheekbones and sturdy nose. She imagined him young and handsome, back in Mexico with his family. Had he ever had a wife and children? He was the most alone person she had ever met. When Manuel finally looked up, he seemed unaware of the commotion erupting all around.

"What are you doing?" she asked, sensing she was disturbing a private moment.

He smiled sheepishly. "Trying to work this little patch but the ground is so hard, like stone. I don't know…might be a good spot for squash though I should have started a month ago when it was cooler."

"Did you hear that the Farm's been saved? You must hear people celebrating by the walnut tree." His nonchalance puzzled and disappointed her.

"Saved for now. That's why I'll work this dirt and plant squash."

"Where are Irma and Josefina?"

"Josefina, yo no se…maybe watching her niece and nephew. Irma must be somewhere."

"Does Parker know? Has he come?" Pomona bit her tongue the moment she said his name.

Manuel leaned against the shovel. "He not come here because of you."

"What?"

"He don't want to bother you."

She stepped back as Manuel peeled off his leather gardening gloves and smacked them against his thigh, dislodging a sheet of dried dirt that crumbled to the ground. Her skin tingled with embarrassment. "I never said he couldn't come to the Farm. He mustn't stay away on my account, especially now that the Farm's been saved. He should be here."

Manuel pointed the shovel down toward the earth and struck it again. For the first time ever in Manuel's presence Pomona felt unwelcome. She turned to leave. "I guess I'll go to the women's plot and read my book," she mumbled.

His next words stopped her cold.

"I want to ask, Pomona, why do we push away someone who loves us? Is it because we are scared or have bad feelings inside? Why do we hurt the people who love most?"

She turned back, rigid with defensiveness. "I didn't tell Parker not to come here. Why are you saying this?"

"Parker? No, I think of people in my life." Manuel pulled a handkerchief from his pocket and wiped sweat from his temple, his neck.

Pomona searched for words. "Manuel, you are one of the good people," she finally said. "You would never hurt anyone on purpose."

"Parker is same as me. Things in the past scare him. I've had times in mi vida when I should have fought harder. Love is worth fighting for. Yes, this land is worth fighting for but I think love is worth more."

Pomona placed a gentle hand on his shoulder. "You have a family in Mexico, don't you?"

Manuel nodded. "Mi espousa. Mi hija, Marisol. Mi familia."

"The love worth fighting for? You should be there with them, not here." Pomona suddenly couldn't understand why he would be in California so alone if he had a wife and daughter somewhere else.

"Not so easy. If I go back, I'm too old to cross the Rio Grande again. An old guy like me is never going to get documents I need to come legal. My work with Parker is good. I send money home." Manuel lowered his head and Pomona understood he didn't want to talk more about his family so far away.

"Oh, Manuel, the Farm has been saved. We should be happy. Instead you and I are here, so alone, so sad."

Manuel reached to the earth, grabbed a fistful of dirt, and held it to her nose. "What do you smell?"

She inhaled. "It's fresh. Sweet. Maybe mushrooms and chocolate."

"I smell la vida. Wakes me from sleeping. Plants have much intelligence. I think they are smarter than people. Some people say plants hold all the wisdom of the world. Where I come from, we don't say, this land is mine like we own a shirt," he said. "Did I tell you that back home we lived in a forest, a coffee forest."

"You mean a coffee farm?"

"Si, a farm in a forest. There I planted corn, beans, coffee. All under tall pine trees that gave so much, how do you say, shadows and shade. The earth gave us maize, for our tortillas. We picked and sold our coffee beans. The forest pulls clouds from the sky so that they drop rain on our fields below. The trees protect the plants, but also give us wood for burning, and different medicines. We had everything – clouds, plants, mountains, rivers, animals." Manuel smiled. The memories clearly energized him. "In Mexico we had mucho land. Here I have un poco, but it's good land. Help me plant my squash, Pomona. I teach you. Important to know how to grow your own food."

Pomona laughed, her spirits lifting. "I want to learn. I love it here in the garden. I've never felt happier."

"Yes, Pomona, because this is real life. Look at the caracols. Some say snails are bad for plants but I don't ever harm them. Just move them away from plants."

Pomona and Manuel worked together for the rest of the day, the sounds of celebrations echoing around them, hoots and hollers, beating drums, laughter, and music.

The South Central Farm has been saved. Viva la tierra!

All the while, without any interruptions and no sightings of Irma, Josefina, or Parker, they planted squash and tomatoes, eggplant and chard. Under Manuel's guidance Pomona pushed the heirloom seeds into the waiting soil, her heart swelling with love for the generous, fertile, and patient earth.

Chapter Thirty-three
Without the Land We Are Nothing

Harsh words came just a few days later and swept across the farm like wildfire.

Ralph Horowitz changed his mind. A radio newscast reported that Horowitz had told the *Los Angeles Times* he had turned down the Annenberg Foundation money. The Los Angeles Times story went into further details: Horowitz would not sell the property to the farmers even for $100 million because of how his name had been dragged through the mud. Plus the farmers had missed his deadline and had never shown any gratitude for squatting on his land as long as they had. For treating him like a bad guy when he was a businessman doing what businessmen do.

It wasn't the best deal for him any longer and he was going to move on. The eviction process would continue and the farmers should prepare to leave.

Leave now or the sheriff would forcibly remove them from his land.

The stunned farmers gathered under the walnut tree the next day. Pomona, Irma, and Josefina were among them.

"It's as if I went into your community and took down your temple. Took down your church. These are sacred things and they are taking away our way of life," said Tezo, tears running down his face.

"This is the end of living and the beginning of survival. Anything that has to do with man's connection to the earth should not be broken," said one farmer.

"I know about struggle," said an older black man with a grizzled beard. "I used to be a Black Panther. I am old now but I have one little bit of hell to raise and that's around these farmers."

"We saved this land, took it when it was dirty and we cleaned it up," a young man shouted. "I've been coming here with my papa since I was ten years old. Now they want to throw us out like animals. It's because we are Latinos."

"You see how much a little piece of dirt means to people. Without the land we are nothing."

"The mayor could still convince him," another voice added. "If the mayor went on TV and asked him to reconsider, it might make a difference."

"Where's our justice?" Irma cried out. She had climbed atop a turned over metal pail, tears trailing down her face as she raised a fist to the sky. "Who are we as humans if we don't have a connection to the earth? "

Parker watched her from afar, from behind a fence blocked by a stand of bamboo. Grieving farmers shouted, cried, and wailed their pain at the reversal of the good outcome they had expected. Tragedy wafted in the air- a smell as strong as a Midwestern summer rain.

It had never occurred to any of them that Ralph Horowitz would so cruelly renege on the deal, thought Parker. He had to admit he hadn't seen it coming either. Yesterday he was willing to believe Mr. Horowitz would play his role as expected in this dramatic story. He had been cast as the cold-hearted villain who forces the farmers to grow in faith and strength until in the third act when he sees the light and redeems himself by doing the right thing.

The farmers are victorious. End of play. Curtain call.

When he first heard news of Horowitz's refusal of the offer, Parker was strangely numb to the farmers' pain. Now, watching them from behind the bamboo, he had an urge to run into the middle of this despairing group and tell them that you cannot appeal to the humanity of men like Mr. Horowitz. The universe does not bend towards justice. You cannot appeal to their emotions. Men like Ralph Horowitz and Amos Wilson speak another language, the language of money and power. Of pride and winning.

Parker did not approach the group. He focused his gaze on Pomona who was now holding Irma's hand and helping her down from the pail. Her black hair shielded her stricken face.

He yearned to run to Pomona, take her in his arms and soothe her with words of love.

Would she resist and push him away? Had she forgotten all about him?

He imagined grabbing her shoulders and shaking her until she cried out that she loved him and was sorry she had made him suffer. He would then push her into the dirt and climb atop her, spreading her legs. He would grab her black hair and pull it away so that he could lay his lips on her neck and make her cry in pleasure.

Parker dropped to the ground. He couldn't eat or sleep or work. He was barely holding on. He had avoided Manuel all week by saying he was sick. He could not climb into a palm. Didn't want to. If he couldn't have Pomona he did not want the palms either.

Parker looked up to see Pomona had turned from Irma to wrap her arms around Josefina who was openly sobbing.

A pang of jealousy hit his gut. He had brought Pomona to the Farm and now she was closer to Irma and Josefina than he had ever been.

But he had never said two words to them. He had been friendly, sure, but had he ever wondered about their lives? He was a selfish bastard. Pomona was right. Why would she ever love him?

A pressure was building behind his eyes, a migraine coming on. Saliva pooled in his mouth. He spit on the ground.

That night in McArthur Park after Pomona had run away, he had returned to his truck and grabbed his climbing backpack. He made his way to the dumpster in the alley behind Mama's Hot Tamales. He had pushed open the heavy metal lid and thrown in his climbing gear. When the backpack hit the bottom with a bang, he closed the lid and went home. It was over. The palms, Pomona, his dreams of finding love.

Driving home through the streets of L.A. he wept for all the palms that would someday be gone. News of their demise was already surfacing though he didn't need anyone to tell him what he already saw in his work. Palms dying from fungus and invasive beetles and simple old age. Almost eighty years had passed since 1931 when the city's forestry division had put 400 unemployed men to work planting some 25,000 Mexican fan palms. Such a hopeful undertaking to plant juvenile palms along 150 miles of city boulevards. They had grown tall and strong, reaching for the sun, lining streets like sentries, but their time was running out.

The palms would be gone same as the orange groves ripped out in the name of progress. Who needs fields of fruit when you could have shopping centers and parking lots? City officials had already said they would replace dead and dying palms with drought-tolerant species that provided more shade. Maybe not in Parker's life, but over time they would disappear and palm trimmers like him would be relics of the past, like railway workers or orange pickers.

At home alone that horrible night, the sun had fallen from his sky. Confronted with the darkness of his soul he tried to force out sobs but he could not break through his wall of self-loathing. He decided then he would go back to Kansas with Virginia. That was his destiny. Why fight anymore? And really, would it be so bad? Virginia was beautiful and strong and her body would forever drive him crazy. He would work for his father and they would buy their own ranch and drive matching Cadillacs and go to fancy parties in Wichita. They would have two kids and he would love them with every fiber of his body. He would be different from his father and let his children follow their own hearts wherever it might take them, even if to the top of a palm and they never came down.

Parker decided then once he left he would never return to California. In fact, best to stay away from any tropical or sunny locale for the rest of his life. They would vacation in Montana and Colorado, the East Coast and parts of Europe, Scotland, and France, but just the north. Places with no palms.

He would choose comfort over meaning and his neck would thicken and he would drink too much because he hated his life and he would think of Pomona all the time and dream of palm trees every night.

He must have dozed off behind the bamboo because when he opened his eyes a guy was kneeling beside him with a tall glass of amber liquid.

"Hey, I'm worried that you're getting dehydrated, laying in the direct sun. Drink this."

Parker eyed the glass suspiciously, remembering the joint he naively smoked in MacArthur Park.

The guy laughed. "It's a special potion of water infused with mint and chamomile. Okay, and some herbs like mugwort. My wife makes it every morning and puts it out for everyone. We all need to stay hydrated these days. Stay positive. Drink up buddy."

Parker drank and couldn't stop. It was so cold and delicious. "Thanks, I needed that. Hey, where did everyone go?" The area around the walnut tree was empty.

"Walking the perimeter of the Farm, making phone calls, planning strategies. Can you believe this shit? This is going down. Going to get nasty. I'd better go help. Take care, man."

Parker shook his head and waved his hand. Determined to return to his truck, he stood and stagger-stepped over to the walnut tree where he leaned against its massive trunk.

"A real tragedy if this beautiful walnut tree gets ripped from the ground."

Parker turned to see John Quigley standing a few feet behind him. John, in his forties, was tall and rangy with graying hair and a sun-lined face. His manner was easy going and Parker felt an instant kinship with the famed tree-sitter who three years earlier had spent seventy-one days sitting in a Santa Clarita oak tree to thwart a developer's plan to fell the 400-year-old tree to build a road. John Quigley and the tree dubbed "Old Glory" had even made news in Garden City.

In the end the sheriff had forcibly removed Quigley who had chained himself to the tree's branches. As protesters booed and children sang, "This Land Is Your Land," firefighters hoisted a platform ladder from their truck and plucked John, holding an American flag, from the branches. But because of John's actions the developer agreed to move the tree, at considerable expense, to a nearby park. John Quigley had won that battle. He was a winner.

"How's Old Glory doing?" Parker asked. With feigned nonchalance, he folded his arms across his chest and tried to act normal despite his spinning head. "Transplanting a mature tree is an iffy proposition."

John's smile was as broad as his shoulders. "So far so good. Still too early to tell if the tree has truly taken root. We'll know for sure in a few more years, but right now it's looking good."

Parker looked dubious. "You really feel optimistic? After all you went through and now this?"

"Hey man, the most radical thing you can do is be optimistic," John Quigley answered with a wink. "If you're hopeless then they've already won."

Parker laughed. He liked people who winked. They seemed to have a playful confidence he admired. He motioned to the tree. "Mind if I climb up?"

"Go ahead, we're just getting ready for tonight. Once Daryl and I climb into those branches we're not coming down until the Farm is saved or the sheriff forcibly removes us. I pray for the first option through we're grasping at straws at this point." John was speaking of Daryl Hannah, the movie actor and environmentalist, who had been sitting in the tree with other activists for weeks now.

As John walked away Parker lifted himself to the tree's first branch. This was easy compared to a palm. He took a few moments to breathe into his body and then he climbed over a few more branches until he was twenty feet off the ground. From this vantage he saw John Quigley crouched on the ground, sorting through supplies. Parker looked upward to the tree-sitters' platform fashioned from an old door hanging from a branch. On the bottom someone had painted in green and red paint: "Save the Farm." The tree-sitters would live on this eight-by-four foot space for hours, days, maybe weeks.

He looked back down at John and wondered, what kind of a man puts his entire life on the line to save a tree?

A man living in the power of his convictions.

Why were some men so driven by their convictions and others not at all?

Parker decided he wanted to know the experience of standing on the platform so he climbed higher, lifting and stepping from branch to branch until he hoisted himself onto the hanging door. A California blue jay above his head chirped. The tree's nutty aroma tickled his nose.

Instead of filling him with a sense of conviction and power, as Parker had hoped, standing on the platform made his mind go right to Incencio. For an entire year the knocker had lived in a prison cell no bigger than this platform.

"Hey, Parker, can't you tell your father to do something about the heat," Incencio had asked him one day while they smoked out back during a break. He knew the workers wanted better ventilation so the sweltering summer temperatures that overwhelmed the kill floor didn't exhaust them day after day. Parker had done nothing.

Parker peered back down at Quigley who was speaking to a group of activists in a voice clear and direct. that moment Parker knew John Quigley had a moral compass Parker had none. He had bet against his own brother.

Chapter Thirty-four
Someday the Palms Will All Be Gone

After leaving Irma and Josefina at the Women's Collective Plot, Pomona walked over to find Manuel. He was in his garden plot sitting on a turned-over pail, cleaning his tools with a rag.

"What are you going to do?" Pomona asked.

Manuel scraped dried dirt off his hoe. "Wish I hadn't planted all my seeds. I should have known better. I will clean my tools and go home."

"But you'll return in the morning in case the sheriff comes?"

He shook his head. "No mas tiempo."

"It's still important to do everything we can. If we put up a fight Mr. Horowitz might change his mind or maybe the mayor will have a plan. I know Irma and Josefina and others are working on what to do next."

Manuel now sorted his hand tools into his pail, his pliers and clippers and spade.

At first Pomona thought he didn't hear her but after a moment he said, "Mija, don't be naive. It's over. You think other people even care about saving this land? Most people never even heard of the Farm."

"Wait a minute. You taught me about plants. Soil. We planted together. You're the one who convinced me this land is worth fighting for. Never give up."

Manuel chuckled. "Me fight a powerful, rich American? A poor man from Mexico? In this country I am no one. Invisible."

"Why are you giving up?" She grabbed Manuel's hoe and held it before him. "You can't leave."

Manuel stood straight and gave her a funny look.

"Stop it, Pomona. Enough." Irma strode into the plot with a fierce scowl, marched over and snatched the hoe from her grip. "Manuel's been fighting alongside the other farmers for three years and you've been coming for what, a few weeks? Hanging out and reading your book?"

Pomona flinched at Irma's rough demeanor but squared her shoulders. "I care about the Farm. I'm at the rallies and protests. But I was never a farmer. Maybe it's not really my fight."

"Not your fight?" Irma glowered with a combustible intensity. "Of course this is your fight. It's everyone's fight. I see you wringing your hands, upset about the situation, but you don't really make a sacrifice. You feel bad for the farmers but when you get tired, you go home to your comfortable Pasadena apartment. If we lose everyone loses."

Pomona bristled from head to toe. "You think I'm some rich girl from Pasadena? Ha! Funny joke. But if I was would it make my involvement less worthy? You accuse me of judging, but what are you doing?"

"Irma, let her alone," Manuel ordered. "I'm not helping either. Not really. Not like before."

"You've already gone through this once before," Irma yelled. "You don't need to do it again."

"Again?" Pomona looked from Irma to Manuel.

"His coffee farm in Mexico. Stolen."

"Stolen by whom?"

"It doesn't matter," Manuel shouted. He grabbed the hoe from Irma's grip, then scuffled over to the plot of vegetables he and Pomona had planted two days earlier.

Good, Pomona thought. Working the soil will calm him down.

But instead Manuel lifted the hoe and attacked the soil, ripping all the plantings apart with its sharp edge.

"Manuel, stop! What are you doing?" Pomona yelled, running towards him.

"Getting the garden ready for the warehouses."

"You're wrecking our plants."

Irma grabbed Pomona's arm and held her back. "Let him be, mija. Let him be angry. He should let it out."

"You're encouraging him," Pomona screamed, turning toward Irma and pulling her arm free.

But it was too late. After tearing up the soil with the heirloom seeds, Manuel moved to the adjacent bed with the sprouting peppers, green onion, beans, lettuce, and radishes. He raised the hoe and dug its sharp edge into the soil, destroying all the plants as Pomona and Irma watched.

When Manuel finished he turned to the women. "I have seen many times what rich men do to poor men like me. I have lost many things more important. Mateo, Dolores, Marisol, our land, our life. That man can take this farm. I don't care. I lost what matters long ago."

"Oh, Manuel, I'm so sorry," Pomona ran to him and took his hand. "What happened to your family? Tell me." But Manuel just stood still as a statue and stared at the ground.

Irma came over and pulled her away. "Let him alone," she whispered as she led Pomona out of the plot, through the gate, and onto the path. Pomona stumbled alongside.

"I didn't know about Manuel's past. No one told me," she cried.

"Don't be so dramatic. We all have a past. Most people here have left behind or lost something somewhere in this world."

"I only care about Manuel. Why did he lose his land, his family?"

Irma sighed. She led Pomona to a log lying along the path. They both perched on its back. "As you wish. Manuel had a coffee farm in Chiapas, just a little one but a good one. It had been his grandfather's and father's and Manuel worked it with his own son, Mateo, and his wife, Dolores. But then bad luck came, a fungus destroyed the crop. He had never seen such a fungus before and he lost his entire crop that year."

Irma grew quiet. Pomona, sensing her heavy emotion, took and squeezed her hand. She knew Irma meant well, cared for Manuel, certainly knew him better.

Irma gave her a rueful smile. "You know, mija, many of us here are just regular folks, Simple people from villages and small town. To us, Los Angeles is a scary beast." She frowned and looked resigned. "Listen, I can tell you that Manuel made a mistake in Chiapas. Took a loan from a man who made many promises, but when Manuel missed just one payment the man took away the land that his family had owned for generations. It's a familiar story."

The revelation hit Pomona like a stone against her chest. "But why is Manuel here alone when his family is in Mexico?"

Irma looked at Pomona as if she couldn't understand life's most basic principles. "Manuel was desperate. No more land. No way to earn a living. Over time, he became angry. Fighting with Dolores. One morning he and Dolores found a note from Mateo, their son. He had left for Los Angeles to find a job. To send money. Manuel went crazy. Mateo was only seventeen and it's a dangerous journey alone through Mexico, crossing the border. Swimming the Rio Grande. Stupid boy thought he could help his parents this way. For six months they waited but heard nothing so Manuel made the journey himself to find Mateo."

Pomona thought of Francisco. He had done the same, had left Tampico, traveled north, and swam across the Rio Grande to find his father. How many people had risked their lives swimming across the powerful river to find their fathers and son, mothers and daughters.

Irma continued: "Manuel found his way to the Farm and showed everyone Mateo's picture, begging, had they seen him? Could they help find him?" As she spoke, Irma's face looked ten years older than even the day before.

"I used to sometimes take him in my car. Driving the streets looking for Mateo. I said, 'Manuel, this is Los Angeles, not your pueblo. We won't just find Mateo walking along.' Of course so many people have lost their own people. So many lost people, what's one more? Little by little Manuel started planting as he waiting for Mateo. He really believed someday Mateo would come to the Farm, but the years passed and nothing."

The afternoon was deepening. A golden light lit the sky. In a plot across from where they sat, a crow landed on a scarecrow's shoulder and cawed out a greeting.

"Mateo never sent word to his mother? He just disappeared?"

"Mija, people disappear all the time. It's a dangerous journey across Mexico, over the border, through the desert. So much violence, robbery, gangs just waiting to steal what little you have. To love is to grieve. Everyone here knows that."

"What about Dolores and Marisol?" Pomona was heartsick to think not just of Manuel's missing son but his wife and daughter.

Irma shrugged. "It's sad, but Manuel had no way to earn a living in Chiapas and here he found work in the palms so he could send Dolores money each month. Better for them. Anyway, Manuel could not face Dolores without bringing Mateo home."

"Go west young man," Parker murmured as he accelerated his truck across four lanes of traffic. The wind rushed into the open windows and blew through his hair.

Sunlight flashed through his windshield. Parker shaded his eyes with his hand. He had left his sunglasses at home. He had left behind everything: his love, Pomona. His friend, Manuel. His business. He blinked against the glare and swallowed hard.

Guess I'm back to my old tricks, he thought. Running away and ruining everything. How ironic to be running back to the place from which I escaped.

That morning, as Parker packed his few possessions for the road trip east, he spotted his blue backpack of gear leaning against the fireplace. "Come on," the backpack seemed to purr. "You know you want to."

He stopped stuffing clothes into his duffle bag.

"Never again," he answered. Once he hit the road and left L.A., he would never again climb into a palm. Stopping cold turkey was his only option.

"That's kind of crazy," the backpack purred back.

Parker rubbed his twitching thighs with open hands. Cold turkey was the only want to quit anything you no longer wanted or couldn't have. Anyway, it was already one o'clock. Parker planned to cross the Nevada state line before dark.

Parker sank onto the sofa. The backpack reminded him of his weakness. The morning after he had thrown his gear into a dumpster behind Mama's Hot Tamales, he had returned, climbed into the smelly metal receptacle and retrieved the backpack. He had convinced himself it was foolish to trash good equipment that he could give Manuel. He had always loved his spurs, safety belt, and ropes. They had served him well and didn't deserve to end up in a landfill.

"What's one last climb," the backpack seemed to say. "If you're never going to scale another palm, at least enjoy your swan song."

Parker stood, overwhelmed by prickles of desire shooting up his legs.

Wait. What did it really matter, as long as he was in Kansas in two days' time for the hearing. Anyway, it was better to drive at night in cooler temperatures. Parker went to the fireplace and grabbed the backpack straps. He hugged it to his chest and inhaled its familiar musty scent that now held an undertone of chili sauce courtesy of the dumpster. Certainly the old Grand Dame at El Matador beach deserved a final goodbye and thank you.

"Then I can honestly know it's all over," he bargained with himself. "I won't have any more regrets."

The 10 Freeway ended and fed into the Santa Monica Tunnel, pulling Parker into shadowed darkness and then, bam, he emerged on the other side and was hit with a spectacular view of the Pacific Ocean. The whole world opened up as he came through that tunnel. The sparkling ocean gleamed before him. He glanced to his left to see the Ferris wheel on the Santa Monica Pier turning against a cloudless sky. He had come to the ends of the earth where land dissolved into water.

He would miss this psychedelic land where plant life grew so abundantly. It gave him total sensory perception overload. The quality of the light, its unceasing brightness burned away all the trauma that people across the world dragged on their backs to this sun-baked land. They came to Los Angeles for the merciless sun. That's why he came, too.

Parker headed north on Pacific Coast Highway. He drove through Santa Monica, past the Getty Villa, the Malibu Pier, and Pepperdine University nestled in the golden scrubby hills. Onward he pushed toward Point Dume State Beach. The two-lane highway was fairly empty at 5 p.m. and it took him ten minutes to drive from Point Dume to El Matador State Beach five miles further up the rugged coast.

He pulled off PCH onto a dirt road that led to the small parking lot above El Matador. He aimed his truck toward the bluff, killed the engine, and settled in. He watched a couple of young surfers peel off their wetsuits next to the only other car in the lot, a blue pickup truck. The two men were twenty years at most and probably best friends by the comfortable way they talked and joked. A slip of a girl in a tiny bikini sat on the pickup's tailgate. Her hair was the color of a shiny lucky penny. As she giggled her ringlets of curls bounced on her small chest. Parker rolled down his window and stared at the three so young, so naively blissful. How lucky to be alive in such an Eden. They would always carry this beauty around on the inside and expect it from the world. As their laughter and chatter echoed around him, Parker sat patiently in his truck and waited for them to leave.

Pomona watched Manuel take his bucket of tools and walk from his plot without a glance back at her or his now ruined garden. Irma was gone too, swallowed up somewhere in the booming activity and chaos that

226

clattered all around. The Farm had become a battleground as people prepared for a showdown.

None of this made sense to Pomona anymore. The Farm was lost. Parker was lost. The cat was lost. She was lost and now Manuel was lost, too. Her heart ached for all the loss. She realized it wasn't Parker who weighed heaviest. It was Nora and Francisco. The little bit of family she once had disappeared into a void. Sometimes she could barely remember her parents' faces. They appeared before her eyes in flashes like hallucinations, then dissolved into thin air.

Pomona walked past the women's collective plot. It was empty, its gate unlocked. She took her usual place in a garden chair beside the Virgin of Guadalupe. They had become fast friends. The garden's meditative quiet was a blessing. She closed her eyes and tried to conjure up an image of Francisco driving his Gran Torino through orange groves blanketed in blue twilight.

She heard a voice. It was her own, speaking in soft tones to the Virgin.

"I never really pray," she confessed to the statue. "Not in a serious way. Usually only when I'm utterly desperate, like now. I'm wondering if there's a way I can bring my parents back? Not from the dead, of course. But somehow in my heart. I miss them so much. Other people say they feel the spirits of loved ones all around. I feel nothing." Her voice cracked. "I mean, I was their only daughter. Could they possibly be watching over me? I just want to know if I'm doing the right thing. Making good choices."

The Virgin shined her beatific smile in her usual steadfast way. In the presence of the Virgin, and surrounded by the beauty of the garden, she allowed herself to let go. What did anything matter anymore? She released every thought and feeling in her body and head. As she fell into complete surrender, an understanding filled Pomona. A clear knowing.

She had been so mad at Parker in MacArthur Park for not facing his past and fears. But was it Parker she was mad at? Or Nora? If she were honest with herself she would have to admit that she had been angry at Nora since the day Francisco left.

"No," she told the Virgin. "I loved my mother. I really did."

The Virgin seemed to smirk.

"Okay, I loved her. But I hated the way she denied her past. Denied my past. Denied me my relationship with Francisco. She never let me talk about him. How heartbroken I was the entire twenty years he was gone. How I missed him and needed him."

Pomona shivered and wished she had brought a sweater. The truth chilled her bones. The moment Francisco disappeared, she had lost the warm sunshine of his love. "I became frozen in place. A sad girl who didn't know how to create her own a life. What am I supposed to do?"

At that moment the book, *Ramona*, dropped out from her bag.

Pomona frowned. "It's *Ramona*," she told the Virgin. "Something important lays within its pages, doesn't it?"

She had read a few chapters here and there but she wasn't even half way through. Her attempt, like most things she did it like, was halfhearted. Pomona picked up the book. Francisco had asked her to read *Ramona*. So had Nora. Why hadn't she done so with passion and urgency?

The Virgin smiled.

Glancing at the late afternoon sun Pomona calculated a few more hours of daylight. She opened the book and began to read.

Two hours later Pomona closed the book and lifted her sights westward to see a tangerine globe hovered above the horizon, completely incandescent as if lit from within. A hot pink aura surrounded this melting orb and from it electric shades of purple streaked out into the sky. She wished Parker was by her side drinking in this beauty.

As she gazed at the sunset she knew Francisco had loved *Ramona* for many reasons. His own mother had given him the old volume. That itself was a link and connection. But was it also the love between Ramona and

Alejandro, so deeply rooted in their need to find and fight for a home, a place on earth where they could be themselves and live in peace and beauty, that called to his romantic soul? Together they had fought for a home. A place of peace and beauty in which to raise their daughter. Was that the kind of love her father had hoped to create with Nora? He certainly gave her the adoration that Alessandro gave Ramona. Pomona realized a place of peace and beauty, love and safety, was all she'd wanted for her and Parker. The same thing that all the people of the South Central Farm wanted.

Suddenly Nora's voice filled Pomona's head as if she were sitting with her in the garden. In the evening stillness Pomona heard the words her mother had uttered when she had pulled the book from beneath her pillow.

"Something about this book scares me. I don't remember. It contains a secret message. That's why I hid it. Because of the secret."

Pomona shuddered. "What secret message, Mommy? What were you trying to tell me?"

Parker woke with a start. Where was he? He ran a finger over his dry, cracked lips. He had fallen asleep in the truck. He peered through his windshield into an electric sunset, hot pink and deep purple. Through it all a golden sun cast a dazzling glow as it melted into an inky blue ocean.

Parker didn't blink those last few seconds as the sun slipped into the ocean, lower, lower, until it was gone. He ached to share this moment with Pomona. To tell her that in the end it can only be love and beauty that will save the world.

"Oh Pomona, what happened to us? Why are you so far from me?"

When the last light disappeared Parker got out of the truck. In the cool night his mood lifted in anticipation of his California swan song. His final lament. He walked along the bluff in the warm blowsy night, comfortable in his T-shirt and shorts, his sights set on the one seductive palm before him.

The Mexican Fan of rare and unequaled beauty rose at least 120 feet into the sky, standing tall and proud as it had for decades, head and shoulders above the other nearby *Washingtonia robustas*. The grand old dame was leaning south, as coastal palm trees do, partially hanging over the cliff that dropped to an outcrop of rocks and boulders.

The whole world fell away as Parker dropped to his knees on the bluff and unzipped his backpack. He took out his spurs and attached them to his boots. With his spurs strapped in place, he approached the tree.

"Hello, old friend," he said with reverence, patting the smooth, slender trunk. Safety belt in place, Parker circled his arms around the palm and took his first step. He drove his spur into its side and then drove in the other. He pulled out the first and took a step upward, then followed with the other. Yes, his arm hurt, his fracture not quite healed, but it was good pain, the kind that made you feel alive. Up Parker walked, hugging the palm, melting into her strength. Slowly he inched up, five feet, ten, twenty, thirty feet off the ground. Within minutes he summited the crown and was high above the bluff within his seaside cathedral. Gusty gales skirted off the ocean and filled his nose with the pungent smell of seaweed.

Across the horizon he saw her black hair blowing about her face, red lips curled in a cryptic smile. Pomona of the Orchards. Roman Goddess of fruit trees. Her right hand bearing a pruning knife.

This was it, everything he lived for, this breathtaking, life-affirming moment alone with the palm. His heart raced with his love for it all. He settled into position, leaned back into his safety belt. With his feet lodged against the tree, he slipped into a hypnotic state and regarded the ocean and the moon floating in a sea of black. In this state of surrender he understood that every moment of his life had led him to this point. To this night and into this palm. Within the fronds he knew he had reached the end of a journey. He shuddered that the truth was so obvious: Denial was his shackle. Not the palm. Not Pomona. He needed to confront at his deeds of the past to be free.

Absorbing this truth, Parker was incredulous that he had almost forsaken the palms that had healed him. Climbing into palms had made his life better. Palms were never a problem, despite what Virginia, his father and brother had said. The palms and Pomona of the Orchards were his saviors.

"Today is the first day of the rest of my life," he told the palm.

He shook his head at the corny phrase. Where had he just seen those words? Then he remembered. The slogan had been splashed across the T-shirt of one of the MacArthur Park guys, the one who had passed him the hash joint. At the time he had inwardly scoffed at the trite words. But the slogan was like the thousands of bits of information that confront you every day, that filter through and bubble to the surface when you least expect them. The hackneyed words now seemed prophetic.

"Today is the first day of the rest of my life," he repeated, and something about it rang true. The sentiment was hopeful. He could start anew. He didn't have to drag around his past. That's what Los Angeles and the palms had given him. The freedom to stop running away.

Parker dug his spurs deeper into the tree and settled in among the fronds that surrounded him like a thatched hut. He watched as waves rose and fell onto the shore as gentle earthly sighs. The wind was picking up, skating off the ocean, and singing through the trees. A silver radiance from the water seemed to float up and illuminate all the broken fragments of his life. He would own them all. Let them wash through his heart. He clung to the palm and closed his eyes.

Pomona opened her father's book to the back inside cover where a nameplate of heavy card-stock bore her grandmother's name in a flourish of cursive:

Hermoine Delphina Gregorio Sandoval.

With an index finger Pomona traced her abuela's name and wondered about this woman she had never known but who had given her the silver necklace with the Virgin pendant for her tenth birthday. She had been old then and was now buried in a Tampico cemetery.

As Pomona's fingers traced the edges she realized the nameplate was loose against the back cover. With a wiggle of her finger, she pushed against the nameplate. She pushed again and it loosened more. She took one corner and pulled it from the book. The nameplate now gone, she ran her finger over the inside back cover and noticed a slight raise, barely perceptible, where the nameplate had been. Pomona looked closer and saw that the heavy end paper glued to the back inside board was glued down on only three sides; the side against the book spine was actually open, like an envelope. She wiggled a finger into the tight space. With her fingernail she extracted from this hidden space a small envelope, its flap already opened. She pulled from the envelope a single page, handwritten letter, dated October 14, 1986. The small cramped writing read:

Dearest Nora:

You can't imagine my regret that we fought, that I hurt you and left our little girl behind. Without your love I sank so low I wanted to drive into the ocean. Instead I spent a terrible week driving like a madman, mostly through the desert, 29 Palms, Joshua Tree. When I crashed the car in Vegas I took the bus to Fresno where my friend Joaquin got me a job picking lettuce. I was a mess, angry at you, at myself, but after some months working myself to the bone and forgetting the bottle, I have righted myself. I can accept the truth, that I love you and Pomona with all my heart. Last week someone stole my wallet. Lost all the money I had saved for us. Soon as I have $ for a bus ticket I'm coming home. Nora, instead of fighting each other let's fight together for our love. Our family is sacred. Kiss our Pomona and tell her I love her. She needs to know, no matter what, her papa will return.

Te amo, su espouso
Francisco

As Pomona read her father's words her heart jumped and she began spinning outside her body. Sobs came next. They tore through her breastbone and exploded in her lungs. She had known that father would never willfully abandon her. Here was her proof.

I knew it papa, I knew you loved me. I knew you would come back.

The heart is a love-seeking missile.

Pomona read the letter three more times, absorbing every word into her bloodstream. Francisco's words. But why had Nora hidden Francisco's letter in the book? Never shared with her this life-changing message from her father? Nora must have waited for Francisco to return after receiving the letter. Or had she contacted him and told him to stay away? Or had he changed his mind?

No. She knew that Francisco would never had changed his mind.

Was another scenario possible? Had something happened that prevented Francisco from coming home? The only thing Pomona knew for certain was that Nora at some point had placed the letter in the book — a secret message she had wanted Pomona to find.

Chapter Thirty-five

Chavez Ravine

By the time Pomona left the Farm it was almost ten. She decided that she would go to Parker's house and apologize. He had asked her to fight for their love. Instead, she had acted no better than Nora. She had pushed him away as Nora had Francisco. As she parked Pearl on Baxter Street she saw his truck gone from its usual curbside spot.

Pomona's heart sank. She couldn't blame him for returning to Virginia. Virginia had been fearless in fighting for her love with Parker. Ruthless. Determined. Even unscrupulous. Pomona, like Nora, had walked away. Pomona saw Parker's limbs intertwined with Virginia's in her bed, skin upon skin.

"Damn. I should have learned something from Virginia." She turned and headed back toward Pearl. She was crazy coming here. And yet her feet stopped. Her heart resisted. An inner voice whispered, stop. Don't leave. Pomona turned and walked back towards Parker's front door. That's when she saw her nemesis sitting on the front porch with an annoyed look on her furry face.

"Son of a gun," she cried. "What are you doing here?"

The feline looked away in boredom.

Pomona ran to the porch and scooped Delilah into her arms. The cat meowed and tried to squirm away but Pomona grabbed the spare key beneath a pot, unlocked the door, and threw her in the house. "I've been worried sick. Where have you been for the past three weeks? Did you sleep in a garage? Go to outer space? You couldn't leave a note?"

Delilah ran to her bowl, swished her tail, and cried for food. Pomona knelt to the floor and petted the cat from head to tail. Delilah ate and scurried back under the bed. Pomona stood before the living room window and looked out onto the quiet street.

After reading the Helen Hunt Jackson biography at the library, Pomona had used the Internet there to read articles about Chavez Ravine.

It was a *Herald Examiner* article from May 8, 1959, that gave the disturbing account of the day Chavez Ravine residents called Black Friday. After years of debate over the public good of a professional baseball team, the remaining residents of Chavez Ravine were forcibly evicted by Los Angeles County Sheriffs. In the article, resident Aurora Vargas vowed the sheriffs would have to carry her from her house. Indeed, the accompanying photograph shows a woman, expression fierce and black hair flying, resisting as sheriffs carry her from her house.

Yes, the story confirmed, bulldozers that spring day knocked over the few remaining dwellings in Chavez Ravine. Four months later, ground-breaking for Dodger Stadium began.

Where had the families of Chavez Ravine gone after they were pushed from their homes by developers and politicians? Who the hell had fought for these residents? Had celebrities held press conferences? Had a foundation promised them financial support? Did Don Normark's beautiful book of photographs make any difference?

Pomona turned from the window, sat on the sofa, and took *Ramona* from her bag. Helen Hunt Jackson had described in wrenching detail how American settlers had come to the long-time villages and homes of California Indians and presented them with papers from the American land-office, far away in Washington D.C., that certified the land was theirs. With no notice Indian families were forced to pack up all they owned and leave, for fear of violence or death. The villages were left in ruins. The Indians with no land, became lost, poverty-stricken, homeless.

Just because the laws are on your side doesn't make it right. Just because a wealthy businessman decides he can rip out fourteen acres of plants and trees and build warehouses, he shouldn't have carte blanche to destroy nature.

With a heavy sigh, Pomona rose and put *Ramona* on the shelf beside Don Normark's book. Maybe someday, someone would write a story about the South Central Farm and it would live on the shelf with these books. Hopefully it would have a better ending than the story of what had happened to the California Indians and the residents of Chavez Ravine. Pomona hoped someday she would read a book about a wonderful place called the South Central Farm that had risen above these challenges and continued to flourish without threat for generations to come.

Suddenly an insight sprouted in Pomona's head. If she wanted the farm to continue, she had to fight. If she wanted Parker's love, she had to fight for that too.

When Parker burst through the door it was five in the morning and the sky was starting to lighten.

"I saw Pearl parked on the street and I was so happy," he said, his voice trembling. She had been dozing on the sofa and he rushed to her side, took her face in his hands, and kissed her deeply on the mouth. "Last night at the beach I saw the most incredible sunset and I could only think of you."

Pomona buried her face in his shirt and wiped her wet eyes against his collar.

"I thought I lost you," he whispered. "We can never lose each other again."

As he spoke she smelled the sea in his hair. She brushed sand from his cheek and said, "I saw the sunset too from the garden and I thought of you and finished my book. I read all of *Ramona*. It's so beautiful and sad but Parker, you won't believe..." She patted her hand against her chest in a fluster of emotion. "I found a hidden letter from my father saying he wanted to come home. He never abandoned us, not like my mother said, at least, I don't think he did."

"I knew it."

Pomona sat up and showed him the letter she still held in her hand.

After he read it through, Parker said, "My darling, of course your father didn't mean to leave. No one in his right mind would leave you, but I still don't understand. He wrote and sent this letter but then never came back? Did your mother tell him not to come?"

"I don't know, but even if she had, he would have come anyway. I know my father. He repossessed cars. He picked lettuce in the sun, crossed the Mexican border as a teenager. Swam the Rio Grande. He was a fighter, and he would have fought for us."

"She never mentioned this?"

A lump lodged in Pomona's throat as she remembered Nora's fierce desire to live fully in the moment. "Two things tripped up my mother. First, she didn't want the past to intrude on her life. She cut it off and never looked back. After my father left I was never allowed to mention him. She didn't understand how much it hurt to never talk about the things I lost. The people I lost. If only my mother had just admitted she had a broken heart she might have found a way to heal."

The morning sun was now filling the room, shining through the east facing window. They leaned into one another and, exhausted from their long nights, dozed. When they both woke, the room was flooded with bright morning light. Parker said:

"Last night, in the palm I confronted myself. My past. My loathing. I could say I'm ashamed of who I am and what I did. Feel sorry for myself. But I'm so tired of feeling bad."

He rose from the sofa and went to the kitchen to make coffee. He returned with two steaming cups and set them on the coffee table. He said, "Incencio's hearing is in two days and I need to be there. Something happened last night that made me believe I've been given a second chance."

Pomona caressed his cheek and smiled ruefully. "My mother had a saying she liked that I always found corny, but it came to mind last night. She would say, 'Today is the first day of the rest of my life.' Yesterday, after finding the letter, I actually understood what she meant."

Parker's laughter boomed through the room. "That makes it official that we deserve each other because I was thinking of that same dumb phrase yesterday. Pomona, come with me back to Kansas. I can face my family with you by my side. We can have a second chance too."

Pomona touched his cheek and brushed sand from his brow. "No. That's your fight. Your family, and who knows. Maybe when you get home you'll realize it's where you're meant to be. There's something about returning to the place you're from, isn't there? Maybe you're really rooted there. Maybe your Los Angeles adventure was just a mirage."

"That won't happen. I'm going to fight for this. For us."

Chapter Thirty-six

Luis Francisco Gregorio Sandoval

P arker left midmorning. Taking only a small bag of clothes, he drove away in Pearl. Pomona had insisted that the old Volvo would take him further than his dilapidated pick-up truck. In the stillness of his absence, Pomona wandered through the house with Francisco's letter, rereading his words that clearly stated his intention to come home as soon as he saved money.

When I have $ for a bus ticket I'm coming home. Nora, instead of fighting each other let's fight together for our love. Kiss our Pomona and tell her I love her.

His words roiled her head. He had mailed this intention and Nora must have read his words. Surely she was eager to see her husband again. Mad, perhaps, but still in love. Did her heart jump with every knock to the door? Every mail delivery and telephone ring, waiting endlessly for her true love to walk back into her lonely life?

The longer Pomona wandered the house the more agitated she grew. Finally, she showered, dressed, and drove Parker's truck down Baxter Street and onto the northbound 110 Freeway. She took the Orange Grove Avenue exit and navigated the streets back to the Pasadena's Central Library.

By now her mission was clear as she marched through the main hall to the research room. There Pomona sat before a computer monitor. She opened an Internet search engine and, with a deep breath, typed in her father's name:

Francisco Sandoval.

The search engine spat back a long list of web pages for all manner of Francisco Sandovals that ran the gamut from real estate professionals and baseball players to businessmen, photographers, chess players, and prison inmates. Many were dead as indicated by a return of numerous obituaries. The world was apparently filled with guys named Francisco Sandoval.

Pomona lay her head on the table and moaned with frustration.

She was a stupid idiot. Francisco had disappeared in 1986 before the Internet even existed. Why did she think she would find news of her father through an Internet search?

Someone tapped her shoulder. "Hey, you okay?"

She turned to see Daniel, her former coworker, standing beside her. "Not really."

"What happened?"

She rubbed weary eyes and decided she had no more secrets to keep. "It's about my dad. Twenty years ago he walked out on my mom. We never heard from him again and the official story was he abandoned us. But I just found a letter he wrote saying he was coming home. At the time he had a job picking lettuce somewhere around Fresno. My gut tells me something prevented him from coming. I thought now with the Internet I could find some information. Maybe he had won the lottery or been arrested for armed robbery."

"That's quite a story."

"I punched his name into the search engine but there's literally hundreds of Francisco Sandovals so good luck trying to find him in the bunch. I'm not good at online sleuthing. Anyway, the Internet barely existed when he disappeared."

Daniel looked intrigued. "I might be able to help. After four years in a doctoral program and five years here, I'm pretty good at research."

"Really? Are you sure? That would be awesome."

"My shift finishes in twenty minutes. Let me call my wife and see if she can get our daughter from school."

Daniel was in a doctoral program and had a daughter? They had worked together for four years and she knew nothing about him. "I'm sorry I wasn't a better friend," Pomona said.

"You were rather guarded. Seemed you didn't want anyone to intrude in your life."

"What life? I was lost. Lonely. I didn't think I had anything to offer."

"Pomona, I've always liked you. Would love to help now. I'll finish my shift and call my wife. Be back in twenty minutes. In the meantime, write down every single detail about your father. When I return I want to see the letter and we'll go from there. It's important we don't start with any preconceived notions or hopeful outcomes. This is a needle in a haystack scenario. We'll likely find nothing. Or we may simply discover some interesting facts about picking lettuce in Fresno twenty years ago."

When Daniel returned a half hour later Pomona showed him Francisco's letter, which he read over several times.

"Was there an envelope?"

"Yes, but there's nothing on it but a faded postmark. I found the letter in an old book my dad gave me when he left, in a hidden space in the back. My mother must have stuck it there. No one else could have."

Daniel's eyes widened. "This is a real Nancy Drew mystery. Where's the book?"

Pomona pulled *Ramona* from her bag, opened the back cover and showed Daniel the end paper with its opening facing the spine. "I presume my mother slipped the letter in there."

Daniel scratched his head. "Where did your father get this book?"

"His mother gave it to him."

"It's a great older edition. *Ramona* is one of those rare books that's never been out of print. I've seen so many editions with different covers." Daniel took *Ramona*, removed the book jacket and set it aside. He flipped through the pages and ran his fingers across the back inside cover. His fingers were larger than Pomona's so they could not slide into the secret slot. "Can I remove this end paper?"

Pomona nodded and Daniel gingerly peeled back the end paper and held it to the light. "There's a piece of paper stuck to this.

Pomona almost fell out of her chair. "What?"

Daniel squinted at the tiny script letters. "Looks like a birth certificate, for Luis Francisco Gregorio Sandoval. Born November 11, 1944. Tampico, Mexico. You say your grandmother gave this to your dad?"

Pomona nodded, speechless. "I didn't know his first name was Luis. He always went by Francisco."

"Was your dad in the U.S. illegally, I mean, without any documents. Undocumented?"

Pomona shrugged, her eyes troubled. "We never talked about it."

"If I had to draw a conclusion now, I'd guess that your grandmother wanted to give him the birth certificate but was worried it would be lost. But I don't think understanding your grandmother's motives helps us learn what happened to your father. So we have this book, the letter, and a birth certificate. We know he was working in Fresno picking lettuce around what dates, Pomona? What was your address at the time? Tell me, was he the kind of guy to hitchhike? Go to bars? Friendly? A loner? Write down everything you remember. No detail is too small."

Pomona watched Daniel's mouth move but couldn't make sense of the words. "I'm feeling faint." she whispered. "I can't understand what you're saying. I think I need to go outside and get air."

"What? Whoa, you're overwhelmed." He took her hand and led her through the research room into the library's main hall and outside to a courtyard with a fountain where she lowered herself onto a bench.

"Are you sure you want to do this? Some things are better left alone."

Pomona nodded her head. "I didn't think about my father for twenty years because my mom forbade it. Told me he had abandoned us and was unworthy of living even in our memories. For me, he wasn't gone and forgotten, but frozen in ice. I was frozen too."

"Take a minute then and write down all you know about Francisco, then go home and get some rest. I have some ideas of where to look but remember, this is a needle in a haystack scenario. Chances are we'll come up empty handed, but I'm willing to give it a go."

When Daniel called six hours later at 9 p.m., Pomona was lying in Parker's bed, within the mint-hued sheets, staring out the window at the clear night sky and imagining Parker driving the open road. Even though he was driving away from her in distance, she felt he was coming in closer to her heart by facing his past. She was ready to face her past, too.

Daniel said, "I may have something. Can you meet me at the bookstore café on Colorado Avenue?"

Pomona raced back to Pasadena and met him fifteen minutes later. "You've been working this whole time? Doesn't the library close at six."

"No worries," Daniel chuckled. "I know people in high places. Listen, this may be nothing, or it may be everything." Over the surface of the table he pushed a white piece of paper her way. He then quickly pulled it back and frowned. "That was insensitive. Damn, there's no way to win here. If this isn't your father we're back to square one and I know you'll be disappointed that nothing was unearthed. If this is your father, it's a tough story."

Pomona looked into Daniel's kind eyes and sighed. "Wait one minute." She rose and walked back outside. She remembered standing on this sidewalk with Parker the morning of their coffee date, before they had gone to the South Central Farm almost five weeks ago. This evening the sidewalk was alive with couples holding hands, people buying tickets at the next-door movie theater, and queuing at a pizza joint. As she watched the street scene a man stopped before her and kneeled down.

She zeroed in on his fingers as they buttoned the sweater of a small girl holding an ice cream cone. Suddenly it all came back, a tumble of memories of her and her father, the perpetual pair. It was always his hand she held. His lap she sat upon. His bedtime story. His cooing words when she fell and scraped knees.

They were thick as thieves, Nora always said. Thick as thieves.

Her mind returned to that last day she had spent with Francisco at the Santa Anita Racetrack when they won $100 on a $5 bet on Ferdinand. On the drive home, seemingly out of nowhere, he had turned to her and said, "Be proud of who you are. We may be brown but we're brown like the earth and the earth is what's real."

Pomona didn't understand what he meant then but basked in her happiness as they sputtered along in the Volkswagen bug, the car he brought home after the Grand Torino engine blew. Not just happiness, but relief that she was more like Francisco than Nora. She had always liked her father better than her preoccupied mother with the vague smile and nose in a book. Nora came alive with Francisco in the room. Pomona never doubted that her parents loved each other. Theirs was a tempestuous passion that simmered and boiled.

Pomona found herself stepping up to the strange man and hearing a rush of words fall from her mouth. "Excuse me sir, is this your daughter? Such a beautiful child and you must love her so much. Pardon me for asking what must seem a strange question, but would you ever leave her for no reason and not come back? I know you might think I'm some nutty lady but I just have to know because I lost my own father."

The man stood and wrapped a possessive arm around the girl. "No, of course not. I never would do that. No parent would unless they were in a terrible bind. Now we really must go."

"Thank you so much. You have no idea how much you helped me," Pomona called out as the two hurried down the sidewalk. "I hope I didn't scare you, little girl. Your daddy would never leave you." She then returned to the café and took her seat across from Daniel. "It's okay," she said. "Either way I'll be fine."

Daniel pushed the paper back her way. Pomona turned her attention to a copy of a short newspaper article from the *Visalia Times-Delta*. Dated November 1, 1986 it read:

MALE BODY FOUND IN DITCH

Visalia police reported a body found in a ditch near Highway 198 and Highway 43, just outside the Hanford city limits. The victim is described as Latino male, approximate age 45. Investigators believe the man was dead for two days and likely the victim of a hit and run accident. The man had no identification but a paycheck stub from a Fresno agricultural company. Other identifying objects include a silver religious pendant chained around his neck. Police are investigating whether the paystub belonged to the victim and will notify next of kin.

Pomona looked at Daniel. "It's him."

"Are you sure?"

"He was wearing my necklace. I gave it to him when he left. He died on the side of the road alone? No one tried to find us. We never heard anything. Why didn't the police contact us."

"Oh, honey," Daniel murmured. "Don't you know? He didn't have any ID so authorities took him as just another undocumented worker among so many. An illegal Mexican who caught a bad break. The fields are filled with them. They might have made some attempt but if no one stepped forward he was forgotten at the morgue."

Pomona began to weep. Francisco, her Papa, dead alone on the side of the road. How many times can a heart break. "How did you find this? What do you think happened?"

"Based on what you told me I thought he might have started hitchhiking home, maybe to save money. He was probably just walking, trying to get over to Highway Five where he could more easily catch a ride with a trucker. But it was nighttime, maybe foggy, and he got hit. Oh, Pomona, this was a mistake to tell you. Some things are best unknown."

She shook her head vehemently. "No, the opposite. After my mother died I almost killed myself. I had no sense of myself. Always scared and unsure. Frozen in time and unable to make a move. You thought I was guarded but I wanted to jump off a bridge, not because I really wanted to die, but because I had no idea how to live. Then, as I was on my knees, with nothing left to lose, a miracle happened. I met a man and fell in love. Now, because of your kindness, I can grieve my father and move forward. Denying that he ever existed is what made it so bad. You can't just deny the past." Sobbing so hard she could barely speak, Pomona choked out her last remaining question. "Why did you help me?"

A tear rolled down Daniel's cheek. "When my grandparents came to the U.S. from Vietnam they had nothing and they were met by unbelievable kindness. People here helped them find jobs, a home, invited them into their churches, their communities. Believe me, the United States government has so many problems, but nevertheless, the country runs on the kindness that regular folks give one another. Whenever I have a chance to help someone, I try, for the sake of my parents. Honestly Pomona, you would do the same."

Chapter Thirty-seven
The First Editions are Worth Some Money

Pomona stood on the Colorado Street Bridge and peered over its railing, down 150 feet into the scrubby landscape of trees, rocks, and bushes. She turned and glanced toward the San Gabriel Mountains that filled her view to the north. Fluffy clouds drifted across a blue sky. The city of Pasadena hummed. A breeze ruffled her skirt. Pomona smoothed the skirt of her sundress. Plump red cherries popped against a crisp white linen background. It was a beautiful day as white sparkling sunshine came pouring over the hills, lighting the tops of palms that were rising across the city, their fronds reaching up and tickling the sky.

Parker had called that morning to say that he had gone to Incencio's hearing and had spoken on his behalf. The judge then released him from jail. It had not been easy. People were angry. They had besieged Parker at the courthouse and he now had to work to make things right with Incencio and his family, as well as his own brother and father. Parker knew convincing Caleb and Amos to reform work conditions for all the employees was paramount. Knowing what Amos Wilson held dear to his heart, he would need to launch a full campaign on why this was the right course of action and how it would ultimately heal the discord between the workers and his family. Parker believed he could convince Caleb to follow his lead. Not through charm or bullying, but by building a real relationship with his brother, and making a clear and honest case about their responsibilities to run the business with integrity.

Parker wasn't sure how long he would need to put his life in order. "But I'm coming back soon," he promised Pomona.

Pomona's knees buckled in relief but with a firm tone she said, "I've got a lot of my plate too. I need time to put my own life in order." The trip to the bridge had been first on her list.

Now, as Pomona stood on the bridge, Manuel waited for her in Parker's truck. He waited for her in the exact spot where Pomona had parked Pearl on that fateful day many weeks earlier. She told him she needed a few moments on the bridge alone. As she slid from behind the steering wheel he handed her a packet of wildflower seeds that she now clutched in one hand along with Nora's canister of ashes.

Pomona took *Ramona* from her bag and stared at its beautiful cover illustration that forever captured Ramona and Alessandro traveling along the California mountain trail on their search for a place to call home. Having finally read the book, it told her exactly what to do.

Return to the Farm and fight for justice. That's what she learned from Helen Hunt Jackson. One person can make a difference. Pomona wished she could time travel back one hundred and twenty years and tell the author that she had not written in vain. Her book mattered. It was a stepping-stone along the way, joining so many other stepping-stones placed by writers and artists and activists on the road to justice. She set *Ramona* on the railing's ledge. "You should have read the book, mother," she said to the tin canister as she unscrewed the lid. She considered that Nora may have well read the book, but she had chosen to interpret it through her narrow lens, as a haunting story of lost and cursed love with Francisco calling to her from every page. But then in every book Nora read she had always found the story she needed. The one that helped her to make sense of her life.

"Perhaps the question, mother, was not whether we were cursed, but rather, whether the curse was stronger than us or we were stronger than the curse."

Pomona opened the tin's cover and with one firm shake, released Nora into the Arroyo. Her mother's ashes swirled and floated in the dry air. Pomona then opened the wildflower packet and shook out the seeds so that they drifted down into the Arroyo, along with Nora's ashes.

"Goodbye, mother. I hope you and daddy find each other in a beautiful field of flowers."

For a flash she saw her parents sitting in the front seat of the old Ford Torino, Nora's head resting on Francisco's shoulder as they drove through a fragrant orange grove, away into a pitch-black night. Pomona turned to the mid-morning sun. She dropped back her head and let the delicious rays warm her face.

She could have stood all day on the bridge, basking in the sun, but she and Manuel had plans. He was going back to Mexico, to Dolores and Marisol. He was going in part because they had made a deal.

"I have these old books I want to give you," Pomona had told Manuel a week earlier, a few days after Parker had left. "If we take them to a book dealer I'll bet you can make a few bucks and have some money to buy more land in Chiapas. Otherwise, I'm donating them all to the library."

Manuel had laughed. "Okay. We sell your books. Maybe I get $50."

Pomona spent the rest of the day sorting through all Nora's books, her excitement mounting as she studied the many titles and editions. It was the box in Nora's armoire, beneath the winter coats, that sent her reeling.

The next day she and Manuel drove together to a rare book dealer in Century City whose card Pomona had found tucked in the front cover of *The Grapes of Wrath*.

"I remember your mother," the dealer said as she lifted books from the box with gloved hands. "She had a good literary nose. My god, she really put together a stellar collection of California authors' first editions. James M. Cain, John Steinbeck, John Fante, Charles Bukowski, Joan

Didion, Mary Austin. You'll need to leave these with me a few days so I can appraise them properly. Are they insured?"

Pomona laughed as Manuel looked puzzled. "I doubt it."

When Pomona and Manuel returned to the book dealers' shop two days later she made an offer: $45,000 for all the books. Manuel stared, stunned, while Pomona whooped and clapped her hands. The lion's share came from the signed first editions of James M. Cain's *The Postman Always Rings Twice* (Alfred A. Knopf, New York, 1934); Mary Austin's *Land of Little Rain* (Houghton, Mifflin and Company, 1903); and Dashiell Hammett's *Maltese Falcon* (Alfred A. Knopf, New York, 1930), but Joan Didion's signed first edition of *Slouching Toward Bethlehem* (Farrar, Strauss & Giroux, 1968) and John Fante's *Ask the Dust* (Stackpole Sons, 1939) along with numerous other notable books added to the pot.

Nora had been savvy, had invested well in her beloved volumes.

At first Manuel had refused the money with absolute force. "It's too much. You need it for your life with Parker."

"Damn it, Manuel. We shook on it. I would have donated the books." She glared at him until her annoyance dissipated. "Listen, this is my mother's doing. I had no idea those books were worth that much. I didn't know she had them stashed away in the armoire. More than anything I want you to buy another farm in Chiapas, for your family. Can you do that? If you don't or can't, then I will donate the books."

Manuel nodded and his voice cracked as he said, "I lost Mateo, Pomona. I lost my son because I was not careful." Tears ran down his face over his parched desert cheeks like a tiny stream of prayed-for rain.

As Manuel's shoulders shook and his chest heaved, Pomona said, "I will visit someday and meet your family. I've always wanted to really see Mexico. The last time I went we had to sell the Volvo seat covers to get home. Oh, Manuel, this gives me the greatest joy of my entire life. Who knew my crazy mother and her box of old books would save the day?"

Manuel bought a bus ticket to San Diego. There he would cross the border and take a bus to Mexico City, then Chiapas. But before he left he helped Pomona clear out Nora's apartment, moving the few things she decided to keep to Parker's place. She wasn't really yet living in his old house in Chavez Ravine. She had bought a tent so she could join the encampment at the South Central Farm. Amparo offered to help her take care of Delilah so she could be part of the ongoing protest.

Now, having deposited Nora into the Arroyo, Pomona slipped *Ramona* into her bag and walked back across the Colorado Street Bridge.

"It's done," she told Manuel at the truck. "Now we'll go to the Farm to release Mateo's seeds."

Manuel had asked Pomona to accompany him on one final planting project. In memory of Mateo he would scatter handfuls of wildflower seeds across the entire city block that encompassed the South Central Farm. Across its fourteen acres he would broadcast poppies, sunflowers, buttercups, and twining snapdragon on every square inch of soil.

"If the Farm is lost and the gardens destroyed, the wildflowers will still bloom next year," he told Pomona. He reasoned developers and builders could not pour concrete over every inch of earth. Surely a blaze of poppies guided by the light and sun and helped along by a little rain will push through the dirt, victorious in their desire to open their petals and bloom, as is their rightful destiny.

"Is it not the rightful destiny for all of us, to bloom where we are planted?"

"Yes, Manuel," Pomona had replied. "And even if they cut all the flowers, they cannot stop Spring from coming."

As Pomona slid back into the driver's seat of Parker's truck she straightened her back and raised her head with conviction, because just as she knew it was time to plant, she knew it was time to fight.

THE END

Epilogue

Los Angeles Times
L.A. Garden Shut Down; 40 Arrested
Protesters are forcibly taken from the site that had flourished for years in
a poor area. The owner refuses the city's $16-million offer.

June 14, 2006
Hector Becerra, Megan Garvey and Steve Hymon | Times Staff Writers

Los Angeles County sheriff's deputies shut down a 14-acre urban
farm in South Los Angeles on Tuesday, arresting more than 40 protesters
as they cleared a plot of land that has been the source of discord and
controversy in the community for two decades.

The evictions occurred during a frenzied morning both at the farm and
at City Hall. Mayor Antonio Villaraigosa and other city leaders continued
negotiations with the landowner even as deputies used bolt cutters and
power tools to remove protesters who had attached themselves to
concrete-filled drums and mature trees.

In an afternoon news conference, Villaraigosa said owner Ralph
Horowitz turned down $16 million -- an offer that met the asking price.
Talks broke down, the mayor said, in large part because Horowitz wanted
the farmers evicted.

"Today's events are disheartening and unnecessary," Villaraigosa said.
"After years of disagreement over this property, we had all hoped for a
better outcome."

For his part, Horowitz said he had no intention of rewarding a
group that included people he said had made anti-Semitic remarks about

him even as they squatted rent-free on land that was costing him more than $25,000 a month to maintain -- in addition to massive legal bills fighting their efforts to remain.

"If the farmers got a donation and said, 'We got $50 million, would you sell it to us?' I would say no. Not a ... chance," Horowitz said. "It's not about the money."

It took authorities nearly eight hours to forcibly clear protesters from the farm. Officials bulldozed vegetable gardens and chopped down an avocado tree to clear the way for a towering Fire Department ladder truck so the final four protesters could be plucked from a massive walnut tree. Among those aloft: protest organizer John Quigley and actress Daryl Hannah, who waved and smiled as supporters cheered her on from across the street.

The farm site -- and the story of how after the 1992 riots residents turned the vacant land into patches of fruits and vegetables -- has become a symbol of hope and self-sufficiency to many, attracting support from celebrities including Martin Sheen, Danny Glover and Laura Dern.

For more than a week, those camping at the site had waited for the end, running
evacuation drills, attending seminars on their legal rights and orchestrating ways to impede any eviction effort.

The evictions began before the sun was even up. A warning cry went out shortly before 5 a.m. Quigley, serving as a lookout, spotted motorcycle police and a phalanx of cruisers approaching the corner of Long Beach Avenue and 41st Street and shouted from his perch.

"I heard John yell: Get up. This is real! Not a joke," Hannah said in an interview before deputies took her from the tree.

As they had practiced, protesters took their positions -- some chained to the concrete drums, others locking arms through pre-erected pipes. Hannah scrambled to her place on a tree branch near Quigley.

In just minutes, sheriff's deputies cut through the chain-link fence perimeter and ordered protesters out. Soon the perimeter was heavily fortified. About 250 LAPD officers secured the area, many in riot gear, as about 65 sheriff's deputies evacuated the farm. Many streets leading into the area were blocked, snarling traffic in one of the area's busiest commercial districts.

Seferino Hurtado, 70, an immigrant from the Mexican state of Michoacan, said he was not shocked that the farm was finally taken. He had tilled at the garden about 10 years.

"We thought it could happen one day. But I'm disappointed," Hurtado said. "I'm older now, and when I spend time there it serves as therapy."

The land, along an industrial corridor in an economically struggling area, has long been a source of headaches for city officials. It was seized from Horowitz in 1986 after the city used eminent domain in an effort to build an incinerator at the site. Community activists defeated that proposal, and residents turned the land into garden plots where low-income families could grow their own produce.

Horowitz, however, sued to get the land back, eventually winning. Three years ago, he paid $5 million -- close to the price he'd gotten for the land 17 years earlier -- to reacquire the parcels.

But the farmers refused to leave.

As the fight continued and got increasingly contentious, some longtime supporters were alienated and dozens of longtime farming families left their plots.

Printouts of a Spanish-language Internet site that accused Horowitz of being part of a "Jewish Mafia" controlling Los Angeles were circulated at City Hall.

Hard feelings continued at Tuesday's protests.

Another battle was going on at City Hall, where a visibly annoyed Villaraigosa said a last-ditch effort to preserve the land fell apart when Horowitz said he thought it was worth an additional $2 million to $3 million. The rejected $16-million deal included a $10-million promise from the Annenberg Foundation, which sent a letter to Horowitz on June 6 affirming its intention to donate the funds.

"We met his price. He set the bar very high. Now the bar has been moved once again," said the mayor, who supported keeping the land as a public garden.

Horowitz said his 11:30 a.m. call with the mayor -- with evacuations in full swing -- wasn't very amicable.

He said he felt that Villaraigosa was trying to blame him for the failure to save the garden.

As far as he was concerned, Horowitz said, the departure of many families from the farm had left only "the activists, the movie stars, the anarchists and the hard-nosed group -- the ones I disliked from the beginning."

Until recently, he said, the group had insisted that he turn over the land without compensation.

"Do you think they offered a nickel for rent? One nickel for insurance, one nickel for anything?" Horowitz asked. "No. They were demanding they be given the land for free. Fourteen years was not enough."

Councilwoman Jan Perry, who represents the area, said Tuesday that she still favors using some of the property to create jobs -- a proposal she said reflects the desire of many area residents.

Horowitz said Tuesday that he was not sure he would sell the land. There has been talk in the past of building warehouses on part of it.

Some still held out hope that the property could be preserved as a public garden despite Tuesday's drama. Lawyers for the farm's leaders are due in court next month in an effort to overturn the resale of the land to Horowitz, but the argument hinges on proving that the city wasted resources in selling the property -- a difficult proposition.

Villaraigosa said the city would relocate the farmers to a 7.8-acre site at 111th Street and Avalon Boulevard that has the capacity to hold 200 garden plots.

Already, 30 farmers have been allowed to begin cultivating that land. The city has also identified 100 other plots around the city for community gardens, the mayor said.

On the garden's outskirts, as protesters gathered for a Tuesday evening vigil, one man took a more practical tack. Jason Keehn, 45, reached through the chain links of the fence and plucked mint, chamomile and cactuses from the earth to replant at his North Hollywood home.

Author's Note

I first heard about the South Central Farm on KPFK, the Los Angeles Pacifica Network radio station. It was Fall 2005 and the broadcast was filled with news about heated protests erupting to save the farm from being sold to a developer. My husband, Michael, our young daughter, Ramona, and I were compelled to drive from Pasadena to South Central Los Angeles to visit the garden oasis on 41st and Alameda streets. When we stepped foot into the fourteen-acre space, we were thrilled to be standing beneath a canopy of trees, our feet planted in nurturing soil. We walked along dirt paths that bordered lush gardens. I was dazed this place even existed. The contrast to the surrounding concrete, asphalt, and metal was shocking, yet the noisy and polluting throng of zooming cars, trucks, and trains was countered by the garden's healing energy.

Our immediate assumption was that of course everyone would fight as hard as possible to prevent this flourishing open space from being destroyed. How could we not when we already knew that climate change was affecting our earth? Threatening our way of life? Our children's future? Surely we would come to their senses. We would protect this heavenly garden.

At this time I was working as a communications writer at the Huntington Library, Art Museums, and Botanical Gardens. The gorgeous oasis in the well-to-do enclave of San Marino spreads across 207 acres, only a few miles from where we lived in Pasadena. Through my work I learned the history of Henry and Arabella Huntington. I absorbed the details and minutiae of how Henry came to build his fabulous gardens in Southern California, funded in part with family money made through the development of the transcontinental railroad.

In another part of my life I was a novelist with two characters living in my head. For years Parker and Pomona had moved in and refused to leave. I had a sense of who there were: Parker was a man obsessed with palm trees. Pomona, a woman who can only find herself once she connects to the earth. When I visited the farm the inspiration for their story finally hit. During this fraught time I discovered the love story that gave them (and me) the freedom to live their truths.

Of course, I couldn't write a novel about Southern California without including *Ramona*. If you grew up in SoCal, as I did, you knew her story. As a young girl, I had attended with my family the outdoor pageant play staged annually in the desert city of Hemet. My immigrant parents, a father from Mexico and mother from Germany, had in our home Helen Hunt Jackson's novel with the elegant and inspiring cover by artist N.C. Wyeth. The story of Ramona is the story of California. It is a place where people such as my parents, both of whom had escaped desperate and challenging lives in their home countries, could create a new life within this natural paradise. The book was so foundational to my origin story that I named my only daughter Ramona.

While Helen Hunt Jackson's book aimed to educate readers about the tragic plight of the California Indians, it had an unintended consequence. Her story of Ramona and Alessandro and its descriptions of California drew people from other places to see the state's natural beauty. They wanted to leave behind their pasts and start anew by the ocean and beneath the palms. Their ability to come West in droves was made possible by the advent of the railroads in which the Huntington family played a hand.

Los Angeles and California are places that I love dearly. A native Angeleno, I am old enough to remember Orange County when it was filled with strawberry fields. When orange groves spread across the San Gabriel Valley. Yes, the orange groves are gone. Yes, the South Central Farm was lost.

As a trained journalist, I did copious amounts of research while writing this book. It was important that I represent as accurately as possible the story of the South Central Farm. With the availability of online video and news reports, I was able to capture the exact words and sentiments from players and activists involved. These include living people such as the lawyer Dan Stormer and Julia Hill Butterfly. They are often quoted verbatim.

To learn more about the South Central Farm, I recommend watching the excellent 2008 documentary, *The Garden*, by filmmaker Scott Hamilton Kennedy. It gives in-depth insight into the political machinations that doomed the existence of the farm. I am indebted to this wonderful filmmaker for creating this important record.

After the violent removal of the farmers and their supporters by LA County Sheriffs on June 13, 2006, the 14-acre space sat empty for years. None of Ralph Horowitz's plans to build warehouses materialized. In 2022 the City of Los Angeles announced its own plan to build warehouses and offices on the still vacant site. Some farmers were relocated to other plots and open spaces around Los Angeles County, but the original farm at 41st and Alameda was never replicated. Its thriving, gorgeous spirit did not survive.

But pieces of it were transplanted to the Huntington. Botanical staff there worked to save some of the farm's threatened trees by moving them onto the estate. Many did not survive. But some did.

As well, Ramona, California's official outdoor play, continues to be staged each spring as it has since 1923. A visit to the Ramona Bowl in Hemet is a lovely excursion. A place to celebrate love and land.

I hope through Parker and Pomona's story, through the evocation of the South Central Farm, that you, dear reader, are inspired to bloom where you are planted. To create beauty and build community. To plant seeds of hope wherever you may be.

Manuela Gomez Rhine
October 2024

M anuela Gomez Rhine is the author of *The Wild Chihuahuas of Mexico*, a story of the Mexican Revolution told through the adventures of a pack of Chihuahuas, and *Power of One: Pasadenans Shaping Our Community*, a photo-essay book highlighting community activists. She has an MA in English from the University of Kansas, a BA in journalism from San Francisco State University and an AA from the Fashion Institute of Design and Merchandising in Los Angeles. She lives in Pasadena, California, and Oaxaca, Mexico. Find out more at Mexicanista.com

Acknowledgements

I am forever grateful to family, friends, and fellow writers for providing the support, guidance, and love that's infused within this work:

To my wonderful Thursday writing group, Gerda Govine, Kerri Kumasaka, and Carla Sameth. We have a special thing going.

To my steadfast writing comrade Margaret Byrne, whose honesty and unrelenting push for me to rework and rewrite always improves my pages. Our ongoing conversations about writing and the state of the world feed my soul.

I am grateful for guidance and encouragement from Linzi Glass, Susan Priver, and my Oaxaca Amigas.

To Susan Turner-Lowe for opening the door to the Huntington and bringing me back over the years to relive the magic.

To Ramona and Michael showing me what it means to be an artist. Thank you for joining the team and giving it your all. And always to Bennie and Bella, Brother and Sister, for the daily love.

Made in the USA
Middletown, DE
14 October 2024

62699496R00158